Also by Caridad Pineiro

AT THE SHORE

One Summer Night

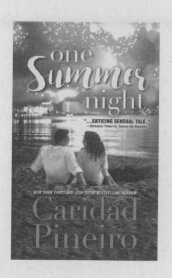

what
happens in
Summer

Caridad
Pineiro

Published by Sourcebooks Casablanca, an imprint of Sourcebooks, Inc.
P.O. Box 4410, Naperville, Illinois 60567-4410
(630) 961-3900
Fax: (630) 961-2168
sourcebooks.com

Printed and bound in Canada.
MBP 10 9 8 7 6 5 4 3 2 1

Prologue

Sea Kiss, New Jersey

PLAYING IT SAFE WAS FAR WORSE THAN TAKING A RISK ON what you wanted.

Jonathan Pierce knew just what he wanted.

He grabbed hold of the gnarly branch of the decades-old wisteria vine that climbed the side of the Sinclair mansion and boosted himself up. He'd made the journey so many times this past summer, he could do it blindfolded.

He scrambled up the vine, finding the familiar foot- and handholds until he vaulted up and over the second-floor railing, and landed silently as a cat burglar on the balcony. It ran the length of the immense oceanfront mansion, with elegant french doors offering views of the sea.

The first darkened doorway was Maggie Sinclair's room. He rushed past it quietly; Maggie belonged to his older brother, Owen. Not that Owen had acted on it yet, but Jonathan had known for years that the two were meant to be together, family feud be damned.

The next doorway was usually Maggie's dad's, but the old man had stopped coming down to the Shore as often as he once had, so it was a good bet that room was unoccupied.

Reaching the third room, he saw the curtains wafting

in the summer breeze and the dim light from behind the partially closed french doors. He smiled, and his heart raced with pleasure.

Connie was waiting for him. Ever-responsible, ever-loyal Connie had broken her own rules to fall in love with him. Or at least he thought it was love. It definitely was on his part. With barely a week left before the girls all went back to college, he intended to let her know just how he felt.

He slipped carefully through the open doors and shut them behind him. He'd gone no more than a step when she launched herself at him, laughing and kissing him as she said, "What took you so long?"

"I missed you too," he said, knowing it was more about the separation to come in a week and not about the long hours since last night.

He bent his head and kissed her, his touch tender and caring, and she answered in kind, her lips soft and coaxing.

Although Maggie had been bringing her friends to the Jersey Shore every summer since they'd met freshman year in college, he hadn't really paid much attention to Connie at first. He'd had his share of girls from his high school class fawning over him.

But when Maggie and her friends had come back the next year, he had finally, gratefully, noticed what a real woman should be. Like Connie: all luscious curves, but also proud, smart, and independent.

As impatient as he might have been to make love to her tonight, he wanted her to know how much this meant to him. How this wasn't just a summer romance for him.

He leaned over her, his gaze locked on her face. He wanted to say the words—Lord, how he wanted to—but they stuck in his throat, so he let every kiss and touch tell her what he couldn't voice.

—✺—

Connie's heart thudded almost painfully in her chest as she wondered how, in a week's time, she could leave him. The ache deepened beneath her breastbone, and she put her hand there and rubbed to assuage the hurt.

What had started as a summer fling with a funny, smart, and beautiful boy had turned into something so much more, with an incredibly amazing man. Falling in love with Jonathan hadn't been in her game plan, but he was just too hard to resist.

She *should* have resisted. He was a Pierce. She wasn't a Sinclair, but Maggie was like a sister, and that stupid family feud was still going strong, as far as she knew.

He was going back to Villanova in a week, and she'd be returning to Princeton. The colleges were not all that far apart, but if she was to execute her game plan, she had to stay in the game, which meant studying and more studying. Not nights spent in bed making love and days spent daydreaming about the nights. But like Eve with the apple, now that she'd had a bite of such delicious forbidden fruit, she didn't know how she could go on a Jonathan-free diet.

At the moment, she could just admire his sun-streaked, light-brown hair waving wildly around a masculine face with chiseled features. A sexy, dimpled grin was on his lips, and his eyes glittered with a blue as enchanting as a Sea Kiss summer sea.

That ache in her heart rocketed to life again together with an almost unbearable lightness in her soul. For so much of her life, she'd been driven to accomplish more and more, but with Jonathan, she could just be herself. No goals or responsibilities. Just…happy.

And so, in the blink of an eye, her game plan altered. She could see it all so clearly, only now Jonathan was there beside her at each step. Finish college. Head to law school. Pass the bar. Get a job in a big New York City law firm so she could help her family financially, as well as others who had legal problems and couldn't afford representation. Become a partner. Marry Jonathan. Or maybe marry Jonathan and then become a partner. She didn't want to wait too long to be with him forever.

Not that she'd ever pictured getting married to anyone before, since her home life hadn't been anything great. But for Jonathan, she'd make an exception.

As she snuggled into the curve of his arm and pillowed her head on his broad shoulder, she sighed and said, "I can't believe the summer's almost over."

He grunted his reply in a typical male way. "Sucks." But then he surprised her by adding, "I'd like to keep on seeing you once you're back in school."

She smiled, pleased by his admission, and glanced up at him. There was a contented smile on his full lips and the first hint of a dimple. The hard line of his jaw had a bit of blond stubble from an evening beard. She ran her hand up to brush away a lock of his hair.

"I'd like that too," she said.

His smile broadened, and the dimple fully emerged, drawing attention to that luscious mouth. She couldn't resist surging up to skim a kiss along that dimple and the corner of his lips.

"What was that for?" he asked.

She wanted to say because he made her happy, but she hesitated. She'd seen what could happen to a woman whose happiness depended on a man, as she'd watched her mother lose herself and her dreams.

"As a way for you to remember me until we visit each other at college," she said instead.

Tension crept into his body, impossible to miss. Enough to worry her. She pulled back from him. "I thought you wanted us to see each other. At least, that's what you said a minute ago."

A chagrined look passed across his features, stirring the worry inside her.

"I do, only… I won't be at college this year. I'm not going back to Villanova."

She searched his face, finding it hard to believe, but he appeared deadly serious.

"What do you mean you're not going back? Did something happen? Are you transferring to another school?"

—◊—

She was freaking out, and Jonathan understood. To someone like Connie, college meant everything, including the stability she'd not had in her early life because her father had abandoned her family. But he wasn't like her. The whole predictable route that she and her friends—and even his brother—were taking was not the path he wanted to follow.

"I liked Villanova. The people. The place. Even some of the classes, but the whole college thing is not for me."

Shock registered on her features, and she shook her head, either not comprehending or, worse, not wanting to. "What do you mean it's not for you? So what do you plan to do? Spend the rest of your life surfing? Or working at the bar?"

Her words were too much like those his father had shouted at him when he'd told him a week ago of his decision. His father, a bitter and angry old man who never had a kind word for either of his sons.

Her words, the look she gave him, stoked the anger in his belly. He tried to keep it banked, because he understood where such anger could lead. In as calm a voice as he could muster, he said, "I have plans, Connie. They're just different from yours."

"Was I ever in your plans? Or was this just a summer hookup?" she asked, the upset evident in her gaze, but his own pain was just as alive. Just as sharp.

He snorted a breath and said more roughly, "You act as if I'm the one who wanted this to be just a hookup, but who's the one who didn't want her friends to know she'd been seeing me?"

She laid her hand over his heart. "It's not what you think."

The pity in her tone unleashed something inside him. Something ugly and hurtful. "Don't tell me what I think, Connie. I think you're ashamed of me. That I'm not good enough for someone like you."

"I care for you, Jon," she said, but it was clear that she was unable to fully commit to what was happening between them. "But I know what it's like to want a man you can't rely on. A man who doesn't fulfill his responsibilities. I won't have that in my life. I *can't* have that in my life again."

The heat of anger rose inside him, and he clenched his hands at his sides. "If that's what you think I am, I guess it's a good thing the summer's over so *this* can be over."

He marched to the door and stood there for a long moment. He delayed there for a second, hoping for a change, but when she said nothing, he turned back to face her. "I love you, Connie. My bad. I should have known better than to give my heart to someone like you."

He stormed through the french doors and slammed them shut but couldn't move away from them as the sound of her tears froze him in place.

From behind the glass of the doors he heard "I love you too."

He was tempted to go back in. Take her in his arms again and tell her everything would be all right, but he knew it wouldn't. With a long sigh and heaviness in his heart, he walked away, hoping he wasn't making the worst mistake of his life.

Superstorm Sandy barreled into New Jersey with a viciousness that hadn't been seen since the 1944 Great Atlantic Hurricane.

Connie hunkered down with her family in their Union City home, praying that the sturdy brick building wouldn't come down around them as it shuddered from the force of the wind and buckets of rain that battered the structure. A constant sound, like that of a freight train roaring by, accompanied the loud bangs and clangs as debris hit their home.

The night was long, especially as the power cut out just a few hours after the storm began. Luckily, they had prepped with candles and batteries, and their gas stove and furnace kept the house warm.

Connie finally drifted off to sleep in the early morning hours. She awoke to a cold, clear day and her grandfather huddled over an old transistor radio, listening to reports about the storm and sipping a *café con leche*. As she joined him and heard the newscast, it was clear that Sandy had caused major damage. Her stomach churned with worry for her friend Emma, who was living in Sea Kiss, and Maggie in her Gramercy Park town house, since there had been massive flooding in the low-lying areas in Manhattan.

Thankfully, she was able to reach both of them via cell phone just a short time later to confirm that they were okay, but by later that day, it was clear that Sea Kiss had taken a serious hit from the hurricane.

When Maggie said that she was heading to the Jersey Shore town in a couple of days to check on her family home and help residents with the cleanup, Connie didn't hesitate, especially since there was zero chance of running into Jonathan Pierce.

She hadn't seen Jonathan in the nearly two years since their breakup that momentous summer when she'd actually considered changing her life plans for him. During that time, she'd heard from Emma that Jonathan had been drifting from one job to another and from one place to another, reinforcing the reasons why she had made the right decision years earlier.

She'd spent too much of her childhood with a father who waltzed in and out of her life with one get-rich-quick scheme after another. She'd seen her mother suffer from his irresponsible behavior, both financially and emotionally. She'd vowed never to be in a similar position.

"You're unusually quiet," Maggie said as they drove down to Sea Kiss in a Jeep Wrangler that Maggie had rented to deal with the possible road conditions down at the Shore.

"Thinking," Connie said but then quickly tacked on, "about the damage to Sea Kiss. I know I don't live there, but I almost feel like it's home sometimes."

"Me too. Emma says there's not much damage to my family's beach house, but I worry about everyone else," Maggie said.

"Hopefully, it won't be that bad," Connie said. They fell silent for the rest of the trip on a parkway that was devoid of the usual traffic since most businesses and schools were still closed due to the aftermath of the storm.

Nearly an hour later, they were pulling off the parkway and heading toward Sea Kiss, but they had to detour for an assortment of downed trees, including one blocking access to Main Street. After a few turns, they were able to reach the Sea Kiss downtown to meet Emma and Carlo, her caterer extraordinaire, who was using his food truck to help feed the volunteers.

They parked and walked over to meet their friends, and as they did so, the mayor and several town council members joined them, as well as Owen Pierce.

Maggie stiffened beside her at the sight of Owen, and Connie understood the tension. She suspected that if things were different between the Pierce and Sinclair families, Maggie and Owen would have been an item.

In no time, the number of volunteers grew steadily. Some people were dispatched to handle various tasks on

Ocean Avenue, where the storm surge had destroyed the boardwalk, pier, and some of the seaside cottages. Other volunteers were sent to deal with the flooded lighthouse and assorted businesses and homes near the inlet.

Connie walked with Maggie down to Ocean Avenue, slogging through growing mounds of wet sand and debris the closer they got to the beachfront. Her breath left her as they reached the area and the full scope of the devastation hit her.

There was no boardwalk left for blocks, and over half of the pier had been swept out to sea. The beachfront was littered with debris, from small pieces of what had once been the boardwalk to immense telephone poles from who knew where. Northward, in the direction of Maggie's home, the dunes had protected the shoreline to some degree but had been flattened in spots. Sand from the dunes covered most of Ocean Avenue for a couple of miles.

Where there had once been some seaside cottages, there was now only emptiness for yards and yards until the remains of the first cottage were visible. It had been uprooted and flipped upside down, while the one beside it had been sheared in half. Others farther down had been a little more fortunate and still stood but were heavily damaged.

Connie's group of volunteers began to help families clear out the cottages that might be salvageable so that deadly mold wouldn't take hold in wet walls and contents. As they assisted with that, the Public Works Department was already at work on plowing sand off the street to make Ocean Avenue passable again.

Connie's throat was tight with emotion as she

worked elbow to elbow with one family to save what they could from their home. Tears streamed down the woman's face as she stood in what had once been the living room and hugged a sea-soaked photo album to her chest. Sucking in a rough breath, Connie tossed broken china and water-logged books into a plastic bag while another part of her crew helped move furniture outside. Eventually, they hoped to take down ruined sheetrock so the building could dry out.

When the bag got heavy, she dragged it across the sand-littered cottage floor and outside. As she neared a growing pile of furniture and bags, a young boy ran across the street and into the path of an oncoming bulldozer.

She called out a warning and ran after him, but in that split second, a man raced across the street, grabbed hold of the child, and hauled him to safety just a few feet away from her.

"Careful there, grommet," the man said as he set the boy back on his feet.

"Sorry, dude," the boy said and hugged the man. Hugged Jonathan Pierce, she realized as she stopped dead and stared at them.

Jonathan released the young child and ruffled the youngster's hair with affection. As the child ran off, this time more carefully behind the wall of furniture and detritus growing along the street, Jonathan smiled and jammed his hands on his hips.

It just wasn't fair that he looked even more handsome than he had two years earlier. His body had filled out with muscle, lovingly shown off by the worn fabric of his flannel shirt. A large rip along one side exposed tanned skin, while faded jeans hugged powerful thighs and lean hips.

Her heart raced in her chest, but it was no longer from the fear of seeing the child mowed down by the bulldozer. As Jonathan turned and saw her, however, his smile faded.

He walked over until he stood barely a foot from her, and his gaze skimmed over her.

Raising her chin a defiant inch, she said, "Jon. I wasn't expecting to see you here."

At his prolonged silence, she wanted to ask where he'd been, what he'd been doing, but the words stayed trapped inside along with a maelstrom of emotions. Fear. Anger. Relief. Maybe even affection, because you never really got over your first love.

Jonathan struggled to find the right words to say. Connie looked so beautiful standing there, wisps of dark hair escaping from the ponytail holding the wealth of her thick hair, a smudge of dirt along one high-boned cheek. But her lips, those full lips he'd loved to kiss for hours, were thinned into a tight slash of disapproval.

He reminded himself that her disapproval was the reason they could never be together. Connie could never accept that he wasn't a nine-to-five guy. That he wasn't the kind to settle down and be home for supper every day because he loved experiencing life too much.

With a shrug, he said, "When I heard where the hurricane was going to hit, I had to come home."

Her eyebrows flew upward. "Home as in the beach house?"

Faking a nonchalant shrug, he said, "Where else?"

But as adventurous as he was, he'd questioned his decision more than once during the long course of the night. As one powerful wind gust after another attacked the house and rain lashed the boarded-up windows, he'd wondered if their home would survive the night. Somehow, the building had ridden out the storm. Somehow, he had as well, but not without realizing that he cared more than he thought for the home he'd escaped years earlier.

Just like the way his clenched heart warned that he was not over what he'd felt for Connie Reyes. Or at least the carefree, laughing, and sensual Connie who had emerged from her über-responsible shell that summer like one of the hermit crabs that lived tucked into the jetties.

"That was foolish. You could have been killed," she said, but her tone was one of concern and not condemnation.

He challenged her on that. "Would you have cared?"

"Don't be a jerk. Of course I would have cared," she almost shouted.

Despite what he'd told himself earlier about the impossibility of their ever being together, he couldn't stop himself from prolonging the encounter. "How's law school going? Heard you got into Columbia."

She nodded and tucked her hands into her front pockets, clearly uncomfortable. "I did. I'm interning at a law firm too." After a long, hesitant beat, she said, "And you? What have you been up to?"

He narrowed his gaze, considering her, wondering if he'd feel like he'd gotten worked after a bad wipeout if he told her, but he decided to press ahead. "This and that. I went to SoCal and hit some surf spots while I worked a couple of different jobs. Came back to Jersey a few months ago. Been doing some car mechanic stuff 'cause I like it."

"Does that mean you're home for good now?" she asked.

He told himself not to believe there was a hint of hopefulness there. "Maybe," he said with another shrug, uncertain to commit to more, even though he knew that was what she wanted to hear. What might bring her back into his life.

She rocked back and forth on her heels, and he waited for her censure, but instead, she said, "I hope you find what will make you happy, Jon."

He told himself to walk away. To resist the urge building inside, but he couldn't, because he could never resist a challenge. Especially one like Connie.

Leaning close, he whispered against her lips, "I thought I had." And then he closed his mouth on hers and savored the heaven lost to him that long-ago summer night.

Chapter 1

JONATHAN PIERCE STARED HARD AT THE MIRROR, wondering what Connie Reyes might see tonight when she and her friends came over for the dinner his brother Owen had arranged. What Connie might think after so much time had passed.

The teen she had known seven years earlier was gone, as was the man she'd run into shortly after Hurricane Sandy. That man had been replaced by one who had known his share of hardship and success. Barely perceptible laugh lines that hadn't been there that last summer bracketed his mouth and eyes. There was a thin scar above one brow thanks to a crash while testing a new vehicle prototype on the Bonneville Salt Flats. Another jagged, white line on his jaw was courtesy of shrapnel when a hydrogen fuel cell had unexpectedly exploded in their lab.

He looked away and leaned heavily on the edge of the vanity, noting the other assorted nicks and scars on his hands. They were the hands of a man who had lived life to the fullest and made himself what he wanted to be and not what others expected. He knew he'd sometimes hurt people with his choices, especially his older brother, Owen, who'd had to shoulder the burden of the family business as well as their father's ire whenever one of Jonathan's escapades caught the attention of the media.

He'd gotten used to the interest the press had in

him. After all, he was the renegade son of a wealthy family, a self-taught inventor who had sold his first small invention for millions. He was now revolutionizing the motor vehicle and battery industries with his innovative designs, unconventional methods, and fearless experiments.

He had brought idea after idea to life with detailed research and hard work. There had been failures along the way, but that had only made the successes that much more enjoyable. He had celebrated those successes with his team, his brother, and a bevy of actresses and models who were only too keen to be seen on the arm of a rebellious multimillionaire who might soon be a billionaire if his company's stock prices continued to climb.

But...none of those women could hold a candle to Connie.

Connie, who he would see in just a few hours thanks to his brother. Owen had finally decided to fight for Maggie Sinclair, and he was happy that his brother was following his heart. But while Jonathan would do almost anything for Owen, he wasn't happy about having to spend time with Connie.

Smart and beautiful Connie, he thought with a sigh and a shake of his head.

He'd managed to avoid her for the last several years. Sure, he'd seen her after Sandy and occasionally from afar when Maggie and her friends had come down to Sea Kiss. Or every now and then when he'd gone to some business event in the city.

He'd tried to tell himself he didn't like the sleek professional woman she'd become. That she wasn't prettier than ever. He tried not to imagine peeling off those elegant business suits to reveal the real woman beneath. But he was lying to himself.

He had never really gotten over the Connie Reyes who had emerged that summer they had shared. The woman who had learned to live for the moment and have fun. Who had been carefree and willing to explore their love. He doubted he would ever forget that woman and wondered if she was still there, trapped inside her very prim and proper suits.

Maybe he'd find out tonight, he thought and prepared himself for what might be a very difficult dinner.

Connie Reyes splayed her hand across the nervous butterflies in her stomach that were beating their wings so violently, she felt like throwing up. She was tempted to beg off from dinner with the Pierce boys, but Maggie needed her moral support, and Connie never disappointed a friend. Especially Maggie, who was like a sister. She'd do anything for Maggie, even suffer through a meal with Jonathan Pierce.

"You feeling okay? You're looking a little..." said Emma Grant, her other BFF. Emma peered at her intently, her green-eyed gaze inquisitive.

"I'm just fine," she lied, but it was clear from Emma's meaningful stare that her friend suspected something was up as they followed Maggie onto the patio and to the long row of tall privet hedges that separated the two Jersey Shore mansions.

She tamed the flutters much as she did when arguing a case before a judge and trudged along behind Maggie as they eased through the hedges and approached the entrance to the Pierce mansion. They had barely reached the front porch when Owen threw open the door, a big, friendly smile on his handsome face.

He welcomed them warmly, but Connie couldn't resist mumbling to Emma, "Said the spider to the fly." As much as she wanted things to work out with Owen, she still worried about how hurt Maggie would be if they didn't.

Emma jabbed her in the ribs, and luckily, it seemed Owen either hadn't heard her comment, or if he had, he was choosing to ignore it. She gave him props if it was the latter, since it indicated he was truly trying to be nice for Maggie's sake.

They quickly walked through the foyer and living room and back to the dining area. Jonathan was in the kitchen, an apron over his jeans and T-shirt. The T-shirt hugged his broad, muscled chest and laid bare the powerful muscles of his arms. His light-brown hair still had the kiss of the summer sun and was tied back from his face, revealing the sharp lines of his features.

He looked older but still so handsome.

She had thought she could handle this dinner for her friend's sake. That she could face Jonathan and not get caught up in the emotions from years past. But it was impossible to forget the way he'd held her in his arms, a dimpled smile on his lips, his sea-blue eyes bright with humor and love. With that memory, the flutters in her stomach were replaced by an ache in the region of her heart.

As they walked into the kitchen area, Jonathan looked up and smiled. He sauntered from beyond the island, over to Maggie, and hugged her. "Nice to see you again, Maggie."

He embraced Emma next, playfully teasing her like he might a kid sister. "How's the world's best wedding planner doing?"

Emma grinned back, apparently totally at ease around him. "Busy making the world less safe for confirmed bachelors like you."

When it came time to greet Connie, his demeanor changed drastically. He kept his distance and provided her with only a quick nod and a forced smile. "Connie."

She tried to understand his reticence, but it didn't make it any easier to handle the pain of his actions. It hurt so much, she lost control and responded out of anger, something she rarely did.

"Jonathan. I almost didn't recognize you. It's been so long since I've seen your face in the news." Her friends' muffled gasps chased her words.

"I should have known you were around when all the sharks migrated to safer waters," he said.

"Professional courtesy," she retorted with a Cheshire-cat smile, trying to hide how much his words hurt. Her eyes grew unfocused with the glimmer of tears, and she immediately regretted that they had gotten off on the wrong foot. This dinner was important for Maggie, and she didn't want to do anything that would hurt her friend's chances with Owen.

"Now, now, children. It's time to play nice," Emma said, trying to soothe the upset.

Connie imagined it was the kind of calming tone her friend used to control unruly situations at one of her wedding events and understood how it worked so well.

"Of course. Sorry. Let me get back to the sauce," Jonathan said and hurried to the stove.

Owen and Maggie walked away to open a bottle of wine while Connie sat down next to Emma.

After Owen and Maggie had poured wine for all of them, Maggie grabbed a glass and ambled over to Jonathan at the stove. Connie watched as Maggie and Jonathan chatted in low tones and wondered what they were discussing. As Jonathan shot a quick, hesitant look at her, it was obvious the talk included her, and she hoped that Maggie wasn't interfering. She suspected that her friend thought that if she and Owen could make things work out, Connie and Jonathan could learn to get along as well. But too many things would have had to change for that to be possible.

As Jonathan finished dishing up bowls of pasta for everyone, Owen and Maggie helped him bring the meal out to the table.

Once they were all seated, Owen raised his glass in a toast and said, "To friendships renewed."

In most worlds, that would be an uncomplicated statement. In their world, it only created a maelstrom of emotions. For Maggie and Owen, it was dealing with a decades-old family feud between their fathers. For Connie and Jonathan, it was the specter of a years-old romance and the hurt that apparently still lingered over the way they'd parted. But somehow, uneasily, their gazes met over the rims of the goblets, and they reluctantly touched their glasses together.

"To friends," Jonathan repeated.

Connie hoped she and Jonathan could at least be civil with each other now that Owen and Maggie were involved.

"*Mangia*," Jonathan shouted out, and in a flurry of activity, everyone dug into the meal.

Connie took her first bite, although it was tough to swallow past the lump in her throat as she imagined how different life might have been if her fight with Jonathan had never happened. If they had been a couple inviting her friends over for a meal as she had imagined in the game plan she had altered so long ago. But she forced those thoughts away, because they were too difficult to bear. Instead, she focused on the now.

Taking another bite of the pasta, she savored the delicate complexities of the meal Jonathan had prepared. The penne were perfectly al dente while creamy at the same time. The Parmesan Jonathan had freshly grated over the dishes was sharp against the sweetness of the Bolognese sauce. The tomato sauce swam with bits of pancetta, onion, and tender veal that just had your taste buds begging for another forkful.

"Amazing," Maggie said, and Emma immediately added, "I need this recipe. Where did you learn to cook like this?"

Connie still knew Jonathan well enough to recognize that he was self-conscious about the praise. Growing up with his nasty father, praise was something to which he was unaccustomed, so it made him awkward with compliments. That clearly hadn't changed.

With a shrug, Jonathan said nonchalantly, "I had to work with some Italian designers and spent about six weeks in Bologna. While I was there, I decided to take some cooking classes in my free time."

She remembered seeing something in the news about Jonathan's company reaching out to the Italians for their new high-end electric car.

"That was for the Lightning design, right? The new

sports car? I thought I saw the prototype in your drive-way," she said, drawing the attention of everyone at the dinner table. As heat blossomed across her cheeks, she avoided Jonathan's surprised gaze by burying her head in her plate of pasta.

"Yeah, it was. I didn't know you were a gearhead," he said, and there was a hint of need in his voice that drew her gaze back to his.

"I like cars. Since we never had one when I was growing up, they seemed so…special. I like seeing what your company is going to do next," she said, but she didn't admit to something else. That she had pored over every article about what he did and had bought stock in his company after their IPO a few years earlier. She had even toyed with buying one of the earlier hybrid sedans they'd made but had held off because it would only serve to remind her of him every time she drove it.

With a humble nod, he said, "Thank you." As Emma asked him another question, he regaled them with stories from some of his other adventures.

As she met Emma's sharp gaze for the barest moment, Connie realized her friend had bailed her out of what could have been an uncomfortable situation. It made her wonder if her friend somehow knew about her involve-ment with Jonathan years earlier, but she still mouthed a silent *Thank you*.

Dinner moved along smoothly, and the tension in her body eased as they finished the pasta. She was grateful the meal had gone better than she could have imagined, but then Owen suggested that they enjoy the midsum-mer night together, especially since the day's earlier rain and fog had dissipated somewhat.

She hoped her friends would skip the offer to hang out on the great lawn. But when Jonathan proposed making s'mores, both Emma and Maggie quickly agreed. Not wanting to seem unfriendly, especially since the sniping between her and Jonathan had calmed down, she agreed, albeit with reluctance.

She understood Maggie's desire to spend more time with Owen, but Emma's chumminess with Jonathan was a little unsettling. Then again, Emma was a beautiful woman. She had nice curves; lush, wavy red hair; and almond-shaped, green eyes that made her look like a sexy water nymph. What man wouldn't be attracted to her?

As jealousy reared its ugly little head, Connie wrestled it to the mat. She no longer had any interest in Jonathan, and Emma would never betray their friendship in that way. Or so she told herself as they headed outside and Owen set aflame the logs in a fire pit while Jonathan placed the chocolate, graham crackers, marshmallows, and the long barbecue skewers on a table by the fire.

She and Emma grabbed the Adirondack chairs that usually graced the large grass lawn behind the mansion. Jonathan plopped onto the chaise longue next to Connie, leaving Owen and Maggie to sit side by side on a second chaise. They were soon roasting marshmallows over the fire, although it might have been better to say that her very nondomestic friend Maggie was busily incinerating her marshmallow.

Owen soon came to the rescue, and Connie looked toward Emma as Maggie shared a sexy moment with the older Pierce brother.

Jonathan clearly wasn't going to let the heat between the two pass without teasing. "If you two are done with your foreplay over there, maybe you want to take a walk on the beach," he called out.

Connie elbowed him so forcefully that it made him grunt with pain.

"Ouch, what was that for?" he shot back, glaring at her while rubbing his ribs.

She leaned closer to him and whispered beneath her breath, "For being an idiot."

Maggie and Owen took the hint, however, bolted upright, and offered their excuses to the group.

Connie breathed a sigh of relief. With them leaving, it was only natural that she and Emma offer their graceful goodbyes, only her friend didn't seem to be in any kind of rush to leave.

"What's up with the inventing, Jon? Did you get past that design problem making you crazy last month?" Emma asked.

The sting of jealousy lashed Connie again. She only had a moment to wonder how Emma knew about Jonathan's struggles before he said, "I think so. Worked out the kinks. I've got my team checking my specs before we go all in on the prototype."

"That sounds sooo exciting," Emma replied.

Connie echoed the sentiment. "It's interesting to see what new thing you've got going on."

Jonathan smiled and chuckled. "Or is it that you're looking forward to seeing what new thing blew up during testing?" he said and absentmindedly ran his finger across the scar on his face.

That he could be so cavalier about nearly losing his life chilled her gut, and in a strangled voice, she said, "That's not funny, Jon. You could have been killed."

With a half smile, Jonathan met her gaze and said, "Thanks for the concern, Reyes, but I promise you that this time, it's not nearly as dangerous."

Emma's phone chirped to signal a text message, and after a quick look, she winced. "So sorry. Carlo says we have a bridezilla problem, and the event is tomorrow night. Gotta run." She shot up, dialed Carlo, and talked to him as she marched toward the privet hedges separating the two mansions.

Thinking that this would be the perfect time to make an excuse and follow, Connie started to rise, but Jonathan said, "Bailing already? Never took you for a coward."

Damn it. He knew just what button to push. She plopped back down onto the chair. "Not running away, Jon. I just don't see the sense of this."

He arched a sandy brow. "This? You mean calling a truce because we don't want to dump more shit on Maggie and Owen?"

Another button pushed. "I don't want to add to their issues. God knows I'm concerned enough about what's going on with them."

"Me too," he said, then pierced a marshmallow with a skewer and placed it over the fire to prep another s'more.

"You don't seem very worried," she said, wondering how he could be so seemingly blasé about the situation.

He speared her with a glance as sharp as the skewer. "You know I'm just a laid-back surfer dude. I don't sweat the small stuff. Or the big stuff for that matter."

She knew all too well. It was why there was no way she'd get involved with him again, even if she still found him way too attractive. "I can't ignore that this thing with Mags and Owen is bound to cause a lot of hurt," she said.

He surprised her with a grimace, but he tried to hide it by meticulously assembling the s'more as he said, "Worrying won't help. You need to chill. And if it goes south, we'll be there to help pick up the pieces."

For the first time in forever, she couldn't argue with him. "I hope we're both wrong," she said and shot to her feet. "I really should go."

He eyed her intently, as if trying to figure her out, only she hadn't changed in all the years, and apparently, neither had he. That he understood that was confirmed by his next words.

"Go find someone safe, Connie. Someone not like me."

Chapter 2

CONNIE NODDED, MUMBLED A QUICK GOODBYE, AND stalked off, crashing through the gap in the privet hedges and over to the patio for the Sinclair mansion.

Emma was inside, still on the phone with Carlo as she paced back and forth in the area just beyond the french doors leading to the patio. As Connie entered, Emma said, "That sounds like a great idea, Carlo. I'll be over tomorrow morning to help out."

Her friend ended the call and faced her as she stormed through the door.

"Wow, is that your happy face?" Emma teased.

"He hasn't changed one damn bit," Connie said and hurried toward the kitchen, needing something to help her calm down.

"Which is totally cool. It's nice to see someone who's stayed true to themselves. Not many people are that strong," Emma said as she followed Connie into the kitchen and snagged two glasses from a rack that hung over the island.

"You mean there aren't that many people who still haven't grown up," Connie said as she brought over the wine bottle they had opened earlier. She split the last of the wine between them, nearly filling the glasses to the rim before she smacked the empty bottle down on the table.

Emma smirked as she picked up her goblet. "OMG, he still manages to get to you. I figured you were over that summer."

Connie glared at her friend, discomfited by the revelation. "You knew?"

Emma's smirk broadened, and her green eyes twinkled with laughter. With her reddish-blond hair and creamy complexion barely dusted with freckles, she looked even more like a mischievous pixie. "You forget that I deal with couples all the time. It was impossible to miss the sparks between you two. Major heat there."

"Amazing you can see that and not your sparkage with Carlo," Connie parried, annoyed with her friend.

Emma wagged a finger back and forth. "No way, Consuelo Maria. You won't avoid me that easily."

She laughed and mimicked her friend's action. "And pulling out the full name won't work, Emma Anne. Everyone can see how much you like being with Carlo and his family."

Emma grew thoughtful, shrugged, and sipped her wine. "His family is totally awesome. They feed you like there's no tomorrow, and we always laugh and have fun. You know what it's like."

"It wasn't always that way with my family," Connie said. Her grandparents had heartily disapproved of her mother's decision to be a single mom and had done little to help her out for a long time. It had taken years for things to settle down between her mother and her family. Years before her unreliable father had finally left and their family life had become more stable.

"But they finally came around. You were really lucky

they did," Emma said, and it was impossible to miss the sorrow in her voice.

Connie reached out and laid her hand over Emma's. "I know it wasn't easy for you either when your parents broke up."

"Maybe even long before that," Emma admitted.

Which was why, between Connie's dad, who had never really been there, and Emma's, who had but had screwed her and her mother, the two of them had commitment issues. Connie was about to respond when Maggie waltzed into the kitchen, a broad smile on her face and a happy gleam in her gaze. A healthy blush that wasn't from the slight chill of the summer night air painted Maggie's cheeks with color.

"Someone had a wicked good time," Emma kidded.

"It was…nice," Maggie said as she slipped into a chair next to Connie.

Connie peered at Maggie, trying to gauge what had actually happened that night. There was an unmistakable flush on her cheeks, and she had slightly swollen lips. Her blue eyes were as bright as a summer sky, but other than that, there was very little else to clue them in to just how far Maggie and Owen had gone.

"Really? Only just nice?" she asked, narrowing her gaze to scrutinize her friend as she answered.

"Nice," Maggie repeated. A heartbeat later, she jabbed a finger in Connie's direction. "That's all you'll get out of me, so you can stop the interrogation."

Connie knew when to quit. Waving her hands, she said, "Far be it from me to push."

"Which means tag, I'm it," Emma quipped. "Spill, Maggie," she said, waggling her brows suggestively.

"No way. I don't kiss and tell. You guys will just have to be patient," Maggie said, and to prove her point, she shot out of her chair and hurried from the room.

Connie and Emma tracked her departure and then glanced at each other.

"Something major happened," Connie said.

"Definitely. Let's hope it doesn't cause major damage when it all goes south," Emma said.

Connie nodded, worry for her friend twisting her gut. "Not *when*, Emma. *If* it happens," she said, trying to be more optimistic than her friend.

Emma waved her off. "Let's agree to disagree, since I have to hit the sack. Carlo needs help in the morning with wedding plans that have gone off the rails."

With an air kiss and another wave, Emma left her alone in the kitchen. Well, alone except for her very full glass of wine and the last few cookies from the batch Emma had made the night before. She grabbed the plate and her wine, shut off the lights, and headed to her room.

After a quick change into her pajamas, she climbed into bed and grabbed her smartphone to scan through her office emails while she sipped her wine and nibbled on the cookies. By the time she finished scrolling through her emails and deleting spam and nonessential ones with a swipe, she was feeling more relaxed, if not downright sleepy. She put aside her phone, glass, and the empty plate, shut off the light, and snuggled beneath the light blanket. The summer sea breeze from earlier had picked up speed, and its plaintive wail sounded outside the french doors at the far side of the room. Something rattled against the glass, and she sat up, listening more carefully, trying to stop the skitter in her heart at the thought that Jonathan might have climbed up the vine much as he had so many years earlier.

But it wasn't him, just the wind kicking up small debris from the potted plants all along the edge of the balcony. She fought back disappointment. There was no room for that emotion in the heart she had walled up so long ago. Except there was a sensation in that guarded space that hadn't been there in forever. A twinge of both loneliness and hopefulness. Hopefulness she strangled, because she would not let seeing Jonathan again open a crack in that carefully constructed wall.

She had seen what loving the wrong man had done to her mother. The tears her mom had shed until she had finally made the tough decision to let her father leave for good. Connie had been eight when her father had walked out the door and never come back. Much like Jonathan's mother had left him when he was only nine.

It was no wonder that the two of them weren't made for a lasting relationship. They'd never had stability in their lives, and yet...

As she closed her eyes and sleep slipped in, so did dreams of Jonathan and of the love they'd shared. Of the way he could make her laugh or make her burn with need or hold her close and soothe her hurts. She hadn't dreamed of him for so long, but for this night, she let herself imagine how things might have been different between them. The dreams she drifted off to were filled with love, hope, and the promise of happily ever after.

~~~

Jonathan had been too wound up to sleep, as worry about his brother and Connie had dogged his thoughts. So he did what he usually did when slumber eluded him: he worked.

He was sitting on the couch, reviewing some specs on a new fuel cell when his brother came in from the beach, much the way he'd come in the night before. A goofy, happy grin was plastered on his face, and contentment shone in his normally steely gaze.

It had been too long since he'd seen his brother this happy, which was a large part of the reason why Jonathan was so worried. He didn't want his brother to get hurt, and being involved with Maggie…

As he'd told Connie earlier, if that relationship didn't work out, it would mean a world of hurt for his brother. But if it did work out, it could mean a world of hurt for him to be constantly thrown together with the woman who'd stolen his heart that long-ago summer. Which was the second cause of his worrying.

"Looks like you had an epic time, Bro," he said in as neutral a tone as he could muster, not wanting to rain on his brother's parade.

Owen was too perceptive not to notice. "Can it, Jon. I know you think this is crazy."

"Totally crazy, but I see how happy you are with her. Maybe crazy is good for you," Jonathan admitted.

Owen's grin broadened, and he shook his head. "You always say I'm too boring and too responsible, so yeah, maybe crazy is good for me right now. What about you?"

"Me?" He avoided his brother's gaze by looking back at his laptop screen and gesturing toward it. "I've still got a gnarly problem with this new design."

Owen snorted and sat on the edge of the coffee table in front of the couch. "You can't fool me, Li'l Bro. You know what I'm talking about."

If there was one person in all the world who got him, it was Owen. So he figured he owed his brother some honesty. But only *some* honesty, because he wasn't prepared to bare his soul.

"So yeah, I still have some feelings toward Connie. Anger. Fear. Disgust."

"Desire. Friendship. Love, even?" Owen challenged, arching a raven-dark brow in emphasis.

Jonathan shut down his laptop and swiveled on the sofa to face his brother. "Look, I can't lie. She did mean a lot to me, and please notice the past tense there. The two of us are like…oil and water. Birthday suits and porcupines. Me and schedules."

His brother shook his head and chuckled. "That good, huh?"

Jonathan forced a laugh, the proverbial clown hiding the tears inside. "That good. We're just too different, and it's a good thing we found that out before either of us really got hurt."

Owen scrutinized his features, as if searching for the truth behind the smile Jonathan plastered on. With a little dip of his head, he said, "I think it's too late not to be hurt, but I understand. You don't want to be hurt again, like when Mom left. You shut off a part of yourself back then, a part I didn't see come back to life until Connie came around, but then you closed yourself off again."

Jonathan hated that his brother could be so intuitive and so right. "I know how you want this thing with

Maggie to work out, but women and the Pierce men—never a good thing. We seem to lose them more than the Broncos lost Super Bowls—"

"Or the Cubs getting to the World Series, only now they finally won, Li'l Bro. So I guess there's hope. You have to win eventually," Owen said and gave him a brotherly jab on the arm.

Jonathan couldn't help but smile at his brother's hopefulness. "Yeah, you can't always wipe out, and I hope you do win, Owen. I promise I'll be on my best behavior around Connie so as not to rock your boat."

His brother considered him for a long, pregnant moment. "Did it ever occur to you that the last thing Connie wants is your *best* behavior?"

Jonathan couldn't contain his snort and shot to his feet. "No way, dude. The last thing Connie wants is the real me. She'd rather have some three-piece suit with a stick up his ass. No offense intended."

Owen laughed harshly, slapped his knees, and slowly got to his feet as well. "I have a suit but can't seem to find my stick. Considering how uptight you are right now, I guess you know where it went."

He didn't wait for Jonathan to respond, and as Owen left, Jonathan felt no anger. He'd deserved the smackdown, because he had to admit that when it came to Connie, he lost his laid-back attitude. Maybe it was because he cared too much. And much like his brother had seen, he'd tried to stop doing that the day their mother had walked out the door and hadn't returned. Adopting that "I don't give a damn, I do what I want" persona had helped him deal with the overwhelming sense of loss and failure. With their father's constant complaints and disregard. With Connie's lack of belief in him so many years earlier.

He wasn't going to open himself up to the same disappointment, but like he'd told his brother, he also wasn't going to make Owen's life harder by fomenting friction with Maggie's best friend. Come the morning, he'd apologize to his brother, and he'd figure out a way to deal with Connie. He'd dealt with way more difficult problems over the years as he'd built his business. Surely, he could figure out a way to deal with one stubborn, opinionated, and beautiful woman.

Chapter 3

CONNIE REVIEWED THE SETTLEMENT OFFER FOR THE case she had taken on a couple of months earlier. The plaintiff was a relatively new and small company with a fast-growing line of organic baby food products that had caught the attention of the public due to their quality and pricing. The products had also unfortunately drawn the interest of a much larger and more established company, which had launched a line whose packaging and name were just too close for comfort.

Her client had been turned down by various firms because they lacked the finances to launch a lawsuit that was bound to be long and contentious and therefore expensive. The partners in her firm had been leery of taking on the case, but she had convinced them to pursue the action on a contingency basis. She had persuaded her firm's partners into taking on quite a number of cases like this one, small clients who might not otherwise have been able to obtain the kind of representation needed for their legal issues. Luckily, her hunches and hard work had paid off for those clients and the firm. Looking at the settlement agreement with the nice eight-figure payment, she smiled at having accomplished yet another satisfactory outcome.

"Don't you look like the cat that ate the canary," said Alfonso Perez as he swaggered into her office without knocking and took a seat.

Her smile chilled, and she closed the file on her desk, since she didn't like or trust her colleague. They were both in the running for a partnership position, and she didn't doubt Perez would do just about anything to get the spot.

"Good morning, Fonzie," she said, using the nickname she knew he hated. With his gelled hair and cocky attitude, the name fit him.

Some of his earlier swagger deflated, but he tried to recapture it by stretching his legs out and crossing them casually, as if he were in someone's living room and not her office.

"Heard you were working on something big and might need some help," he said and motioned to the thick file on her desk. "Is there anything I can do to assist?"

She shook her head. "I appreciate the offer, but no help needed, thanks." As much as she detested the man, she reminded herself she had to keep it civil between them.

Perez narrowed his gaze and almost sneered as he said, "I know you don't want my advice, but I'll offer it anyway. You should recognize that it's still an old boys' club here. I could help you once I make partner."

Even though he'd managed to slip past her armor with his remark, she shrugged it off. "I guess it remains to be seen which one of us will make partner."

Perez likewise shrugged, but he sat up and leaned toward her. "Rumor has it one of our biggest clients has decided to acquire another equally huge company."

"Who doesn't know that?" she said. The office had been abuzz about the news since Monday morning when the client had called to discuss the possible acquisition with the partner handling their cases.

A sly smile crept onto his face. "Guess who they already asked to be on the team?"

If he'd managed to stick the knife into her before, this question twisted it around painfully. She prided herself on how well she could manage all aspects of mergers and acquisitions, having assisted with several since joining the firm.

Attempting to deflect his hit, she said, "Congrats, Fonzie. But since they're a *smart* old boys' club, it should be obvious to them to include me on the team as well."

To avoid continuing the discussion, she rose and grabbed another file from the cabinet behind her desk. "You'll have to excuse me. I have clients who are waiting for my advice," she said.

Luckily, her colleague took the hint, but not before trying to supposedly be helpful again. "You might want to try and not be such a hard-ass, Reyes. We both know the old guys like that in men but not women."

Rage rose up in her and had her almost shaking as she replied, "You may think that being a man is enough, but that's no substitute for hard work and intelligence, two things with which you're not acquainted."

Perez stormed out of her office, leaving her to her work, but she was just too wired to sit there. She needed to dispel some of the angry energy. Locking away the file that had snagged his interest, she slipped on her suit jacket and grabbed her wristlet. A quick walk to get some food before heading back to eat lunch at her desk was just the thing to wipe away the slimy feeling of a visit from Perez and forget his insinuations.

She hurried out of the office and jumped on the

elevator but was surprised to find it slowing to stop at another floor. Since they'd installed a new system a year ago, it was rare to ride either up or down with anyone else. She wasn't sure the antisocialness of it was a trade-off for the supposed efficiency of the system. Although as the doors opened and Jonathan Pierce stood there, she suddenly wished for greater efficiency.

That he was as shocked was proven by the fact that the doors started to close on his face, but instinct had her reaching out to hit the "Door Open" button. As the doors jerked to a stop and popped wide, he stepped on with a wary smile.

"Connie. I totally forgot this was your building," he said, surprising her again. She hadn't thought he'd kept track of her, and she battled the pleasure that brought.

"And you? I thought your company was downtown," she said and winced, hating that she'd likewise given away that she'd been following the news about him.

As the elevator doors shut and they began to move, he motioned toward the floor they'd just left. "My bean counters are here. I had a meeting with them about financing something new."

"Anything interesting?" She covered her mouth with her hand, a little too late, since the words had burst from her before she could control herself.

A dimpled grin erupted on his face, and his eyes, as blue as the Sea Kiss ocean, glittered with amusement. "I assume that's the gearhead asking," he said.

She was grateful for the out he had provided. "Of course. Who wouldn't covet a car like the Lightning?"

―◦◦◦―

Jonathan wanted to tell her that all she had to do was say the word and he'd have one built and delivered to her, but he knew Connie's pride would never let her accept such an extravagant gift. She had worked hard for everything in her life, and if she wanted a Lightning, with its nearly $200,000 price tag, she'd pay for it herself.

"Thanks. We're stoked about how it turned out," he said as the elevator doors opened and they stepped into the lobby of the building. She hesitated, almost as if she might actually want to extend this chance encounter, and he'd never been one to not seize the moment. "I was just going to grab a bite. What are you up to?"

She fiddled with the wristlet in her hands. "I had planned on working through lunch."

He grinned and pinned her with his gaze. "And that would be more fun than lunch with me because?"

She met his gaze directly, the green of her eyes looking more blue today thanks to the deep midnight color of the suit she wore. "You really are sure of yourself, aren't you?" she teased.

He wanted to say that he was never sure of anything around her, but he wasn't ready to give her that kind of power. At least not yet. "How about it? I promise it will be quick and good—"

"Two words that don't seem well suited together," she shot back, and a becoming stain of color erupted across her cheeks.

"Why, Reyes. Are you flirting with me?" he said, which upped the color on her cheeks exponentially.

"Never. But I did need to get out of the office, and I hate eating alone."

He clasped his hands together and brought them

close to his chest. "How could I refuse an invitation like that?"

"*You* invited *me*, remember?" she said and jabbed him playfully, the way a guy would jab another guy. A defense mechanism, but he wouldn't pass up this opportunity, because he had to restore order to this relationship. For Owen and the relationship with Maggie that was still blossoming nearly two weeks after the dinner they'd all shared in Sea Kiss. For himself, because he felt like this part of his life was incomplete.

"I did invite you first. So is that a yes?"

Chapter 4

THE ITALIAN RESTAURANT WAS ONLY HALF A BLOCK away on Forty-Second Street. It was a place for business lunches and special occasions with colleagues. Definitely not a romantic venue, especially at midday, and Connie was thankful for that.

The eatery was on the busy side, but the host quickly seated them at a corner table in the large, noisy back portion of the restaurant. The ambient chatter toned down the intimate feel of the cozy corner location. The host held the chair closest to the wall out for her, and Jonathan took the spot across from her, but even with that, the table was so small that their knees bumped. She shuffled her chair back until it hit the wall, ending the contact, which, despite its innocence, was way too distracting.

She hid behind her menu while she gathered herself, but when she put it down, she found herself staring into Jonathan's too-intense gaze.

"You seemed a little…angry when I first got on the elevator," he said.

Shrugging, she averted her gaze. "A little. Just some typical office bullshit."

"Care to share?" he asked, but luckily, the waiter came over at that moment to take their orders.

As soon as the orders were placed and the waiter walked away, she shifted the topic to Jonathan, because most men she dealt with were generally more interested in talking about themselves. "What projects were you discussing with your accountants?"

He wagged a finger and shot her a lopsided grin. "Not until I hear what pissed you off."

She'd give him points for that, as much as she didn't want to share. But she shared anyway. "A male colleague who thinks his dick and ethnicity should move him up the corporate ladder."

"Totally wrong on both counts. Besides, you have more balls than he does," Jonathan said as he snagged a slice of focaccia from the bread basket the waiter placed on the table.

She arched a brow, examining him, but he clearly had meant it as a compliment. "Thanks," she said, but just in case, she tacked on, "I think."

"Just telling the truth and definitely a compliment. I know that whatever you want, you'll work hard to get it. Right?"

She nodded, and it made her wonder about him. Whether he had changed despite her comment days earlier to Emma. "What about you? Have you been working hard or hardly working?" she said in a tone that was half-kidding, half-serious.

He broke off a piece of the focaccia and munched on it thoughtfully, scrutinizing her features. It was long moments before he finally said, "Working hard, even though you might doubt that."

She hated that he could read her so easily. Grabbing her water glass, she took a sip before she replied uneasily, "I don't doubt it, but…"

He made a face and looked away for a moment before returning his attention to her. "You're confused, right? Maybe because you don't want to admit that I've changed a little?"

"Maybe," she said quickly and decided it was time to move away from the personal, since it could only bring hurt. "But the gearhead in me definitely wants to know what you're working on."

—⁓—

Jonathan saw through her ploy but didn't challenge her. Despite what she might have thought, he was a patient man, and it would take time to break through the barriers Connie had erected against him. If he even wanted to move past those walls, because being with her was a risky proposition. One that could bring them both a lot of pain.

"I've been talking to an AI company about buying them."

"AI? Artificial intelligence?" she asked to confirm.

He nodded and dipped a piece of the bread into the olive oil he'd poured onto his bread plate. "They've done some epic work, and we need to up our game in that department. I like programming, but it's really not my thing."

"What is your thing? I mean, how did you get into what you do? School was never something you liked," she said.

Her words brought back memories of how they'd parted and the many times his father had chastised him about his grades, which had always been middling but not failing. He clenched his fist on the tabletop, fighting back the pain and anger the memories brought. To his surprise, she laid her hand over his, the gesture comforting. Soothing.

"I'm sorry. I didn't mean it to be accusatory or condemning. The last time we talked, you were working with cars. I really want to know how you decided to do such amazing things with them."

Pleased that she had remembered a bit of that talk after Hurricane Sandy, he decided to accept the olive branch she had offered. He nodded but slipped his hand from beneath hers, because her touch was rousing too many emotions. Too much need.

The waiter whisked in at that moment with their meals. She had opted for a traditional piece of lasagna while he had gone for a less predictable white pizza with prosciutto and a baked egg nestled in the center. The differences spoke volumes about their personalities.

After he had taken a bite and swallowed, he answered her. "School didn't do it for me. All I had to do was look at something and I understood it. So I decided to bail."

—◦◦◦—

"Because you were bored to death," Connie said. As long as she had known Jonathan, he had always been all action guy, and now, she kind of knew why.

He nodded. "It was like sitting in the ocean when it's glassy and you're just stuck out on your board, doing nothing but waiting. I couldn't wait anymore."

"Why cars? There are so many companies out there already," she said and ate her lasagna while she waited for his answer.

With a nonchalant kind of shrug, he said, "Why not? I loved souping up my Jeep, and for some reason, I understood them—how they worked or didn't."

"The car whisperer," she teased and was surprised when he blushed.

"I guess you could say that. After I got back from SoCal, I got my hands on as many books as I could find and started tinkering with various models, trying out different things. I figured out a way to reduce heavy metals in catalytic converters—"

"I know you sold that idea for big bucks," she jumped in.

He nodded and smiled. "With that money, I lined up people who knew more about things like fuel cells, and that blew my mind open to all these sick ideas. The next thing I knew, we were going into business together."

She swallowed the last little bit of her food and said, "And the rest is history, as they say."

With a reluctant bob of his head, he said, "History and the future. We want to improve what we're doing and maybe even expand into other areas."

"Expand?" she wondered aloud, worried that his constant search for new things was Jonathan's way of not staying put.

A hesitant shrug greeted her. "You know what I'm like—a rolling stone. Always on the move. Always chasing something new—"

"So that you won't get bored," she said, which confirmed her earlier fear. She hated the reminder that he wasn't one to stick around. That she shouldn't allow him to get close again, because he'd just get tired of her and move on. Just like her father had moved on time and time again.

Tension crept into the laugh lines around his lips, and shards of ice glittered in his blue gaze. "It makes it easier for you to think that, right? That I'm like your dad? That I'm going to bail on you."

Her heart stuttered a beat, and her throat choked tight. Somehow, she managed to draw a breath and then another. Her voice thick with emotion and her gut chilled with fear and anger, she said, "Does running away make your pain disappear, Jon? Does it make you less afraid of being left behind the way your mom left you?"

She didn't wait for his answer because she didn't want to hear it. No matter how he responded, it would only confirm that any relationship between them was doomed from the start.

———

Jonathan gripped the tabletop to keep from going after her as she dashed out of the restaurant. It would do no good. Worse, it would only make things harder when Maggie and Owen became more involved. He had no doubt now that that was going to happen, and if it did, he'd have to keep a neutral, if not civil, demeanor around Connie, because his brother was too important for him to stay away. Contrary to what Connie thought, he was done running. He was staying put this time.

With a sharp wave at the waiter, he requested the check, paid quickly, and hurried out to Forty-Second Street. It was a lovely early August day, and even if lunch had ended on such a sour note, he intended to make the most of the beautiful weather. Jaywalking across the street, he handed the hotel valet his parking ticket, and within a few minutes, a young man wheeled around his vintage Willys Jeep. He had lovingly restored the vehicle and added a few improvements in the engine and suspension based on the work they had done on the Lightning prototype.

To take advantage of the sunshine, he rolled down the canvas top and secured it. He hopped into the Jeep and took off into Manhattan traffic, tires squealing on the cement. With a quick turn onto Second Avenue, he maneuvered his way to FDR Drive, intending to ride it to his loft in Chelsea. But as his exit neared, he found himself pushing onward, needing to put distance between himself and the city. In no time at all, he was traveling through the Battery Tunnel and into Brooklyn. From the road, he caught sight of Governor's Island and later the Marine Terminal. Farther along, he switched over to the Belt Parkway with its amazing views of the Upper Bay and, in front of him, the Verrazano-Narrows Bridge. As he climbed up and over the bridge, he finally acknowledged that he was escaping to the one place where he always felt at ease: Sea Kiss.

The wind blew in and around the open Jeep, and the sun was strong. Too strong, and he fumbled beside him for his sunglasses and slipped them on. With every mile that he got farther and farther away from the city, the tension left him, and contentment crept in. He reached forward to the tablet he'd worked into the dash of the Jeep, and with a swipe of his finger, music spilled out of the speakers.

He tapped his fingers and sang along to "Losing My Religion" by R.E.M. That song segued into Billy Joel's "Piano Man." The rest of the mix that followed during the hour-plus drive to Sea Kiss was as eclectic but apropos, especially as the sounds of the Beach Boys blasted into the ocean-scented air the second he turned off the parkway. He lowered the volume while he cruised past the edge of Sea Kiss and onto Main Street with its many shops. Thanks to the beauty of the day, the sidewalks were teeming with pedestrians going in and out of shops and toward the beach.

When he reached the boardwalk and Ocean Avenue, he steered away from town and toward the inns, cottages, and homes that sprang up on the beachside once the boardwalk ended. Soon, the Pierce and Sinclair mansions were just a short distance ahead. He smiled, and the heaviness in his heart was lifted away by the sight of the sea and surf and the warmth of the sun on his face.

He pulled into the circular drive of his family's mansion and shut off the engine, then sat there for a long time, staring at his home. Glancing from it to the Sinclair mansion next door. The two houses shared so much history, and yet, to look at them, they seemed so far removed from each other.

Over a hundred years earlier, the two buildings had been small beach cottages used for only three seasons, since they didn't have heat and were boarded up for the winter. Over the years, the cottages had been expanded and heat added, but the real change had occurred during Prohibition. The cottages had been razed and the larger homes had been built, prompting some to speculate that the families had been in cahoots with the bootleggers who brought rum up from the Caribbean or whiskey down from Canada and Ireland.

The small mansions had survived the financial downturn of the Depression and been lovingly maintained by the subsequent generations of Sinclair and Pierce descendants. For a while, the homes had looked rather similar, even after the start of the family feud. But that had all changed when Maggie's mother had died.

The Sinclair mansion had been repainted in bright, lovely colors in honor of Maggie's mom. Months later, the Pierce family home had been redone in shades of deep eggplant and dark charcoal, almost as if the house had gone into mourning. Jonathan and Owen's mother had left a few years later, apparently tired of their father's bitterness, and they had been barred from coming down to Sea Kiss. It had taken nearly a decade before Owen and he had returned, but in all that time, as far as he knew, his father had never once again visited their Jersey Shore home.

As he hopped out of the Jeep and walked to the front door, he kicked at the low edge of neatly trimmed box-wood along the walk, remembering when the beds had once been filled with rolling waves of colorful flowers and not the ruthlessly manicured shrubs. If he'd owned the home, he'd have put the flowers back in and, while he was at it, get rid of the funereal colors.

He entered and went straight to the french doors at the back of the house to get a better look at the surf. It had seemed to be pretty good from what he'd spotted as he drove, but he wanted to confirm it. Sure enough, there were some nice sets of waves breaking, and a few surfers were already out there, floating on the ocean's surface while they waited to catch a wave.

Hurrying to his room, he changed into his board shorts and dashed down the stairs and to the garage to get his board. Within minutes, he was out on the water, flying along the crest of a wave. Sea mist spritzed his face, cooling the heat of the summer sun. As he kicked out, the board went one way, and he sank into the water. He let himself drift below the surface, savoring the refreshing temperature of the midseason ocean before the leash's tug on his ankle reminded him to get his board.

He swam back to the surface, secured his board, and paddled back out to float, waiting for the right wave. He watched the other surfers catch a ride before he paddled into a wave, jumped to his feet, and flew across the sea until the wave died beneath him and he escaped into the ocean again.

Over and over, he surfed until the cold of the water ate into his body heat and his wrinkled fingers warned him that it was time to go in. On shore, he grabbed the towel he had tossed on the sand and rubbed it over his head and chest as he walked to the house. Since he planned on going back out tomorrow, he left the board in the mudroom and strolled to the kitchen table where his smartphone was buzzing away like a swarm of angry bees.

He grimaced, well aware of what that meant. He chastised himself before he picked up, because he should have called to let his partners know how the meeting had gone and that he had decided not to return to the office. Skimming through the messages, he did triage and decided it could all wait until he called his partner.

Dialing Andy, he wrapped the towel around his waist to stop dripping on the floor. His partner answered on the second ring.

"Glad to know you're still alive," Andy said, but there was no sting in his words.

"Sorry, dude. I ran into an old acquaintance at lunch and needed some space afterward."

"I'm guessing a female acquaintance," Andy kidded.

"You guessed right," he said but swept aside further discussion of Connie. "The bean counters agree with our valuation for the AI company. They think we can swing it without selling off any of our shares."

"That's good. Are you down in Sea Kiss?"

Andy had always been able to read him. "Yeah, I am. I'll probably stay through the weekend. Take advantage of being down here to look for a spot for the new research and development center."

There was a long hesitation across the line before Andy said, "Are you really sure about doing this, Jon? About settling down in Sea Kiss?"

He knew his partner meant well, but considering what had happened just hours earlier, it was like having someone pick at a scab that had barely healed over.

"I've never been more sure of anything," he said, his tone determined.

His partner's relieved sigh erupted across the line. "Thank God. While you're at it, please pick up some of those home-buying magazines for me. My wife is already bugging me about finding a place," his partner said.

"Sure thing, Andy. Let's meet with Roscoe on Monday. We need to discuss how we want to approach the AI guys. I know Roscoe has doubts, but I think we should move on them before someone drops in before we do."

"I agree, Jon. See you on Monday. Enjoy the surf," Andy said and hung up.

Monday. Nearly four days away, and at one time, he would have relished so much time off with nothing to do but surf. But lately, lots of free time wasn't as rewarding as it used to be. Especially since he'd sworn off women in the last few months. Like too much free time, the ladies he'd been seeing had been lame.

Connie would probably laugh to know that. Prickly Connie who always seemed to think the worst of him, although he had sensed some softening today at lunch. Some, but not enough. Despite that, she intrigued him far more than any of the women he'd been dating off and on. Mostly off.

The air-conditioning kicked on, raising goose bumps on his damp skin. Time to change and get clean. He lingered in the shower, chasing the chill of the ocean and AC from his body. He ran soapy hands all along his torso, wincing as he skimmed across a raw scrape earned from misjudging the sandy bottom when he'd wiped out.

His mind wandered to years past and Connie. Imagining those days made his knees go weak, but he drove those thoughts away. Satisfying himself with memories of making love with Connie wouldn't fill the empty space inside him that demanded more than physical release. A space that demanded real passion and a real woman with whom to share it. For now, that was still out of reach. But he hoped that was something he could remedy in the future.

I only have to find the right woman, he thought and ignored the little voice that said that he already had. Connie was a part of his past, and he wasn't quite sure that she could ever be part of his future.

Chapter 5

AFTER HER DISTURBING INCIDENT WITH PEREZ AND her confusing lunch with Jonathan, Connie had gone home after work and vowed to relax. Instead, she found herself mindlessly watching television and needing to unload her problems before she exploded. Normally, she would have called Maggie, but her friend already had enough on her plate. She'd had a meeting with Maggie just the day before to discuss whether Maggie could take charge of saving her family's stores, which were on the brink of bankruptcy. Unfortunately, her legal review had only made her friend's life more difficult. Given what was going on in Maggie's personal life with Owen, any mention of Jonathan was impossible. Not to mention that when it came time to talk about men, both Maggie and her other best friend, recently married Tracy, had blinders on and believed that the happily ever after was possible. Unlike Emma and her, who knew better.

She wished that Emma wasn't so far away in Sea Kiss. Sometimes, she even wished she could spend more time there, since she loved the place and the people. There was something about life in a quaint shore town that occasionally appealed to the city girl in her, but it just wasn't in her game plan. Especially now, when she was so close to the partnership she'd been working toward for years. Maybe once she'd earned enough money to finish paying off her family's house and put aside a little nest egg for herself. She had vowed as a child never to be in financial straits again.

Needing to talk to someone, she video-called Emma and was relieved when she picked up.

"Hey, Connie. How's the hotshot lawyer doing today?"

"Not so good, Emma. What about you? Tame any bridezillas lately?" she said with a laugh.

Emma chuckled and shook her head. "Luckily, no bridezillas, so I didn't have to get out the whip. But I can see your day sucked. What's up?"

Connie rolled her eyes and said, "You wouldn't believe." She went on and gave Emma the blow-by-blow on her run-in with her despicable colleague while she finished the last few sips of the wine she'd poured to help herself unwind.

"He sounds like a total dickhead," Emma said when Connie finished. Narrowing her gaze, Emma probed further. "But I can tell that's not the only reason you called, Con. Spill. What's bothering you?"

Drawing in a shaky breath, Connie leaned back against the pillows on her bed. She hesitated before she blurted out, "I had lunch with Jon today."

Emma leaned closer to her phone, as if by doing so, she could get a better picture of her friend. "Jon? As in Jonathan Pierce? Are you freakin' kidding me?"

Connie shook her head. "I wish I were. It's almost like Fate is out to kick my ass. Here I am on the elevator, and *whoosh*, it stops on another floor. It *never* stops on another floor," she almost wailed and went on to tell Emma about the lunch and the miserable way it had ended.

"I accused him of running away, but I was the one

who ran out of there like the place was on fire. *I'm* the one who's afraid of *him*."

Her friend sat back, and Connie realized that Emma was still in her office at the bridal shop where she worked. Guilt slammed into her. "I didn't realize you were stuck at the shop. I don't want to keep you."

"You're not keeping me. Besides, I always have time for a friend. I'm sure you'd be there for me."

She would. Just like she'd come running if one of her other friends needed her. "Thanks, Em."

"You're welcome, but I have to ask: Why does he scare you, Con?"

Dozens of reasons rampaged through her brain, but none of them made it to her mouth. At least, not at first, but then one snuck through. And then another. "Because he makes me want to forget everything I want. Everything I've worked so hard for. And because I'm not sure I can rely on him."

Emma, ever-perceptive and intuitive Emma, was quick to cut to the chase. "He's not your dad, and you're not your mom. Besides, I don't think that your mom regrets the choices she made."

Connie glanced away from her phone, considering the statement. She'd never talked to her mother about her father. About the difficult decision that her mother had made that had changed her life—and Connie's—forever.

At her hesitation, Emma forged ahead. "Trust me, Con. Talk to her about it. You might be surprised at what she says."

I might be. Nodding, she said, "Thanks for listening."

"I wish I could help more, but I'm the last person on the face of this earth to give advice about men."

While Emma's comment was not all that far off the mark, Connie recognized when her friend needed a pep talk. "You may think that, but you're a great wedding planner because you can see past all the bullshit to what people really feel."

Emma chuckled, raised a finger perfectly manicured in Barbie pink, and wiggled it back and forth. "Are you this obvious in court? Do you get a lot of objections about leading the witness?"

Smiling, Connie mimicked someone walking with her fingers. "Leading you right to your fabulous partner Carlo."

"He's not my partner," Emma shot back.

"Friend?" Connie pressed.

"Well, yes, but in a platonic way," Emma clarified.

Connie shook her head. "A shame. He's prime, Emma. I'm assuming you've at least noticed that about him."

With a huff and a glare, Emma said, "For sure. I'm not dead, you know."

"Glad to hear that. Maybe you should take some of your own advice and talk to your mom about what happened with your dad."

Connie waited for the explosion that usually followed any mention of Emma's father, but surprisingly, her friend's reply was measured and controlled. Only a slight nervous tremble in her voice provided any clue to her real emotions.

"Not possible. I'm still too hurt and angry."

"Which is keeping you from moving on." Connie did the walking fingers again and added, "And going right to Carlo. He loves you. Or at least he would if you let him."

Emma's long silence was worrisome, but then she nodded and said, "I promise I'll think about it, but only if you swear you'll talk to your mom."

She would. Eventually, but not now, when her feelings were so unsettled. "You're a tough negotiator, Em. I promise."

An impish grin erupted on her friend's face. "Score another one for the bridezilla tamer. Love you, Con."

"Love you, Em."

—⁓—

Jonathan paced back and forth across the kitchen, edgy energy racing across his nerve endings. A morning spent surfing hadn't help tire out that energy. Skipping his morning coffees hadn't either. That had only made him grumpy and given him a massive caffeine withdrawal headache. He was craving a huge mug of java, and while he could make it at the fancy coffee machine Owen had purchased because Maggie was a coffee addict, he had to get rid of his restlessness and the feeling that the house was just too big and too empty. For a second, the walls started closing in on him the way they had when Owen told him that their mom had left. But only for a too-long second as he wrestled back the desire to escape.

It was time to stop running. It was time to settle down for a bit, if only to be there for his brother if it all went south. He hoped for Owen's sake that it didn't, but if it did, he planned on supporting his brother just like his brother had taken care of him.

He grabbed the keys for the house and stuffed them into the pocket of his khaki shorts. Snagging a pair of sunglasses to guard against the intense midday sun, he hurried out the french doors, across the great lawn behind the mansion, and down the short boardwalk, over the dunes, and to the beach. It was just a mile or so walk to the jetty and lighthouse that marked the farthest part of Sea Kiss. Barely ten minutes later, he'd worked up a healthy sweat thanks to the hot summer day, but a sharp breeze sweeping along the river inlet by the jetty quickly cooled him down.

He strolled past the Main Street inns and houses nearest to the beach and boardwalk and up to the center of the business district and the shops there. The enticing smell of burgers grilling wafted out of the corner luncheonette, making his stomach growl, but first, he had to have his coffee. Pushing past the restaurant, he walked by a real estate office, hardware store, and the local surf and skate shop where he got his wax, clothes, and shoes, as well as his favorite longboard. He should have ridden that skateboard to town. Maybe he'd pick up a new one on his way back.

A cheese shop came next, tempting him yet again, but like his brother, he had a dangerous sweet tooth and walked into the adjacent bake shop. He fixed himself the largest coffee they had and added a glazed donut and chocolate cigar to the mix. He munched and sipped as he kept walking up to Fireman's Park in the center of town, where he sat on a bench and watched the various dogs and their pet parents who were out enjoying the glorious day. At one corner of the park square, a local animal shelter had set up a stand, and after he finished his sweet treats, he strolled over. A trio of cages held an assortment of kittens for adoption, but as cute as they were, he had always been a dog kind of guy.

"They've got all their shots and are ready to go home with a special someone," one of the shelter ladies said cheerfully.

He smiled but demurred. "I'm not really into kittens." Basically because they grew up to be cats, not that there was anything wrong with that.

"It's your lucky day then. We've got quite a number of puppies and dogs available at the shelter today. It's just a few blocks away," she replied, still bubbling with happy.

It made him wonder if it was an animal thing, the joyfulness and optimism. He'd read more than one article about all the benefits of having a pet. As one kitten peered at him from the cage and meowed playfully, he had to confess that something inside him lightened a little, which for some reason had him saying, "I know where it is, thanks."

He pivoted on his heel, and instead of heading back through town, he found himself walking in the direction of the shelter where, a few minutes later, another perky volunteer was guiding him past a row of cages filled with puppies. Cute, fluffy, hyper, little puppies yipping and yapping as he strolled by.

Despite his sudden and unexpected desire to not feel so alone, not that he was ready to acknowledge that emotion outright, something about the puppies failed to call to him.

"Aren't they sooo cute?" the too-energetic young woman said with a barely contained squeal in her voice that he was certain would shatter glass at full volume. The perpetual happiness of everyone connected with the shelter only seemed to reinforce that maybe the pets were responsible for the constant state of joyfulness.

Which kept him advancing along the aisle to the pens with the older dogs that had been given up for adoption. The sad looks on some of them had his mind playing a woeful Sarah McLachlan soundtrack in his head until he got to one cage where a small, cream-and-white terrier ambled to the cage door. The dog leaned one paw on the wire and climbed up into a jaunty kind of position. With what looked like a wry grin, the dog gave one short, demanding bark.

"This is Muffin. His owners only had him for a few months when they had to give him up on account of allergies, so he's kind of still a puppy."

With a yip, Muffin confirmed her statement, only he didn't seem much like a Muffin to Jonathan. He had too much attitude to be called Muffin. *And what kind of name is that for a boy dog anyway?* Jonathan thought as the volunteer, sensing interest, opened the cage and set Muffin on the floor.

The pup took one look at him, obediently sat at a spot right beside his feet, and peered up at him in an adoring way that filled him with warmth and all kinds of gooey feelings that he refused to admit. He bent and rubbed the dog's head. The fur was soft and curly beneath his hand. As the dog continued to gaze at him, brown eyes gleaming with admiration and possibly love, he was a goner.

"I don't have to call him Muffin, do I?" he said as he scooped up the terrier.

"Actually, some people recommend changing the name to get past the dog's past history, which may be negative," the young woman said as she petted Muffin, but then she finally gave Jonathan her attention. Her very female attention if he was reading the vibes right.

While she was a looker, he had no interest in responding to her subtle invitation.

"Thanks. I guess there's some paperwork we need to do," he said and shoved off, eager to finish the adoption and be on the way.

At the front desk, he filled out assorted documents and bought a collar, ID, leash, and squeeze toy. A different young woman at the desk handed him a can and a few small packets of dog food to hold him over until he got settled.

Muffin obediently sat there as Jonathan secured the collar and ID around his neck and clipped on the leash. "You're a good boy, aren't you?" he said and rubbed a spot behind the dog's floppy ear.

The dog barked what sounded like a yes, and Jonathan smiled. "Come on, boy."

In no time, they had walked the few blocks back to Main Street, Muffin strolling beside him as if they had done it dozens of times before. He felt so secure with the pup that he walked with him into the surf and skate shop where the young owner, Sammie, immediately gushed over the dog.

"He's adorable," Sammie said and glanced at Jonathan as he stood beside the dog. "What's his name?"

"Muffin," he said, deadpan.

Sammie rolled her eyes in disbelief. "No way, Jon. He's *so* not a Muffin."

"For sure," he said and gestured to the handcrafted longboard hanging on a wooden display stand. The maple and mahogany board with the deep-red wheels had caught his eye on another visit. "Can you ring that one up for me, Sammie?"

"My pleasure. Do you want to keep those wheels, or can I change them out for you?" she asked as she walked over to the register.

"These are good for now, right, Dudley?" he said, surprising himself with the name that sprang up in his mind and with the happy yip the dog gave in reply.

Sammie laughed as she rang up the purchase. "I guess he's got his new name."

"I guess," he said. Once they were out on the sidewalk, he placed the skateboard down to try it out, and to his surprise, Dudley jumped up onto the very front of the longboard. Dudley gave a look over his shoulder that seemed to say *Come on* and Jonathan jumped on the board and pedaled off for home.

Home.

He almost stopped short, since it had been a long time since he'd thought of the shore house as home, although he was always drawn there to find peace. His loft in Manhattan was, for the most part, a place where he spent time between trips for work and time in Sea Kiss. With new insight, he said, "Come on, Dudley. We're going home."

Chapter 6

WHEN THE PATIO OF MAGGIE'S NEW YORK TOWN house started spinning into an Impressionistic blur of emerald grass, rusty brick, and pink, purple, and blue flower petals, Connie decided that maybe the last margarita had been one too many. Especially when combined with the cosmos she and Maggie had shared over dinner as they lamented the state of their lives.

After a few weeks of dating that had been leading up to the big moment, Maggie had blown off the all-important first weekend alone at the Shore with Owen.

Connie's firm had blown off her participation in the big acquisition Perez had rubbed in her face days earlier. It was the second time in as many months that she'd been passed over to work on an important matter.

"Fuckin' men," she said after a prolonged silence where she suspected Maggie might have passed out or fallen asleep. Either was a possibility given the liquor they'd imbibed and the lateness of the hour.

"We've got to cut the Pierce boys some slack," Maggie said drowsily.

"Really? Says the woman who bailed on the very delicious Owen Pierce this weekend," she parried, leaning forward to search her friend's features in the dim light in the garden. A mistake, since that only made the world around her spin even faster, creating nausea-inducing blobs of colors. Taking a deep breath, she tamped down the whirl and found her friend scrutinizing her intently.

"Jon is no slacker in the looks department either."

"Just all the other departments," Connie said and leaned back in the Adirondack chair that was too much like the chairs they'd shared with the Pierce boys just a couple of weeks earlier.

"Liar," Maggie retorted.

"Not lying. Hotness is no substitute for someone who will be there for you. I need someone who isn't always looking for any excuse to leave."

Maggie turned in her chair and cursed when she knocked her knee against the wooden frame. "Darn it, that hurt."

"Just like it'll hurt if I let myself have any feelings for Jonathan Pierce," Connie emphasized.

"Or if you let yourself fall for him *again*," Maggie said.

"No way! You knew too! When? How?" she said, the shock of her friend's revelation like an ice-cold bucket of water, driving away some of her alcohol-induced numbness. She'd never suspected that both Emma and Maggie had been wise to her summer fling with Jonathan.

"Owen told me the night he climbed up the wisteria vine to see me a few weeks ago. He said Jon used to do that when the two of you were a thing. Back in college. What happened?" Maggie asked. It was clear she was truly interested in helping and not just having Connie relive old hurts.

"Shit happened. I was going back to college. Jon wasn't. I had plans for my life. Jon didn't," she said matter-of-factly, although there was nothing so cut-and-dried about what had occurred so long ago.

"He's changed," Maggie said in defense, both surprising Connie and annoying her that Maggie would be siding with Jonathan.

"He hasn't changed, Mags. He's still a rebel even if he owns a billion-dollar business. Just look at everything in the papers. At his escapades. The only thing he's changed is the magnitude of the trouble he gets into." Her volume had risen with each word, to the point that by the time she finished, her head throbbed from the sound. Rubbing her temple, she said, "I'm sorry. I think it's time I got some sleep. And it's getting chilly out here."

The mid-August day had been warm, but after the sun had gone down, the temperature had done an unseasonable drop. With the cold as an excuse, Connie didn't wait for Maggie to respond and rushed into the house and up to the room that was usually hers when she stayed over. Since she had changed into comfortable clothes when they'd first gotten to her friend's town house, she just plopped onto the bed and closed her eyes. She willed away the sensation of spinning and wished she could just as easily force away thoughts of Jonathan.

Only it wasn't as easy. Especially as she recalled the way he'd looked as she'd stormed out of the restaurant. There had been pain there. Hurt she hadn't meant to cause, but of course, it seemed like that's the one thing that always happened when they were together. They caused each other hurt because neither of them was really, truly whole. Neither of them really knew what it was like to have a healthy relationship with someone of the opposite sex. It was why she'd avoided commitment for so long by dedicating herself to her career. She suspected, based on the many photos of Jonathan with an assortment of women on his arm, that he'd avoided relationships in a different way—by skipping from woman to woman.

Regardless, Jonathan could only bring her pain, so it was best that she plan and adapt to keep her life on course. But as she drifted off to sleep, a little voice in her head that sounded way too much like Jonathan said, "God laughs at those who make plans."

"Those who fail to plan, plan to fail," Connie retorted, which effectively silenced that annoying little voice but left her feeling empty inside.

—◆◇◆—

Jonathan watched as Owen devoured most of the grass-fed steak they'd bought at the butcher earlier that day during their stroll through town. The stroll had led to an enlightening talk after his brother had arrived on the doorstep, moaning about having been stood up by Maggie for their weekend get-together. After weeks of dating, spending a weekend in Sea Kiss was supposed to have moved their relationship to the next level.

Or at least, that's what Owen had been expecting. Maggie not so much apparently.

"Hungry?" Jonathan teased and sipped his wine. He put down his glass to cut a piece off his perfectly done, incredibly tender steak and offered up the little bit of meat to his pup, who was sitting at his feet patiently. Dudley yipped excitedly and wolfed down the treat, then sat there patiently waiting for another piece. His furry little face was so hopeful as he gazed up at Jonathan that it was impossible to resist. "You know too many table scraps aren't good for you," Jonathan said as he cut off another piece of the meat, hoping Owen would let it pass that he was apparently having a conversation with his dog.

Jonathan had prepared the steak flawlessly, if he had to say so himself, since his brother had barely mumbled a word during dinner. At least Owen's appetite hadn't been affected by Maggie canceling their weekend plans, but there was no denying based on their earlier talk that Owen was bothered by her desertion.

Like you're bothered by Connie? his annoying inner self asked as he fed Dudley yet another bite from his plate.

Finishing his steak, he pushed away his plate and grabbed his wine. He reached down to stroke Dudley's head. Jonathan could have sworn that his little dog smiled at him before lying down by his feet with a contented sigh. Peering over the rim of the glass, he considered his brother before he took another sip and then asked, "So she bailed on you. What are you going to do about it?"

Owen finally looked up from his food and paused with his fork halfway up to his mouth. "It?" he asked obtusely.

"Maggie. Dad," he said. "Seems to me it's a lose-lose situation any which way."

"I cannot argue with that, Li'l Bro," Owen said around a mouthful of steak. Then he jabbed his fork in Jonathan's direction. "You know what that old bastard said to me about Maggie? That I should fuck her, marry her, and get the properties he thinks they cheated him out of. All he ever thinks about is getting even with the Sinclairs."

"And you? What's your plan for one Sinclair in particular?" Jon kidded.

Owen arched a dark brow and laid down his fork. He picked up his glass and took a big swallow. His hand shook as he settled the glass on the tablecloth. "I'm almost afraid to say this, but I want to do forever with Maggie. Maybe it seems too soon to say that—"

Jonathan shook his head. "Negatory. Even as kids, you clicked. I had a hunch you'd end up together."

Owen blew out a harsh chuckle. "Wishful thinking when I can't even get the lady to spend some serious time with me."

"Patience, Bro. Rome wasn't built in a day," Jonathan urged.

His brother snorted even louder. "That's rich coming from you. You never wait to go after what you want. Do you know that the old bastard even said I should be more like you that way?"

"No way!" Jonathan said, surprised his father thought he had any redeeming qualities. But regardless, he had been itching for something different in his life lately. "That was the old me. The new me is going to be more like you," he reminded Owen.

"Boring and responsible?" his brother challenged with another arch of his brow.

Jonathan laughed. "More chill. Settled, you know."

His brother wagged his head so hard, Jonathan worried he might give himself whiplash. "You say you're doing that," Owen said.

"I *am*. Why the hell do people think I can't?" Jonathan replied, sudden anger laced through his words. At that, Dudley's ears perked up, and the pup sat up in an attitude of alertness. Jonathan thought Dudley was gazing at him with a worried look, wondering where the threat was, so he patted the dog's head to reassure him all was okay and resolved to stay chill in front of the dog. He'd never imagined that being a pet parent was going to require so much mindfulness.

Shame filled his brother's features. "I'm sorry, Jon. You've always done what you've said you'd do. And I appreciate that I'm part of the reason you're staying put."

"Damn straight. You've always been my wingman. I am going to be here for you in case things don't work out," he said, echoing what he had told his brother earlier that day as they'd strolled through Sea Kiss.

Owen stared at him intently, a weird kind of look on his face as he said, "And what if things do work out?"

He was taken aback for a second about what his brother meant, but then it hit him as hard as a speeding freight train. "You mean Connie."

Owen nodded. "I mean Connie. After all, if it gets really serious with Maggie, you're bound to have to spend time with her. They're like sisters, you know."

He knew, Lord, how he knew. From the night of the dinner that the group had shared weeks earlier, he'd suspected that he was doomed to spend time with Connie when this thing with Maggie and Owen became more permanent.

"It may get a little gnarly, but I can handle her," he said, but even as he uttered those words, it was almost like he was trying to convince himself of the truth of them. That he could handle a woman who alternately made him angry as sin, weak with need, and joyful as the summer sun in a crystal-blue sky.

"It's only fair, considering all that you've done for me," Jonathan added, thinking of the many times Owen had offered support after their mom had left. Remembering how, time after time, his big brother had stood up for him or deflected his father's anger until the day that Jonathan had finally decided to leave. Even after that, Owen had been supportive, handling the family business and his father, both difficult jobs.

"I'm your brother. I'd do anything for you, Jon. You should know that."

Jon grinned. "I do, Bro. Now how about those cannolis we picked up for dessert before this gets way too serious?"

Barely a week earlier, Connie had counseled Maggie to stand up to her father so she could save the family retail stores that were almost on the verge of bankruptcy thanks to his mismanagement. Maggie's father, Bryce Sinclair, had been running the stores just like he imagined his dear departed wife would. Only, times had changed, but Bryce refused to do so, which had severely impacted the viability of the business.

The one way Maggie could take steps to save the stores was to confront her father. She had done so and was already implementing a wide series of ideas to save not only her legacy, but also the hundreds of jobs for the people who worked at the stores.

Just like her friend had done, it was time for Connie

to face the partner for whom she worked and convince him that she belonged on the team responsible for their client's acquisition. Which was why she'd scheduled a meeting with him to discuss the project.

"Mr. Goodwyn will see you now," his assistant advised.

Connie rose from her chair, straightened her suit jacket, and entered Mr. Goodwyn's office.

He was seated at his massive desk in his even more massive corner office. Size apparently did matter in the legal world.

"Connie. What can I do for you today?" he said, barely raising his gaze from the file in front of him. As she walked toward him, he continued flipping papers and didn't rise as she approached him. With a half glance, he gestured to one of the chairs in front of his desk.

She went to sit on the chair, but she kept on going lower and lower, since the height of the chair was anything but normal. It took only a second to realize that the chair's configuration forced her to look at her colleague the way a penitent might gaze skyward at salvation. A power play for sure, but she'd deal with it.

"I wanted to discuss the VCZ project," she said, her tone measured and neutral. Nothing set Goodwyn off faster than the thought that he was being challenged.

He finally gave her his full attention. He leaned back, placed his elbows on the arms of the leather chair, and steepled his hands before his mouth in what she knew to be his carefully rehearsed pensive pose. The one that said "I'm listening to you" when, in general, he rarely listened to anyone.

Despite that, she still had to try to get her point across.

"I know you've chosen a team, but I think I have a lot that I could contribute on this particular project."

"Do you now? Please go on," he said, his gaze skewering her as if she were a butterfly pinned to a collector's board.

"I've worked on a number of VCZ's past projects and am well aware of their concerns about possible acquisitions. I'm familiar with their due diligence requirements, and I believe I could be an asset with this particular third party, since I interned in a lab environment when I was doing my double major in college. It may provide an edge in some situations."

"And you believe Mr. Perez lacks your experience?" he said, deadpan.

While she would like nothing better than to throw Perez under the bus, that was just not her style. She intended to prove herself the worthier candidate for partnership. It was up to Perez to do the same or fail on his own.

"I'd rather discuss my experience, sir. VCZ is an important client, and I know that what you want is for them to be well represented."

"And you think you're a better choice than Mr. Perez?" he pressed, but she refused to take the bait.

"I am not questioning your choice, sir. All I'm asking for is a chance to prove—"

"That you're a worthy candidate for partnership. Isn't that what we're really discussing here?" he replied, anger growing in his voice.

She was blowing it big time, because she'd underestimated the size of Goodwyn's ego and that he'd view her request as a challenge. "I didn't intend for this to be that discussion, and I apologize if that's the way I came across. I understand that we'll have that discussion when the time is right."

"Rather presumptuous of you, isn't it? That we'll ever have that discussion?"

Damn it, she was crashing and burning. Worse yet, the sting of tears warned her not to let him get to her.

"I had hoped we would," she said, her voice choked as she fought back disappointment.

"Getting emotional, Ms. Reyes? Displaying emotion in the legal world is never good. It's a sign of weakness."

Displaying emotion like a woman, because women were weak, was what the dumb-ass was saying. And while she might be a woman, she was anything but weak. Stiffening her spine, she drew in a long inhale and slowly rose from her chair. "I'm sorry that you can't see my worth to the firm. I hope the other partners will. As for the VCZ project, I *am* a good candidate to assist, but if that's not your desire, I'll abide by that choice. I am a team player after all."

Goodwyn surprised her by shooting out of his chair, his face growing a deeper shade of red by the second as he jabbed a finger at his chest and said, "It is *my* choice, because it's *my* client and *my* firm. If you think the other partners will dare to challenge me, you've made a serious miscalculation."

She raised her chin a defiant inch and nodded. "Understood, Mr. Goodwyn. Thank you for taking the time to speak with me."

Pivoting on her high heel, she ignored his sputtered protest about her insolence and marched out of his office, head held high even though what she wanted to do was curl into a ball and cry. She would not cry. There was no crying in the legal world.

But as she entered her office and closed the door behind her, the tears cascaded down her cheeks. She leaned against the door, the only place for privacy in her glass-walled prison, and let the tears come. When the flood finally abated, she dashed the evidence away. After a few deep breaths, she mustered enough control to be able to return to her desk and the work waiting there.

Work was what she did. It was what would get her to what she wanted: a partnership and financial independence. But after the meeting just minutes earlier, she doubted whether that would be possible at Brewster, Goodwyn, and Smith. But she wasn't a quitter. Partnerships weren't generally announced until the end of the year, so she still had time to make her plan work.

She had to, because she had no backup plan, and that was totally unlike her. In her brain, she heard challenging laughter and decided that maybe it was time she made one.

Chapter 7

ON MONDAY MORNING, JONATHAN PATIENTLY WALKED Dudley along the edges of the great lawn, waiting for him to do his thing. Over and over, the pup sniffed and explored, but nothing happened.

Jonathan wasn't normally one to live by the clock, but he had committed to a morning meeting, and between feeding Dudley and walking him, he was running late, but he also knew his pup couldn't keep it in for the nearly two-hour drive back to the city.

He sucked it up, and after another fifteen minutes of Dudley darting around, the little dog finally relieved himself. As Jonathan scooped it up, he grimaced at the smell.

"Dude, what did you eat?" he kidded. *Besides one of my fave pairs of flip-flops*, he thought.

Dudley looked up at him and seemed almost upset by his comment.

"Just kidding, man," he said and petted the pup's head, earning a grin and lick of his hand, easing his concern that Dudley was somehow upset.

He wondered if this uncertainty and worry was what new parents felt—without the shoe eating of course.

It's called being responsible, the annoying voice in his head that sounded too much like his father said, but Jonathan ignored it.

He disposed of the poop bag in the garbage can and

walked Dudley around to the driveway where the Jeep was parked. He quickly harnessed Dudley into the passenger seat. The pup grinned and leaned out the open window, tongue lolling, already eagerly anticipating the ride.

Jonathan smiled and sped off for the return to Manhattan and the meeting with his partners. Reluctantly leaving, but also filled with a sense of relief. He hadn't wanted to abandon Sea Kiss quite so soon, and yet the place that had brought him such peace in the past seemed empty at times.

Dudley's presence and Owen's had abated that hole in his heart to some degree over the last few days. But there was a growing sense of restlessness inside him when he was in Sea Kiss. Maybe it was the memories that the family mansion brought. Memories of the time spent there with their mother before she'd just up and left, never to return.

He forced away that negativity as he sat in his office after he arrived in the city, closed his eyes, and brought back a happier picture of him, Maggie, and Owen playing on the beach. Racing through the wash of the ocean before returning to salvage a sand castle being threatened by the waves. The picture morphed, and suddenly, it was him and Connie, chasing each other at the water's edge. Falling into the surf and coming up wrapped around each other, laughing. Kissing. He smiled and held on to that happy tableau and added one of Dudley playfully chasing a tennis ball into the ocean.

"Daydreaming?" said his partner Andy as he walked into Jonathan's office where Dudley was tucked into a new doggie bed behind Jonathan's desk.

At Andy's entrance, Dudley's ears perked up, and the pup got to his feet and let out a little bark as if saying hello. He trotted right over to Andy and began to sniff his shoes.

"Yep," Jonathan said with no trace of guilt, because Andy wasn't normally judgmental. It was one of the reasons why they worked so well together.

"And who's this guy?" Andy said as Dudley rolled over for a belly rub and whimpered in bliss as Andy complied.

"My new sidekick. His name is Dudley," Jonathan said and smiled.

"So besides picking up this chick magnet, any luck on finding a location for the new building?" Andy asked as he stood and then plopped into a chair before Jonathan's desk.

Jonathan ignored the comment about Dudley as the dog settled back into his bed. He leaned forward and yanked his smartphone from his back pocket. "My brother gave me the name of a local real estate agent, and they sent me some possible properties this morning. I'll send you and Roscoe the email so we can discuss them later."

"And then you'll go back down and take a look at them?" Andy asked.

"I'm stoked about finding a place," he admitted without hesitation.

"I'm truly sensing something different here. I know you said you were serious about this, and I kind of think you truly are," his partner said, but with no hint of censure. They knew each other too well for that, and besides, Andy and Roscoe knew that it was his ideas and drive that put bread on the table. Not that he'd ever use that to get his way.

"It's time to get a little more settled, and I'm a surfer dude at heart. Sea Kiss is home to me," he said, finally admitting out loud what had been in his heart for a long time.

His partner shook his head from side to side and ran a hand through the ginger-colored springs of his curly hair. "All I can say is that I'm looking forward to some time on the Jersey Shore."

Jonathan chuckled. "Believe me, dude, you're going to love it."

"I guess we'll have to figure out how this is going to work. There are some folks who'll want to join you down in Sea Kiss, like me. But some may want to stay in the city, like Roscoe."

He nodded. "It's totally up to each person what they want to do. Whatever positions are changed by the move, we'll hire to fill the vacancies. It's time to expand in any case, now that we're adding the AI company to the mix. Maybe we can even meld the two workforces. Offer more work from home for some of the programming people."

Andy smiled and nodded. "It sounds like a plan, Jon. We can discuss it more at this morning's meeting."

Without waiting for his reply, Andy strolled out of Jonathan's office, leaving him to firm up his plans for all that was happening in his life.

Plans, he thought with some chagrin. Some people might say that his life so far had been one big, unscripted joy ride, and yet he knew that even chaos had order. It was just that some people couldn't see past the apparent randomness.

Like Connie hadn't been able to see it so many years

earlier. He drove that thought away, because it was use-less to think about her. She was in the past, and while the future might throw them together again, he held out no hope that she could see his determination and under-stand it as well.

———⁊⁊⁊———

The plans in Connie's life were like soap bubbles lately, floating haphazardly along the wind until the most delicate of touches made them burst. She had barely formulated a campaign for what she would do about Goodwyn and her seemingly diminishing partnership chances when Maggie had popped yet another bubble by announcing that she was going to marry Owen Pierce barely a couple of days after skipping out on their week-end plans. Only it wasn't your everyday "we love you, we want to be together" kind of marriage plan. It was more like a loan agreement, with lots of crossed *t*'s and dotted *i*'s involving Maggie's lawyer.

Connie recognized the logic of a prenuptial agree-ment, but despite that, she worried that there was some-thing inherently wrong and problematic about starting a marriage based on a business deal. Marriage was sup-posed to be about love and respect, and the romantic Connie who rarely emerged feared that Maggie was headed for heartache. But there was little she could do as she sat in Maggie's Sea Kiss home a week after the announcement and the signing of the prenup. Maggie stood in front of a cheval mirror and modeled the wed-ding dress that had been her great-grandmother's and that Maggie's mom had worn over thirty years earlier to get married.

"You look just like your mother on her wedding day," said Mrs. Patrick, who was not only the mansion's housekeeper, but also like a grandmother to Maggie. The older woman covered her mouth with her hand, tears glimmering in her eyes.

Maggie looked into the mirror, and her gaze skipped to Tracy, their other best friend who had driven in from Princeton to help with all the wedding prep, and then to Emma and finally to Connie. "What do you think?" Maggie asked.

"Perfect," they all said in unison.

"Perfect," Maggie repeated, and Mrs. Patrick shooed her out of the kitchen and into her private quarters so she could pin the dress in order to make some minor alterations to the vintage wedding gown.

As Maggie walked away, Connie peered at Emma and noted she had the same forced happy face that Connie had plastered on that morning for the wedding planning meeting with new fiancé Owen and best man Jonathan, as well Emma's partner, Carlo. Worse, pressure was building in Connie's head and threatening to release the emotions she had managed to dam up so far. Sucking in a deep breath, she blurted out in a choked whisper, "She looked so happy and so beautiful."

Emma nodded and swiped at a tear as it escaped. "She did, and it's all going to work out."

Tracy wrapped an arm around Emma's shoulders and hugged her tight. "She's going to be just fine."

Tracy's platitude overloaded Connie's dam and opened the first crack. The words spilled from Connie in a rush. "Says the woman who's only been married for a few months and is already in marriage counseling."

Tracy's lips thinned into a knife-sharp slash. "I'll forgive your bitchiness because I can only guess at what you're feeling right now. You and Maggie have always been like this," she said, held up her hand, and crossed two fingers. "Maggie's a smart woman, and while this all might seem a bit rushed—"

"That's an understatement. Engaged in just a few weeks. Wedding in less than a month," Emma said.

"She'll be fine," Tracy insisted.

Connie didn't share Tracy's certainty, and as she glanced at Emma, it was obvious her other friend felt the same.

Mustering her reserve, Connie tried to shore up the dam keeping her emotions in check and managed to somehow last through dinner that night and the wine they shared afterward out on the patio beneath a starlit sky on the warm summer night. After one glass, Tracy excused herself to drive home, since she and her new husband had early morning plans for the next day. As she hugged Tracy goodbye, Connie whispered, "I'm sorry for what I said before. I know you're really trying hard to make things work."

"Thank you. If you need to talk, you know I'm here for you," Tracy said.

Emma, Maggie, and Connie lingered on the patio for a little longer, but Emma was next to go, since she had to get going on the wedding plans the next day. While she would normally have stayed over, this night, she was going back to her Sea Kiss cottage so she could get an early start in the morning.

Which left Connie and Maggie, her best friend in the whole world, sitting out on the lawn. Maggie, her best fuckin' friend forever. A woman whom she thought she'd understood. Because her friend had a lot to lose besides her heart, she couldn't ignore the worry in her gut about what Maggie planned to do. Leaning close, she twined her fingers with Maggie's and whispered, "Are you sure about this, Mags?"

Her friend smiled almost indulgently. "I am, but I know you have lots of doubts."

"I do, and I hope you know it's only because I love you and want you to be happy."

Maggie offered a sympathetic squeeze of Connie's hand. "Owen's a good guy. I trust him. I care for him, and he makes me happy. I've been afraid to admit it to myself for a while, but I haven't been happy in a long time."

"Until Owen," Connie chimed in.

"Until Owen," Maggie repeated, but then quickly added, "Just like you haven't been happy since Jon said goodbye that summer. After he left, you set a course as straight as a ruler, and you haven't detoured once, but sometimes, you have to. Sometimes, your happiness lies along a different path."

In the almost infinite moment that followed her words, the truth in them broke open the dam, and the feelings swirling inside Connie cascaded free. Somehow, she managed to choke out, "I love you, Maggie, and I hope it all works out for you. But what I want is way different from what you think I want."

Maggie squeezed her hand again and said, "No matter what, I'll be here for you."

She'd never doubted Maggie's word or her resolve, but she'd seen too many women drift away when the demands of marriage had left them with little time for old friends. A wave of emotion swept over her as she thought about losing Maggie, and she reined herself in to keep control.

"I have to get some air. See you in the morning," she forced past the knot in her throat and hugged Maggie hard.

"Good night, Connie," Maggie said and held her for a moment longer, as if to say *Believe in me*.

But a second later, Connie was charging across the great lawn and toward the boardwalk leading to the beach, her body silently shaking as she held herself together. As she reached the sand, she glanced around and was thankful that despite the breathtaking late-summer night, there were few people out. Only one lone couple several houses down, strolling hand in hand toward the jetty and the end of Sea Kiss.

She found a spot along the edge of the dunes that provided a bit of privacy, plopped down, and finally freed her tears. The force of them created a whirlpool of emotions that threatened to suck her under and drown her with their weight. She tucked her head against her knees as huge, shuddering sobs wracked her body, almost violent in their intensity. She let them come, hoping to wash away all the doubts and fears that were plaguing her.

Little by little, the sobs became intermittent hiccups and sniffles. Connie dashed away the remnants of her crying jag, swiping at the tears wetting her cheeks. As she did so, she heard a rustle in the dune grasses above her, and suddenly, a curly-haired ball of cream and white crashed through the grasses and virtually landed in her lap.

The dog squirmed and spun around to face her. The pup gazed at her with a look that seemed knowing in a gamin face. With a doggie grin, it laid its paws on her chest and licked her face, dragging a watery chuckle from her. The dog yipped what she assumed was a greeting and settled into her lap as if that was where he was supposed to be.

Pounding footsteps rushed down the boardwalk to the Pierce home before silence suggested that the person had hit the sand before calling out, "Dudley!"

The dog barked again, and Connie poked her head from around the protection of the dune to see who it was.

God, please take me now, she thought as Jonathan strolled toward her.

Chapter 8

JONATHAN HEARD DUDLEY'S HAPPY BARK AND WALKED toward the sound. A second later, Connie stuck her head out from around the edge of one of the dunes.

Fuck me, he thought and called out Dudley's name, only to have another happy yip confirm that the terrier was with her.

He sucked in a deep inhalation and slowly ambled toward her. So far, amid all the rushed wedding prep, they'd managed to stay cordial. But they'd also managed to keep their distance, well aware that being too close produced a combustible mix. The last thing anyone needed was a messy explosion on top of all the hectic, last-minute wedding arrangements.

When he reached the almost foxhole-like spot where she was sitting, he stopped short. Dudley was in her lap, happily providing dog kisses, and while it dragged a chuckle from her, he had no doubt that she'd been crying. The sheen of tears on her cheeks shimmered beneath the moonlight, and her eyes were red rimmed.

"Hi, Jon," she said, her voice husky from the tears she'd shed.

"Were you crying?" he asked and kneeled close to her. He could handle her stubbornness and the temper that she luckily kept leashed for the most part. He could even handle the iciness that warned him to stay away. But the thought of her crying just shredded his heart.

"No," she answered way too quickly and rubbed Dudley's head as he kept up his enthusiastic loving.

"What's that on your cheeks then?" he pushed, needing her to admit it, not so that he could rejoice, but because he wanted to help.

"Dog spit. *Your* dog's spit, because I'm assuming this little guy belongs to you," she said and urged the terrier down into her lap again. The dog squirmed and presented her with his belly, jonesing for a rub.

As she obliged, Jonathan's gut tightened. He hated that he was suddenly wishing he could get that kind of attention as well. But wishes like that were best kept secret, because Connie had made it clear she wanted no part of him. And yet, something inside made him try to change things between them.

"He's mine. When I saw him at the shelter a few weeks ago, I couldn't walk away. Now that I plan on moving to Sea Kiss—"

"You're moving to Sea Kiss? To the mansion?" she asked with surprise.

He shook his head. "I only stay here because I know my father never comes down. As much as I love the family home, I need to find my own place. I've started searching for a house nearby."

There was no doubting the look on her face and her obvious worry. With Maggie and Owen getting married and him right in the neighborhood, they'd be constantly thrown together.

"Don't worry, Connie. I won't make it hard for you to see Maggie. I know how close the two of you are."

A guilty splotch of color erupted on cheeks already ruddy from her tears. "It's not like that. We're two mature adults. We can handle being around each other."

"Yes, we can. Like now. We're talking. No anger. No worries."

She huffed out a breath and looked away. "Right, no worries," she said, but despite her words, something major was going on with her.

"If you want to talk about it—"

"I don't."

He didn't give up. With a smile, he said, "Or if you just need a shoulder to cry on."

She tilted her chin up in a defiant gesture that was achingly familiar. "I wasn't crying. Like I said before, it was just your puppy's kisses."

"Really?" He couldn't resist the challenge. He leaned forward and cradled her chin with his hand.

Her gold-green eyes widened in surprise as he came ever closer. When he kissed the corner of her right eye, her eyelashes fluttered against his lips as she closed her eyes.

"Sweetest," he began and shifted to her other eye. "Dog spit," he said and didn't wait for her protest. "Ever." He kissed her lips, a gentle coaxing kiss that had her tilting into him and grasping his shoulders for support. As they moved closer, Dudley, who had been sitting in her lap, squirmed and barked a complaint as he got sandwiched between their bodies.

They slowly shifted apart, and even in the dim moonlight, the flush of color across her cheeks was obvious. She grabbed Dudley, thrust the dog against Jonathan's chest, and shot to her feet.

"I have to go," she said and raced away without waiting for his reply.

As Jonathan watched her rush off, Dudley slathered his face with kisses, either in apology for ruining the moment or in sympathy for the loss he felt at her departure. Jonathan rubbed the dog's head and set him on the ground. He talked to him as they walked back to the mansion. "Silly pooch. I knew you had the right name since it seemed like you always did the right thing."

He stepped up onto the boardwalk, Dudley dutifully at his side. "And now you go and run away and to her of all people. And damn, you interrupted at the worst possible time, dude. I thought I was finally breaking through that wall of hers."

Dudley gave a combo growl/bark, making Jonathan pause on the edge of the great lawn.

"What? You don't like that idea?" he asked and shook his head in wonderment. He was truly losing it. He was talking to his dog, for God's sakes.

Dudley barked again, looked toward the Sinclair mansion, and whined loudly. Beyond the row of privet hedges, Connie's silhouette was visible through the tiny leaves and thin branches. It was almost as if the little dog wanted him to go after her, but Jonathan knew that was crazy, just like it had been crazy to kiss her before.

Only she had looked so sad and so alone. He had never been one to ignore someone in need. Even if it had been Connie. Smart, beautiful, prickly, stubborn Connie.

"Come on, Dudley. Forget about her," he said, but inside of him, a spark of hope ignited. He didn't rush to extinguish it.

~~~

Connie was grateful that no one was around when she slipped back into the mansion. Mrs. Patrick had left a light on in the kitchen, not that Connie needed it to navigate her way around the table and island and to the stairs that led to the second floor. Thankfully, nothing had changed in the house in the nearly ten years she'd been visiting, so she could do the walk blindfolded. *But so many other things have changed*, Connie thought as she trudged up the stairs and marched to her room.

Tracy was married. For now at least, since the marriage was off to a rocky start. She hoped her friend could make a go of it, since she was truly trying hard to be a better person and set things to right. A very different attitude from Tracy's usual drama-queen persona.

Maggie was getting married. That still had to sink in some more, since it was all too new and uncertain.

Emma…Emma never changed. She was essentially the same woman who Connie had met in college. Hardworking, bright, and beautiful. Still denying that there was a Prince Charming out there for her, even though Carlo was standing right before her eyes.

Just like you can't see what's right in front of your face? the little voice in her head challenged. *Just like you haven't changed at all?* it tacked on cheekily.

Connie shut down that annoying voice as she walked into her bedroom, undressed, and got into bed. She lay there, staring at the ceiling and listening to the normally calming rumble of the surf, and let her mind wander. Or at least tried to let it wander, since it seemed to circle right back to her earlier thoughts.

Contrary to the little voice's challenge, she had changed. She was not the frightened little girl she had been, always worrying about her parents fighting. Time and time again, her father had left to chase one unrealistic dream or another until the day he had walked away for good and the fighting had stopped. Then it became worry about how little they had and how hard her mom worked to earn it. It was why she'd been good. Her mother deserved some respite when she came home.

And they both deserved a better, easier life, which was why she'd worked so hard to get straight A's and a scholarship for college. She'd wanted to provide for herself and her mom. She hadn't wanted to be that scared little girl all her life.

But as much as she had changed, here she was, afraid again. Fearful of not getting the partnership for which she'd worked so hard and worse, losing it to someone like Perez, who'd always coasted through life. She was also worried about whether her best friend would have her heart broken. Worried, just a little, about how that marriage might impact her. Which led to her next biggest fear: Jonathan.

She raised her hand and brushed her fingertips across her lips. Recalled his gentle kiss, filled with tenderness. His humor, which could always draw her out of the darkness, like where she'd been tonight. His caring, because he hadn't just asked her to talk about it as a platitude. He'd meant it.

And even though she'd told her friends weeks earlier that Jonathan hadn't changed, she had to confess that there had been something different about him lately. She'd sensed it during their impromptu lunch that had ended so badly. And again earlier that day when they'd all gathered to discuss the wedding preparations. It had even been more apparent tonight as he'd talked about buying a house in Sea Kiss. *Not to mention his adorable little terrier*, she thought with a smile.

It was almost as if he was truly trying to settle down, but Jonathan had always been someone wildly alive and free. Like anything wild, it wasn't easy to domesticate him.

Like you wanted to? said the little voice as it emerged again.

Maybe she had wanted to, but the last thing she wanted to do was destroy the spirit that had attracted her to him in the first place. Now, with the advantage of maturity and hindsight, she recognized that the plans she had made for them so many years earlier would have done just that. But despite all the little changes that said he was a tamer version of the Jonathan she'd fallen in love with, she didn't dare take the chance. It was too easy to see him growing tired of the everyday and leaving for one of his adventures, just like her father had come and gone until the day when he hadn't returned.

Some people weren't meant to be contained. She was wise enough to know that wild animals that had been caged for too long either lost their spirit or turned on their masters. Neither outcome would be good for her or Jonathan.

Chapter 9

THE PRENUP HAD BEEN SIGNED AND THE WEDDING plans finalized a few weeks earlier. In a flurry of activity, Connie, Emma, and Tracy had gotten their bridesmaids' dresses. Emma had muscled the men into choosing their tuxes. Earlier that day, they'd met at the Sinclair mansion to walk through what would happen when Maggie and Owen walked down the aisle together tomorrow.

It had been difficult to stand by Jonathan and stroll across the great lawn with him to the arbor that had been assembled on the beach for the nuptials. Her mind had betrayed her, making her wonder what it would be like if it were the two of them doing the walk. A happy walk instead of one that had felt like they were death-row prisoners on the way to their execution. Somehow, they'd managed to get through it.

Now Connie had to survive the rehearsal dinner. Luckily, there were a good number of people there. Beside some long-distance members of the Sinclair and Pierce families, there were about half a dozen or so close friends. Since the wedding itself had been rushed and people were flying in anyway for tomorrow's wedding, it had seemed to be a good idea to give them this one night to toast the soon-to-be newlyweds and get to know each other before the big event. Not a traditional rehearsal dinner, but it seemed like everyone was enjoying themselves so far.

Connie circled the floor of the ballroom in the large Sea Kiss inn where the affair was being held, making sure that everyone was enjoying themselves. At various other spots, Emma and Tracy were doing the same thing while Maggie and Owen went from table to table, greeting their guests. At one table with a gathering of men she recognized from their college days, Jonathan sat, apparently regaling them with tales of his exploits as the men laughed out loud and one of them congratulated Jonathan with a sharp clap on the back.

Jonathan did an "aw shucks" kind of shrug that was too damn endearing and had her heart constricting painfully. He'd always downplayed his accomplishments, maybe because of his dad and the man's constant criticism. After their talk at lunch weeks earlier, she knew that he'd hidden a lot, including the fact that he was a genius behind that laid-back surfer-dude persona.

She tore her gaze away from him because he looked just too damned good. His blue eyes were bright against skin tanned from his time on Sea Kiss Beach. The custom suit he'd put on emphasized his broad shoulders, and she'd noticed earlier how the suit pants hugged his muscular legs and fine ass.

Damn, she said to herself as heat spiraled through her. She really had to stop looking at and thinking about him and how he'd tamed his sun-streaked light-brown hair into a man bun. She hated man buns and those silly bad boy bracelets. Thumb rings too, but as she glanced at him again from the corner of her eye, it was only to wonder why he carried them off so well and why it affected her so.

"Are you okay? You look a little flushed," Emma

said as they crossed paths and then walked together to their table.

"Just fine," Connie said, but another round of loud laughter drew her attention back to Jonathan's table. Damn if he wasn't smiling that dimpled grin that did all kinds of things to her insides.

"Oh, I see," Emma said as they sat. She reached for an icy glass of water and handed it to Connie. "Take a sip. It may help you cool down."

"Fuck you, Emma," she playfully murmured under her breath.

Emma chuckled out loud. "Don't blame me if you have no control," she teased and picked up her half-finished glass of champagne. They'd done a toast and brought out dessert about half an hour ago, and the dinner would be winding down soon.

"I so have control," Connie said, trying to convince herself as Jonathan rose from the table and went over to the side of the room where Owen was standing next to Carlo. Carlo seemed to be giving his staff final instructions as the affair ended, but once he was finished, he turned his attention to the two brothers. Jonathan reached into his pocket and handed something to Carlo.

She risked a glance from the corner of her eye at Emma, whose gaze was set on the very handsome man who was her caterer extraordinaire. She might have been fantasizing about Jonathan, but her friend was likewise fixated on Carlo.

"Ladies, you two seem to be interested in something," Tracy said as she joined them and glanced over at the men. "Ah, I see," she said, earning protestations from both Connie and Emma.

"It's not what you think," they said, almost in unison.

Tracy barely contained her laughter. "Right. I may have made a mess of my romantic life, but you two... It's really sad, you know."

As Emma began a spirited defense, Connie focused on the men across the way again. It was impossible to miss the look on Carlo's face as he gazed at Emma. It was filled with disappointment and yearning. Despite Emma's protestations, she knew her friend had feelings for him. It was good to know those feelings weren't unrequited.

A second later, Jonathan also peered in their direction. As his gaze locked with hers, the emotion on his face was raw. Needy. Luckily, Owen wrapped an arm around his brother's shoulders and drew him back into the discussion with Carlo.

"Connie. Earth to Connie," Tracy said, but Maggie returned to their table at that moment, beaming with such happiness that it was impossible not to get caught up in it.

"It looks like you're ready for the big day," Connie said.

"Totally," she said and glanced lovingly in Owen's direction.

That made Emma smirk and say, "Still think it's a good idea not to see Owen until the wedding tomorrow?"

"For sure. It'll make tomorrow night that much more special."

"That's the spirit," said Tracy, who of all of them had always been the one to embrace romance with both hands.

Because Connie didn't want to rain on Maggie's parade, she added, "It will be wonderful."

Maggie smiled and hugged her. "You know it will, and tonight, it will be wonderful for all of us. Let's go back to the mansion and have our last girl's night with me as a single lady."

———

Jonathan raised his glass of beer and toasted his brother. "To Owen. I know I'm supposed to say something more, but to be honest, I'm still trying to figure out what to say tomorrow, so for now, I'm glad we have this excuse to get drunk tonight."

Not that he planned on getting drunk, since he was driving all of them home, but he truly was struggling with what he'd say tomorrow as the best man. Especially since he didn't have a clue about marriage or finding the right woman. Or maybe it was more appropriate to say keeping the right woman. Obviously, he sucked at that, he thought as Dudley trotted over and sat by his feet. Since the pup had been home all alone for most of the day, he'd decided to bring him along for their impromptu bachelor party. Dudley had happily gone along with them, trotting beside him jauntily as they'd packed up the car and headed out.

Owen laughed and playfully punched his arm. "Come on, Li'l Bro. You're going to have to do better than that tomorrow."

"I'll try," he said and glanced at Carlo, who had joined them at the home Jonathan had borrowed from a friend for Maggie and Owen's short weekend honeymoon. "You must have some tips. How many weddings have you done with Emma? Hundreds?"

Carlo rolled his eyes. "Definitely hundreds, and you

think that they'll get easier, but each one seems to have its own drama."

"Like Tracy wanting to make Bill a eunuch at her wedding?" Owen asked.

"For real? I didn't notice that," Jonathan said, earning a loud laugh from his brother and another punch on the arm. This time, Dudley shot to his feet, growled at Owen, and bared his teeth.

"Wow, Jonathan. You've got quite a little guard dog there," Owen teased.

Jonathan smile and rubbed the pup's head. "He's just playing, dude."

"Right, just playing," Owen said to the little terrier, who cocked his head at Owen but finally seemed to understand and settled back down at Jonathan's feet.

Owen quickly continued their earlier conversation. "You didn't notice Tracy's craziness 'cause you were too busy ogling Connie."

Jonathan thought that Owen had obviously had enough alcohol to loosen lips that should have stayed shut. He didn't need even more people wondering what was up with him and Connie.

After a chug of beer, Carlo considered him in light of Owen's slip. "I guess I didn't mistake the vibes I've detected the last few weeks."

Damn, Jonathan thought. "A long time ago, dude. There's nothing happening there now. What do you expect for Maggie and Owen's big day tomorrow?" he said, trying to deflect attention away from himself.

Carlo inclined his head in a noble kind of way and pensively drank his beer. With another little dip of his head in Owen's direction, he finally said, "I see a perfect day for two people who are thoroughly in love."

Owen smacked the oak table and shouted, "That's my man. That's what I want to hear." He pinned his gaze on Jonathan. "Maybe you should do the catering and Carlo should be my best man. I'd have him walk Emma down the aisle like he'd like to do," Owen teased, then he raised his glass and finished off the rest of his beer in one long chug.

Jonathan shared a glance with Carlo, and the other man grabbed another beer from the bucket they had on the table next to the remains of the heroes they'd assembled earlier that night. Carlo had brought the ingredients with him after the rehearsal dinner along with the remainder of the food he'd prepped for Maggie and Owen's stay at the home.

"Like I said at the dinner, Emma is a hard nut, but I think that if anyone can crack that shell, it just might be our man Carlo here," Jonathan said and squeezed the other man's shoulder in a conciliatory gesture. He hadn't realized Carlo's interest earlier and had stuck his foot in his mouth. Maybe more than just his foot, come to think of it.

Carlo handed Owen the beer and smiled. "I'm a patient man, Jon."

"You have to be, considering what you do for a living. All those bridezillas," Owen said with a shudder and started in on the next beer. Since his brother wasn't much of a drinker, Jonathan suspected this one would be enough to push him over the edge, which was what Owen needed, to just let go, because Jonathan knew that it wasn't going to be as easy tomorrow as Carlo had suggested.

"If you think the brides can be bad, the families can be worse. Arguing about who pays for what and who sits where," Carlo said.

It earned a very drunk "If they even bother to show up" from Owen.

Their mother had departed long ago and was no longer a part of their lives. They didn't even have any idea where she was, and in truth, neither of them wanted to know. Or at least that's what Jonathan told himself. And his father had disowned Jonathan a decade earlier, but even though his father was bitter and angry and never acknowledged either of them in a positive way, Owen somehow had a relationship with him. A complicated and unrewarding one as far as Jonathan was concerned, but his dick of a father should have at least bothered to come to the rehearsal dinner. He hoped that the old man would do the right thing and come for the wedding tomorrow, but he doubted it.

But he'd be there for his brother. He wrapped an arm around Owen's shoulders and gave him an intense bro hug. "The only thing that matters is that Maggie doesn't bail on you. Anything else is icing on the cake."

"Or beer in my belly," Owen said and sucked down the rest of the bottle.

Jonathan and Carlo shared a look, but with a shrug, Carlo snared another bottle from the bucket and started to pass it down, but Jonathan held up his hand to stop him. Carlo nodded in understanding. A hungover groom was never a good thing.

Owen tried to set his bottle on the table, but as it tipped over, it occurred to Jonathan that maybe it was a little too late to avoid a hungover groom. He righted the bottle and said, "How about we get you some water and an aspirin."

Carlo jumped up from the table to find the items, leaving the two brothers alone.

Owen unsteadily grabbed hold of Jonathan's shoulder, and with a sniffle in his voice, he said, "He's not going to come, is he?"

"I wouldn't count on it, Bro. But it doesn't matter. I've got your six, and you have Maggie. That's all that counts, you know," Jonathan said, his own voice wavering with emotion. "That's all that counts."

Chapter 10

CONNIE SAT ON THE DAIS THAT HAD BEEN SET UP ON the great lawn parallel to the privet hedges that separated the Pierce and Sinclair mansions. Ironic, since this wedding united the scions of the two warring families, although Maggie's dad was here and had given his blessing. The only one still fighting apparently was Owen and Jonathan's dad.

The sharp squeal of feedback on a microphone warned it was time for the start of the speeches. The master of ceremonies was the female singer from the live band Emma had hired for the wedding. She walked over to the dais and introduced Jonathan, who stood, took the mike, and faced Maggie and his brother.

"It seems like so long ago that the three of us used to hang out on this beach. Building epic sand castles. Chasing each other in the surf. My bro and I always hated leaving Sea Kiss and having to wait months until we could come back, but I think Owen hated it more, because it meant being away from Maggie." He stopped to draw a ragged breath before he continued. "There was something special between the two of you. Something strong and yet malleable enough not to break when things get gnarly, but I hope you will have only joy. As I see the love and respect between you, it makes me think that if there really is a secret to a happy marriage, the two of you have discovered that secret."

He paused again, a sheen of tears in his eyes, picked up his glass of champagne from the table, and held it high. "Maggie. Like summer, you bring warmth and joy and lightness to my brother. May you share that eternal summer with him for the rest of your lives."

Connie raised her glass and took a sip. She sucked in a deep breath to contain the emotions Jonathan's speech had roused and prepared to give her toast in honor of the groom. As the applause died down from Jonathan's speech, he walked over and held out his hand to help her from the chair. She slipped her hand in his, rose, and accepted the microphone as he handed it to her. He stayed beside her, his hand at the small of her back as if sensing that she needed support.

She gifted him a smile and faced the wedding guests. "When I met Maggie in freshman year, I didn't just get a best friend. I got a sister." She glanced at her friend and smiled, fighting the threat of tears. "We've shared so much over the years, and I know I will share many more joyful times in the future with you and Owen, because I see how happy he makes you. I see that he understands you and will support you in whatever you do. That's a rare gift and one you totally deserve."

As her throat choked up, she hesitated to gather herself. Jonathan ran his hand up and down her back in a soothing gesture, and after a moment, she continued, buoyed by his presence. "Owen. From the first day you kissed Maggie on a long ago summer night, I knew that there was something special between you. I hoped it was just a matter of time before you found each other and your love, and you have. May you never say goodbye again. May you always keep the magic of that one summer night in your hearts."

She raised her glass and sipped the champagne. The chill of it slipped down her throat, soothing the rawness of the emotions she'd kept bottled up. Turning, she offered Jonathan another smile, and he grinned, nodded, and took the microphone. As she sat, he walked away from the dais and to the table with Maggie's father. He handed him the microphone and then returned to the dais, but not before sharing another smile and friendly nod with her.

While she appreciated his caring, she wasn't sure she could deal with him tonight on top of all the feelings that Maggie's wedding was creating. But she had to handle it for her friend's sake and for her own. She was so engrossed with her thoughts that it took Emma's poke in her ribs to realize Maggie's dad had finished his toast. She raised her glass and sipped again. Unfortunately, there would be no toast from the groom's father, since the old bastard had not shown up for his son's wedding.

Just a few minutes later, the MC announced that it was time for the bride and groom's first dance. Maggie and Owen shared a smile and a kiss before heading to the floor. They stepped into each other's arms, and Connie's heart skipped a beat at the love and joy on their faces as they danced to the band's cover of Lifehouse's "You and Me."

Emma grabbed both her hand and Tracy's, and the three friends shared a moment, fingers intertwined, celebrating their friend's happiness as well as the bond that they hoped would last beyond this marriage.

As the song neared the halfway point, the band

finished one chorus and then began a longer rendition. The singer invited people to join the happy couple on the makeshift dance floor on the great lawn. Various couples joined Maggie and Owen in their dance. A second later, Jonathan sauntered over to Connie and held out his hand.

She stared at it in surprise and sat there, but then Emma elbowed her forcefully, leaned close, and whispered, "Go for it."

Go for what? she wanted to say, but with another jab from her friend, she slowly stood and eased her hand into Jonathan's.

Her hand was smooth but icy cold with nerves. Jonathan laced his fingers with hers, and with a playful shake, he said, "We can do this for Maggie and Owen."

Her head did a wobbly bobble, and she repeated, "For Maggie and Owen."

Together, they walked onto the dance floor, and he smiled at Maggie and his brother as they passed by, not that he thought that Owen noticed. His brother was totally enraptured with his new wife.

His heart filled with joy at his brother's happiness, but as he drew Connie close, that joy morphed to longing for the woman in his arms. A woman who refused to believe that such happiness was possible for them. A woman who was tense as a high wire in his arms as they moved on the dance floor.

He tucked his head against hers, rousing the smell of the orange blossoms woven into the fancy braid of her dark-brown hair. The skin of her temple was smooth against his jaw, since the heels she wore made her almost his height. With a slight shift of his head, he brushed a kiss across her temple and whispered, "Relax."

She did, her body softening against his, allowing all those luscious, womanly curves to come into contact with his body. Her full breasts pressed against his chest while the soft flatness of her belly cradled him. As his body reacted, he shifted away slightly and met her knowing gaze. He couldn't avoid seeing the soft swells of her breasts above the edge of her bodice. He hardened even more and stiffened in her arms, fighting the need rising in him.

"Relax," she said with a Mona Lisa smile and the ring of amusement in her voice.

With a nod and a strangled sigh, he settled her back against him, closed his eyes, and drummed up what little restraint he could. *Think golf*, he told himself. Dull. Boring. Nothing at all like the vibrant woman in his arms. As passion rose up again, he thought, *Think paint drying. Mowing the lawn. Taking out the trash.* All things he hated to do, and somehow, he managed to survive the dance without totally embarrassing himself.

As the song wound down and the band leader invited Maggie's dad to come up for the traditional father-daughter dance, Jonathan led Connie back to the dais and then took his spot on the groom's side but not before sharing a glance with her that said that she knew just how much she still affected him. As a blush blossomed on her cheeks, it was clear he wasn't the only one feeling the desire.

The question was: What did he want to do about that?

The answer eluded him through the courses of the

amazing dinner Carlo had whipped up for the Victorian-themed wedding. There had been some kind of fruity soup to start the meal. He wasn't normally a fan of fowl, but the duck breast that had come next was delicious. The duck had been seared and served in a red wine demi-glace. It was followed by one of his favorites, a grilled foie gras. Meat had been the next course in the meal, and he was definitely a steak kind of guy. A fork-tender filet mignon, roasted fingerling potatoes, and asparagus delicately drizzled with hollandaise sauce had been delicious. In between each of those courses, a chill lemon ice had helped to clear the palate.

Although he could typically eat anyone out of house and home, he was grateful for the break that came before the remaining courses. He took advantage of that time to walk around and greet the various guests to make sure they were all having a good time. As he crossed paths with his brother at one table, Owen gestured with his head to take him aside.

Together, they walked over to the far side of the great lawn, and when they stopped, Owen shoved his hands in his pockets and jerked his chin in the direction of their beach home. "You'd think, since he's here, he'd bother to come down and watch his son get married."

Shock filled Jonathan at his brother's words. He looked back toward the beach house and noticed the lights were on in the third-story rooms. A shadow crossed by one of the windows. His father had come down for the wedding. Or at least he'd watched the celebration from afar. It was surprising on various levels.

Nearly twenty years earlier and right around the time that Maggie's mom had died, his father had stopped visiting Sea Kiss. He'd forbidden his sons from coming down as well. It was only once they'd gotten into their teens and had been too much trouble to handle that his father had deigned to let them return to the beach house, but he had never returned. Until tonight.

"He's here to gloat. To think about you finally screwing the Sinclairs, figuratively and literally," Jonathan said, holding out no hope that his father had changed his mind about why he thought Owen married Maggie Sinclair.

"He's going to be very disappointed," Owen said without hesitation.

Jonathan didn't doubt that, but there had been worry niggling in his mind for weeks, ever since his brother had announced his plans and explained to him the reason for them.

"You need to tell Maggie the truth, Owen. You need to explain to her what you did and why," he urged, not wanting anything to taint the love his brother had for his newlywed wife.

Owen nodded. "When the time is right, I'll tell her."

"You need to do it before she finds out some other way," he pressed, fearing the worst.

His brother shot him a quick look from the corner of his eye and said, "And when are you going to tell Connie how you still feel about her? It's obvious, you know."

"When the time is right," he said and walked away, wanting no part of that discussion for the moment.

He detoured on his way back to get another glass of champagne from an intricate fountain on the patio that burbled a copious shower of bubbly. He filled one glass and downed it. Topped off a second glass and debated what he'd do next as the servers brought out a fruit and cheese tray before the traditional cake cutting.

Connie was still sitting on the dais with her friends, laughing and smiling. He recalled how they'd once shared such laughter and joy. It made him realize how much he missed being with her. Draining his second glass, he refilled it and grabbed another champagne flute. Filling the empty glass, he headed over with both to the dais, but instead of resuming his original place, he sat beside Connie, since Maggie and Owen were still making the rounds of the guests and would soon be cutting the cake.

He handed Connie the champagne, and she stared at him quizzically before accepting it. "Thanks," she said.

The server came around at that moment to place the fruit and cheese tray before them. As if that was her cue, Emma rose from her chair and said, "I have to check on something with Carlo."

Tracy likewise stood. "I need to connect with Bill. He's been alone for too long," she said about her new husband who had already strayed from his vows months earlier.

As her two friends hurried away, Connie hissed beneath her breath, "Traitors."

Jonathan grinned. "To smart women," he said and raised his glass in a toast.

―――⁂―――

Smart women, foolish choices, she thought, since it was something she and her friends discussed often, but to keep the peace, she clinked her glass to his and took a sip. Only a sip, because she needed to keep her wits about her, since Jonathan was totally a foolish choice. *Beyond foolish, downright crazy*, she thought but couldn't control the skitter of desire that raced down her spine as he grinned at her lopsidedly. The dimple to the right of those delicious lips tempted her to run her finger along that indent and then over to those very masculine, very capable lips.

She snared her glass and cooled her lust with a less-than-ladylike chug of the champagne. The chill and bubbles caused an ache in the middle of her chest. Or at least that's what she told herself as she pressed her hand there. Another mistake, as he followed the movement with his summer-sky gaze and lovingly ran it all along the exposed swells of her breasts.

Beneath the heavily beaded bodice of the gown, her nipples tightened and rubbed against the fabric. Each tiny movement sent a tug of need to parts south.

"I need some air," she said and jumped out of the chair.

Jonathan did the same and, looking around, he said, "We're outside."

"Shut up, Jon. Just shut up," she said with an angry slash of her hand.

He followed, but as they reached the edge of the dance floor, the MC announced that it was time for the cutting of the cake.

Before she could take a step onto the great lawn to head down to the beachfront, Emma and Tracy were there, grabbing her elbows and propelling her back toward the dais.

"You know what comes next, Connie. You can't miss that," Emma whispered.

Connie cringed. Yes, she knew. The dreaded hauling out of the old maids and having them battle for the bridal bouquet for the privilege of being groped by a drunk-ass bachelor hoping to get lucky.

"No way," she said and jerked her elbows free.

"Way. If I have to do it, so do you," Emma replied.

Tracy held up her hand to show her wedding band. With a shrug, she singsonged, "Married."

"Traitor," Connie said again, but she patiently waited as Maggie and Owen cut their cake and ate it. Moments later, Carlo came out onto the dance floor and called for his staff to assist and wheel the cake aside so it could be served.

The lead singer from the band walked over to Maggie, grabbed her bouquet, and waved it in the air. "All you single ladies, come on up," she called out.

A gaggle of teens raced up, followed by some reluctant millennials. Tracy pushed Connie and Emma out onto the dance floor, and to appease Connie, they hung out at the back of the pack. From the corner of her eye, Connie noticed Jonathan standing by the dais, an amused grin on his face. She kept her hands fisted at her sides, having no intention of catching the bouquet, but as her gaze connected with Maggie's, it was obvious her friend was calculating how to accomplish just that.

As the new bride turned her back and the countdown began for the toss, Connie quickly sidestepped Emma and, with a subtle hip check, shifted her friend to where she had been standing seconds earlier. As Maggie had planned, the bouquet flew through the air and straight at Emma's head, giving her no choice but to catch it or be beaned by the tussie-mussie.

Realizing what Connie had done, Emma whirled on her and whined, "I thought you were my friend!"

"Totally," she said and waltzed off to the side to grab Carlo and pull him onto the dance floor for the next part of the ritual.

He protested at first, and all eyes settled on him as he balked. Jonathan came over to haul him onto the floor, and Carlo finally relented, although clearly reluctantly. The handsome caterer stood by Jonathan, and as Owen prepared his garter toss, Emma closed her eyes and mumbled something beneath her breath.

It sounded like a prayer to Connie, but apparently God wasn't listening (or maybe he was), since the garter flew across the air, and like a horseshoe tossed at a ring, the garter encircled Carlo's index finger, earning hoots and shouts from all gathered there at the perfect shot.

As Emma opened her eyes and saw Carlo standing there, dangling the baby-blue garter for all to see, a bright-red flush erupted across her face and up to her ears. She half glanced at Connie and said, "I will kill you for this. When you least suspect it, it will happen."

Connie couldn't stifle her chuckle, and when Jonathan came to her side, she high-fived him for his assistance with the plot but asked, "How did you know Emma and Carlo—"

"I didn't until yesterday and then it was damned obvi- ous," he said.

She guessed that there was more that he wasn't saying. She wanted to pry but suspected there was some kind of bro code that would keep him from telling her, much like she wouldn't share her friend's secrets. Or her own namely that, deep inside her, she still cared for him. Still wondered at times what it would be like to be with him.

The band launched into a sexy riff to assist Carlo with placing the garter on Emma. Ever the gentleman, he kept it clean, his touch deferential while he slipped the lacy fabric past her shoe and ankle. Up a little higher to her calf where he paused to look up at Emma, who was staring skyward, her color deepening. With her fair skin, it was impossible to hide the flush.

Carlo grinned and inched the garter past her knee but stopped there despite the entreaties of the single men to go ever higher. He wagged his head, shook his finger in a no-way gesture, and draped Emma's gown back over her legs.

Emma finally met his gaze, thankful, but then Carlo did the totally unexpected. He wrapped an arm around her waist and slowly drew her close. Keeping one hand at her waist, he cradled her jaw and kissed her like there was no tomorrow.

When Carlo finally ended the kiss, Emma stood there, dazed and a little unsteady, until Carlo bent and whispered something in her ear and she playfully shoved him away.

That prompted yet more catcalls from the single men, and with a shrug, Carlo left the floor and started giving instructions to his crew again, while Emma stomped toward her friends, her green eyes blazing fire.

She thrust the tussie-mussie bouquet against Connie's chest and repeated her earlier warning. "You're a dead woman."

But Connie could only chuckle, and Jonathan joined her with a full belly laugh and a clap of his hands. "Oh man, she's got it bad for him," he said.

"Yep, she does," Connie replied. Caught up in the lighthearted spirit of the moment, she didn't refuse him when he led her out on the dance floor for a fast number.

Chapter 11

CONNIE STOOD BEFORE JONATHAN AS THE WEDDING guests lined up to say goodbye to the newlywed couple. After Maggie and Owen emerged from the Sinclair mansion, Maggie hugged both Tracy and Emma, then came over to the other side of the stairs to embrace Connie. The two women shared a heartfelt hug and for a second, Maggie met Jonathan's gaze as if to say *Take care of her*. His brother followed, enfolding Connie in his arms and then shaking Jonathan's hand. He dipped his head toward Connie as if to repeat his wife's entreaty.

When Jonathan leaned forward to get a better look down the line and toward the Pierce Lightning prototype his brother was driving, his chest brushed across Connie's back, and it was impossible to miss her trembling. He stepped closer and wrapped an arm around her waist, and she leaned back into his support.

A few short minutes later, the Lightning pulled away soundlessly, thanks to the electric-powered engine. As it did so, the crowd gathered along the steps of the mansion and the driveway dispersed leisurely. Some walked back toward the patio and great lawn, where a Viennese table held dozens of different sweets. Others drifted toward the cars parked along Ocean Avenue, ready to go home.

Connie stood there silently, as did Emma and Tracy opposite her. Scattered tremors still drifted across her body, but they'd abated somewhat as she marshaled her control. Tracy was the first to move, wrapping Emma in a one-armed bear hug and holding out her other arm for Connie to join them.

Jonathan released her, and the three women embraced, heads tucked tight, until Tracy finally straightened and said, "You did good, Emma. Everything was absolutely perfect."

"Thanks," Emma said, her voice husky with emotion, then she looked back toward Carlo. "Thank you. I couldn't have done it without you."

Carlo smiled and brushed a lock of Emma's strawberry blond hair back from her forehead. "I'm always here for you."

Jonathan hoped Emma would one day realize that and make Carlo a happy man, but he wasn't sure about it, just as he wasn't sure about Connie and whatever was going on with them. But as she stepped back toward him and didn't protest as he wrapped his arm around her waist again, it occurred to him that maybe it wasn't a hopeless cause.

"Why don't we go get some dessert?" he said, but Tracy and her husband demurred, saying they had an early morning date with other friends.

"Carlo and I need to give the staff some final instructions," Emma said.

Carlo confirmed it with a nod and said, "Maybe later."

"How about it, Connie?" Jonathan held his breath and waited for her to bail on him, but she surprised him yet again.

"I could use some sweets to help me deal with the last few weeks," she said.

He held out his hand, inviting her to lead the way, and she did, cutting through the house to the patio, where the Viennese table had been set up. They walked around the display of sweets together, piling a plate high with an assortment of pastries. He carried the dish to the dais where they'd been seated earlier, laid it down, and excused himself to get them some coffee.

At the hot beverage service, one of the waiters was prepping Irish coffees, and Jonathan ordered two, thinking that a little alcohol would also go a long way toward soothing Connie. When he returned, he noted the tiny dollop of cream on Connie's upper lip that said she hadn't waited to attack the sweets. After he placed the large mug with the coffee before her, he swiped away the cream and licked his finger. Teased her with, "Delicious. I see why you couldn't wait."

Connie's insides twisted with desire at the thought of him licking assorted parts of her body. Especially since she had never forgotten the wicked things he could do with his tongue and mouth. A part of her was wondering if he could still bring her such intense pleasure.

Needing to prop up her failing reserve, she grabbed her coffee and took a bracing sip, only to sputter as she got past the whipped cream to the whiskey-laced java beneath the surface. A trail of warmth from the liquor worked its way down her throat.

"Holy shit, that's strong."

"Is it?" He took a sip and shrugged noncommittally, but all she could see was the whipped cream sitting at the corner of his mouth, right by where his dimple would emerge when he grinned. As if on cue, he grinned when he noticed her attention and licked away the cream with a catlike swipe of his tongue.

She grabbed her mug with both hands to hide the tremble in her hands and drank some more. She placed the mug down and reached for a napoleon on the plate, but Jonathan had already taken hold of it.

"Never let it be said that I'm not a gentleman." He offered it up to her, and she took a tentative bite. He took the next, substantially larger, and then offered it to her again.

As she placed her lips on the pastry, she wondered if she would taste him there and chastised herself at her foolishness. If she wanted a taste, he was right before her and obviously willing, but was she? Could she give herself this one night with him and then walk away in the morning?

He popped the last little bit of napoleon in his mouth, chewed, and then washed it down with some of the spiked coffee. He picked up another treat, a chocolate-covered cream puff, and offered her a bite.

She bit into it, and as she did so, cream burst from the other side, all over his thumb and forefinger. With inordinate attention, she fixated on him as he ate the rest of it and licked the cream from his fingers.

Beneath her gown, her nipples tightened once again, begging for his attention. Between her legs, damp heat gathered, warning her that she was balanced on a razor-thin edge that would only bring pain if she fell.

She shot to her feet and said, "It's getting late. I really should get going."

With a wry grin and a jerk of his head in the

direction of Maggie's beach home, he said, "Yeah, that walk up the stairs is a long trip. Don't want to get stuck in traffic."

"Your trip isn't much longer," she reminded him, feeling awkward, because she really had no reason to cut the night short other than her own fear of what she was feeling around him.

He shrugged, and his grin faded. "Actually, I may have to drive back to the city tonight."

Confusion filled her, since she knew he'd been staying next door for days. "Work on a weekend?" she asked while jealousy reared up inside and silently added, *Or a hot date?*

He looked over his shoulder at the Pierce mansion and then pointed upward. She followed the line of his gesture to the third floor, where lights blazed and a shadow passed in front of one window and then another. It didn't clear up her confusion at first, until the most obvious answer hit her. "Your dad? He's here at the house and didn't come to the wedding?"

"Looks like that," he said, but it was obvious there was so much more he was holding in. The lines of his face were tight, and his body had tensed up. He shoved his hands in his pockets and rocked back and forth, obviously uneasy.

She understood. The Pierce brothers had always had a complicated relationship with their father. In the many years since Jonathan had decided not to return to college, that relationship had only become even more intricate and rancorous. With Owen marrying Maggie and defying their father... She couldn't even begin to imagine how much worse it could get.

She laid a hand on his chest and stroked it back and forth lightly, trying to offer comfort. "I'm sorry. I know how hard it is for you to be around him."

He huffed out a laugh. "That's an understatement. I haven't seen or talked to the bastard in nearly eight years."

"Sometimes that's not a bad thing." Since the day her father had left and not come back, things around her house had gotten decidedly better. But at least she'd had a loving mother and eventually grandparents who loved and cared for her, as well as Maggie, Emma, and Tracy, who were like sisters. Jonathan had only had Owen.

He pursed his lips and nodded abruptly. "I should get going."

Trying to lighten the mood, she smiled and said, "That's my line. Besides, you don't really want to do the nearly two-hour trip to New York tonight, do you? And what about your stuff? You're going to leave your laptop here? And Dudley?"

Jonathan narrowed his gaze and scrutinized her. "You think you know me, Reyes?" he teased as some of the tension left his body.

"I know you and your laptop have a deep and abiding relationship, and you wouldn't go anywhere without it or Dudley," she kidded right back.

He shook his head and looked away from her, not daring to dream about what she might be proposing. "And what am I supposed to do? It's too late to walk into one of the inns in town. Besides, they're probably all full, between the tourists trying to hang on to summer and the wedding guests. I guess there's always the beach and a blanket. It's still warm enough, and it wouldn't be the first time."

His words brought back a memory of the two of them, making love at midnight while wrapped tight inside a blanket on the beach. As he met her gaze and saw it darken from that unique gold green to almost emerald, he realized she was remembering that night as well.

"No, it wouldn't," she said, her voice rough with desire. "But you'd be more comfortable bunking out on the settee in my room."

He would, since sand wasn't nearly as comfortable to sleep on as people thought. But the two of them, in a room, all alone…

Gesturing toward the Sinclair home, he said, "What about the other rooms? There must be one that's free."

She shook her head. "All filled with family, even Maggie's room. One of her cousins decided to attend at the last minute and didn't have a place to stay."

"Your settee, huh? You really don't mind?" He wanted to be certain that she was sure about the offer she had just made.

She shook her head. "I don't mind. Come on. It's getting late," she said and held out her hand to him.

Certain Dudley would be okay until the morning, since he'd set him up with a fancy new device he'd accessed with his smartphone to give Dudley food and water as well as wee-wee pads so he could relieve himself, he twined his fingers with hers, and together they walked toward the french doors off the patio that led into Maggie's home. The event staff was clearing up the Viennese table and the bars on the patio. As they passed one bar, Connie grabbed an open bottle of wine. With his free hand, he snared two glasses.

It was quiet inside the house, and they tiptoed up to her room. Once inside, Connie led him to the sitting area at the far side of the space. The settee, a chair, and a small table were right by the doors leading to the balcony that ran along the length of the house and faced the ocean. Although there were lights by the entrance to each bedroom, they were off, and since Connie hadn't turned any on in the room when they'd entered, the settee, chair, and table were in intimate darkness.

She placed the bottle of wine on the table and kicked off her heels. A second later, she plucked the orange blossoms from her hair, undid the intricate braid, and let her thick, brown hair cascade to her shoulders. With a relieved sigh, she sank onto the settee and curled her legs beneath her.

Taking his cue from her, he set the glasses on the table, shucked off his jacket, vest, and ascot, and undid the first few buttons on his shirt. "I hate this monkey suit," he said and tossed the wedding attire onto the nearby chair.

"I know. Believe me, I'm not a fan of all this dress-up stuff either," she said as he poured a glass of wine and handed it to her.

"But you looked beautiful. You all looked beautiful."

The dark failed to hide the splash of color on her cheeks. He found it delightful that a woman as poised and professional as Connie could still blush.

"Thank you, but Maggie stole the show in her great-grandmother's gown. Did you know her mom wore the same gown when she got married here at the mansion?"

He hadn't, and he tried to drag up a memory of Maggie's mom. When they were kids, she'd often join them on the beach. As he recalled her vibrant smile and her kind eyes, it occurred to him that Maggie looked a lot like her mother. "I remember her. She was a nice lady." As other memories surged forward, he added, "She was the only one who ever seemed to be able to make my father smile. I even remember her convincing him to help us build a sand castle once. He had just come down from the city and was still in his suit pants and starched white shirt, but he got down on his knees and did it."

The memory brought a smile to his face, something that didn't happen often in connection with his father. But it also made him consider something else. "I was little when she died and don't remember much about it. But things were different afterward, and not for the better."

"How so?" Connie asked and sipped her wine.

He struggled to recall what had made him feel that way, but he'd only been six at the time. There had been grief. Anger. Loneliness. With an uncertain shake of his head, he said, "I can't say. We stopped coming down to Sea Kiss after that. We hated that, Owen especially. I think even back then he was in love with Maggie."

That earned a strangled laugh from Connie. "Seriously, Jon. They were, like, what, seven or eight?"

He glanced at her over the rim of his glass of wine and said, "Sometimes you just know."

―⁓―

Connie had never been one to believe in love at first

sight. She'd always been too practical and level-headed. Driven, some would say. And while she might scoff at Jonathan's fanciful belief that her friend and his brother had fallen in love as children, there was no doubting the look in his eyes that said Jonathan thought she might be "the one."

She stared down at her glass and swirled the wine around as if searching for some truth there. Didn't they say *in vino veritas* after all? But the only thing that came to her was something he wouldn't want to hear.

"Sometimes 'the one' is the totally wrong person for you," she said softly.

"You mean like your dad and my mom? People who were supposed to be there for us but just up and left?"

It was impossible to miss the raw emotion on his face or the tightness in his voice. She scooted over on the settee and cradled his jaw. Her gaze grew misty at his pain, and she said, "You still miss her."

It was hard for her to understand, since his mother had been gone nearly two decades. She had been barely eight when her father had left, and her memories of him were not good.

As he examined her features, the side of his mouth turned up in a nascent grin. "Why, Reyes. I might just think you care."

She gave in to a whim and ran her index finger along the line of the dimple that emerged as his grin broadened. "I'm afraid that I care too much," she said.

He grew serious and reached up, brushed a lock of hair away from her face. Rubbed a thick strand gently between his fingers as he said, "Caring takes courage, but the risk is worth the reward."

"She who dares wins," she murmured and traced the line of his lips with her thumb. Closed the distance between them to drop a kiss on the corner of his mouth. She felt his smile grow ever larger and shifted to the other side of his mouth. Placed a kiss there before covering his lips with hers, her kiss hesitant at first.

Courage, she told herself, afraid of so much, but she didn't want to waste this night with a man who she had been unable to forget for so many years.

He eased his hand to the back of her head and kept her close as they kissed over and over, but it just wasn't enough. She needed to be closer. Needed to feel his hard body against hers. The touch of his hands.

She straddled his legs, and he wrapped an arm around her waist and urged her toward him until her breasts were pressed tight against his chest and his growing erection was nestled at her center. The feel of it there, hardening and pressing against her, drew a ragged sigh from her.

He ended their kiss and shifted away from her, his gaze questioning, tender, and full of concern. "Connie?"

"Touch me, Jon. Please touch me."

Chapter 12

Jonathan's hands shook as he reached around, located the zipper on the back of the gown, and slowly drew it down. The bodice of the dress gaped and slipped away. As it did so, it revealed the lush curves of her breasts and the first hint of her dusky-rose nipples, hardened with passion.

As he finished lowering the zipper, he grabbed hold of the yards of satin and beads and drew the gown up and over her head. Let the dress slide to the ground in a puddle of navy.

"God, you're so beautiful," he said as he cupped her breasts and then kissed her again, swallowing her murmur of pleasure at his touch.

He ran his thumbs along the sensitive tips, entering into a familiar dance, because he hadn't forgotten what brought her pleasure. As her lips parted with a sigh of satisfaction, he slipped his tongue past the seam of her mouth and danced it along the perfect line of her teeth. Tasted her sweetness before retreating to skim a kiss along her jaw and neck and then lower.

She rose up on her knees to give him unfettered access to her breasts, and he feasted on the tight nubs of her nipples, licking and sucking them deep into his mouth. He wrapped an arm around her waist to steady her, and she cradled his head to her, urging him on with her soft cries. As she shifted her hips, rocking against him, he reached down, shifted aside the almost nonexistent scrap of lace covering her, and caressed her damp lips before finding the sensitive nub at her center. He stroked his finger across her clit and gently bit the tip of her nipple, dragging a rough shudder from her that said it wouldn't take much more to send her over the edge.

But he wasn't about to rush. Not when he'd waited so long to be with her again.

He rose from the couch, and she wrapped her legs around him and held on as he walked across the room to the bed. He fell down onto the bedspread with her, earning pleased laughter and a complaint.

"You've got too much clothing on," she whispered in his ear, and in a flurry of activity, she helped him remove his shirt and pants while he toed off his shoes and socks.

He covered her body with his, pressing her down into the mattress, leaving a playful trail of kisses from her neck to her breasts, where he leisurely built her passion, nipping and sucking until she was keening and bumping her hips up into his. Wanting to savor every second, he dipped one hand down and below the edge of her lace panties. Wrapped the fabric around his fingers and eased it lower to expose the dark, trimmed curls at her center. She lifted her hips to help him draw the panties off, leaving her naked on the bedspread.

He took a moment to appreciate the sight. Connie all grown-up, her womanly curves tempting him almost more than he could bear. Her gaze darkened as she licked her lips, murmured his name huskily, and spread her legs in invitation.

Easing between her legs, he wrapped his arms around her thighs and held her to his mouth as he explored her nether lips, flush with passion. Her breath hiked in her chest as he parted them to lick her and then nibble at her center.

Her body jerked upward, and she cupped the back of his head, urging him on.

He sucked and gently teethed her while stroking her toward a climax. The heat and wet of her there had his erection swelling and jerking with anticipation. As she neared the precipice, she shifted away slightly and cried out, "Come with me, Jon. I want you to come with me."

He was so, so ready, but as she guided him to her center, he realized that he hadn't prepared for something like this tonight. "Fuck, Connie, I'm so sorry. I don't have protection."

She caught him off guard with a sexy laugh. "That's okay," she said and reached into the nightstand beside the bed to pull out a strip of condoms. "Mrs. Patrick always wants her girls to be prepared," she said, referring to Maggie's housekeeper, who watched over the girls like they were her own.

"God bless Mrs. Patrick, only I'm not sure I'm up for so much preparedness," he said with a surprised look at the long length of the condom strip.

Connie grinned and took one out of the foil. She sexily caressed him as she rolled it down his length, and a shiver of desire tracked down his spine. "Seems to me you're up for it quite nicely."

He laughed, enjoying the mix of play and passion, recalling that making love with her had always been a meld of emotions that had made being together fresh and exciting. Keeping things in that spirit, he said, "I promise I will do my utmost not to disappoint."

———

Connie didn't doubt that he would do just that. As he dipped his head and kissed her breasts, she guided him to her center, sucking in a breath as his hard length brushed her sensitized lips. She released her breath shakily as he slowly, almost hesitantly, entered her inch by amazing inch until he was buried deep.

The pressure of him filling her nearly undid her. Her body shook from his possession and the tug and lick of his mouth on her nipples. She arched her back, wanting every inch of their bodies closer, savoring the hard muscle and lean body of the man he had become.

She offered herself up to him, cradling his hips with her knees to deepen his penetration until with one powerful thrust, she tumbled over the edge and he fell with her. He threw his head back, cried out her name, and ground himself even deeper as his body shook from the force of his release.

When he dropped onto her, he brushed a kiss across her lips before rolling onto his side and cradling her against him as he remained joined with her. He stroked his hand lightly along her cheek, his gaze searching her features. Uncertain of what he was looking for, she offered him a satisfied smile and a kiss. She tucked her head just beneath his jaw and wrapped her arms around him, content to share the peace that she felt in his arms.

She wouldn't read too much into that feeling right now. It was both too early and too late to think about it. She hadn't recognized that emotion when they had been together in college, and now, she wasn't sure where this night would lead.

"Relax," he said and stroked his hand down her back, sensing the growing tension in her body.

She took a deep breath and unwound the growing spiral of doubt inside her. Tonight was about enjoying all that was good between them. Worry could wait until tomorrow.

—⁓—

Jonathan woke to the warmth of her mouth on him and a teasing lick all along the sensitive underside of his erection. He groaned, tilted his hips upward, and brushed his fingers through her hair, gently guiding her as she made love to him.

As she took him in deep, he sucked in a breath to fight back his release. "Connie, I want to be with you," he said and reached toward the nightstand for protection.

Her husky laugh nearly undid him, and as he glanced at her, she held up the packet in her hand and grinned. "I've got this under control."

"Do you now?" he said with a grin, but he shook as she unrolled it down his length while caressing him.

"Fuck, Connie. Don't be a tease." Despite his complaint, he loved the leisurely way she straddled him and sank onto him. She stretched out over his body and ran her hands up his arms to twine her fingers with his. She pinned their joined arms above his head, bringing their bodies flush together. The soft hairs of his chest against her smooth skin. Hard muscle to curvy softness.

It felt so good, he didn't want to move. Didn't want to end the moment.

"Jon," she said and met his gaze. She let out a long sibilant sigh and brushed her lips along his over and over. Deepening the kiss, she urged his lips open to taste him.

He accepted the slide of her tongue and teased hers until she moaned into his mouth and shifted away slightly.

—///—

Connie searched his features, needing to understand what he wanted. How to finish what she had started but didn't want to end alone.

He smiled lopsidedly. "You're in control, Connie. Whatever you want. Whatever you need."

I want you, she thought. *I need you*, but the words stayed trapped inside along with the maelstrom of feelings for him.

She brought their joined hands down and placed his hands at her waist, inviting him to guide her as she slowly raised her hips before plunging back down, starting another dance. Savoring the rhythm as she rode him and their bodies glided ever closer to a release.

As the meter of her movements became more erratic, he tightened his hold on her and helped set the pace. She leaned forward and splayed her hands on the hard wall of his chest, the sun-bleached hair on his body soft beneath her palms, his erection rigid, the thickness of him an erotic fullness inside as she moved ever faster, climbing toward a climax.

"Jon," she keened as she rocked against him, and he moved beneath her, joining her in the duet until with one deep grind, she came, but he wasn't done.

———ᴧᴧᴧ———

Her body contracted and vibrated along his length, inviting him to join her in her release, but Jonathan wanted so much more from her. He wanted her to remember this time together in case they never had another night of loving. He wanted her wild and out of control to match what he was feeling inside.

Rolling, he trapped her beneath him, leaned forward, and kissed the tip of her breast before drawing it into his mouth. He shifted his hips and began to move again, gliding in and out of her, lifting her back up to the edge and keeping her there with his caresses and the powerful thrusts of his body.

Beneath him, she cried out with her passion and grabbed hold of his shoulders, bit into his skin with her nails, the pleasure and pain challenging his control. As she raised her knees and wrapped her legs around his waist, he drove in deep, barely keeping his own climax at bay. But as she arched her back and screamed out his name, he lost it and joined her in passion.

He held his weight off her as his climax raced across his body. Sucking in deep breaths, it took him long minutes to finally feel in control, and it was no different for Connie. Her body was still shaking from her release as he eased to his side and tucked her against him.

The morning sun was just rising past the ocean's embrace, and the first fingers of a rosy dawn leaked in through the open french doors along with a gentle early fall breeze. As the sun rose, it stretched those fingers toward the bed, warning that it was time to rise, but he was hesitant to move. He dreaded leaving her. Again.

She sensed the tension creeping into his body, cradled his face, and said, "Look at me, Jon."

He met her gaze but told himself it wasn't love he saw there. He didn't dare believe, as much as he wanted to. He didn't dare say the words, because it was too soon and there was too much history there. Too much pain.

She offered him an enigmatic half smile and said, "Let's not color this moment with anything dark. Not when it's such a lovely morning filled with light and promise."

In spite of her words, he couldn't help fear where this interlude would lead. But maybe it was best to leave it as is. Filled with light and promise. "It is truly an epic morning," he said and turned his face to place a kiss on her palm.

Her smile brightened, and she settled back into his embrace, laid her hand against his chest, and began a slow, soothing caress there. He let himself relax into the moment, enjoying the easy morning as the sun crept ever higher and called for them to rise and begin the day.

They dressed in silence, but not alone, helping each other pick up the pieces of clothing that had been tossed about the night before. He dressed in his wedding clothes but left the vest and top few buttons of his shirt open. She tucked the ascot into the breast pocket of the tux with a loving caress along his chest.

He reached down and tightened the belt on the robe she had slipped on before taking hold of her hand and guiding her down the stairs and to the front door of the mansion. He paused there and faced her, unsure of how to say goodbye, but she kept him from saying a word by rising up on tiptoes and skimming a kiss along his lips.

"It's too soon, Jon," she said.

"I get it, Reyes. You want this to develop organically," he said with a grin.

She narrowed her gaze to scrutinize him. "That's genius talk for 'we're going to fly by the seat of our pants,' isn't it?"

He tucked his hands into his pockets, and his grin broadened. "It sure is. Can you deal with that?"

He held his breath as he waited, because Connie never did anything that spontaneous, but then she shocked the shit out of him by saying, "Maybe."

Not wanting to push, he nodded and brushed a featherlight kiss across her lips. He turned and walked away and told himself not to look back, because if she was still there, he'd be tempted to return and stretch a night and morning of loving into an afternoon of loving. But he did, only to find that she'd already closed the door.

Don't read anything into that, he thought. *Last night was more than you could ever have hoped for*, he reminded himself and smiled, filled with light and promise in the early morning sun. But the closer he got to his front door, the more the feeling fled as he realized that he'd have no choice but to finally face his father.

He paused at the front door, girding himself for the confrontation, wondering what he'd say after nearly a decade of separation. But if he and Connie could somehow find their way together, maybe he and his father could as well.

He grabbed hold of the knob, opened the door, and marched in.

Chapter 13

DON'T LINGER, CONNIE THOUGHT, SHUT THE DOOR, AND then leaned back against it, wondering what she'd just done.

Maybe? Really? Had she, the person who'd had a plan for every part of her life, actually just given the green light to a no-rules, here-goes-anything relationship with him? Could you even call it a relationship after only one night and a promise of maybe?

The sound of someone padding down the stairs drew her attention. Emma, almost skipping along the steps, an immense smile on her face. Her friend paused as she saw Connie by the door, and her smile faded.

"Oh no. I've seen that look on your face before, and it wasn't good," Emma said.

Connie shook her head, but it was half-hearted with her confusion. She finally pushed away from the door and toward her friend, wrapped her arm around Emma's shoulders, and hugged her.

"You seem better today. Not like last night," Connie said and urged Emma to the kitchen where the sound of Mrs. Patrick's joyful humming filled the air. As they entered the kitchen, Mrs. Patrick turned away from the island where she had all the fixings for waffles.

"Good morning, my girls. How are you today?" she said. She settled her wizened gaze on Connie, and that made Emma examine Connie's features again.

"You and Jon? Last night? This morning?" her friend said.

Heat erupted across Connie's cheeks, and she covered them with her hands. "Do I have a scarlet letter *A* on my chest or something?"

Emma peered at her, as if searching for additional evidence confirming last night's loving but apparently found none. That didn't keep her friend from pushing for more. "Did you have too much to drink? Get carried away with all the wedding stuff? Or did you just go insane?"

Connie rolled her eyes and walked over to the island. Bowls of assorted berries and mascarpone sat beside a shaker with cinnamon sugar and a small jug of maple syrup. Mrs. Patrick handed Connie a plate with a duo of waffles straight off the iron, but she handed it back and said, "Please, you go first. I can make the next batch."

The older woman didn't argue, but as Connie took over making the waffles, Mrs. Patrick passed by and whispered, "She won't let go of it that easily."

Connie grabbed a ladle, filled it with batter, and went to work on another batch, but as the housekeeper had predicted, Emma stood across from her at the island, leaned her hands on the edge, and said, "Spill, Connie. What happened with Jon?"

With an exasperated sigh, she adopted a pose similar to Emma's, hands braced on the counter. She arched her brow and said, "Do I look like the kind to kiss and tell?"

Emma laughed out loud. "OMG, the fact that you even say that tells me there was not only kissing involved but a lot, lot more."

A flush warmed her cheeks again, but she tilted her

chin up and met Emma's gaze directly. "I wasn't drunk, and I didn't get carried away. Whether I'm insane is up for grabs. It kind of developed…organically," she said a smile.

Emma barked out a laugh, and the tone of her voice had the ring of rising worry. "Organically? You mean like bullshit? That's organic, isn't it?"

Connie leaned across the island counter and grabbed hold of Emma's hand. "It just happened, okay? I'm not sorry it did, and I'm not sure where it's going to go. We're going to play it by ear."

Emma's eyebrows shot up. "Play it by ear? Con, you never do anything spontaneous. Seriously, you even plan spontaneity."

She chuckled because she couldn't deny her friend's statements. "I *do* plan everything, and it's *not* easy to think about just going with the flow. It scares the shit out of me, especially with someone like Jon."

"Because he broke your heart last time and you don't want him to break it again," Emma added and gave Connie's hand a reassuring squeeze.

She nodded, and as she noticed the light on the iron go green, she took the waffles off it, put them on a plate, and passed it to Emma. "Yes, because of all that and more, but enough about me. What about you?"

Emma accepted the plate from Connie and blew out an exasperated sigh. "Carlo is a friend. Just a good friend," she said while she loaded up the waffle with the mascarpone, berries, and a generous drizzle of maple syrup.

"A very handsome friend, Emma. Very responsible and caring as well. If I were younger, I'd be sure not to let a man like that get away," Mrs. Patrick chimed in from the table where she was eating her waffles.

"Yes, he's all those other things," Emma replied as she sat down with her waffles.

"And you like his family too, and they like you," Connie said and poured more batter onto the waffle iron for her breakfast.

"I do like his family," Emma said reluctantly, but then she quickly tacked on, "But Carlo and I work together, and we've even talked about becoming partners. It would totally complicate everything if we got involved."

Connie walked over to the nearby coffeepot, grabbed the carafe, poured cups for the three of them, and then sat down by Emma. "But *he* wants to be involved. Surely you can see that, Em. You see everything about the couples in your weddings, so you have to see how he feels about you."

Emma laid down her fork and stared at her plate. Her tones were soft and tinged with pain as she said, "I see it. It hurts me to see it. I can't be what he wants. There's something broken inside me, and he deserves more than someone who can never be whole."

Connie wrapped her arms around her friend, brought her close, and dropped a kiss on her temple. "He wants you. He understands you. And I know that he can fix whatever you think is broken inside."

Emma sniffled and nodded. "I'll think about it. It's all I can promise."

Connie smiled and hugged her hard again. "No matter what, we'll be here for you."

"And I'll be here for you, Con. Don't be afraid to

give Jon a chance. He's a good guy, and I don't think he ever stopped loving you."

And maybe I never stopped loving him, she thought. But that didn't make it any easier to think about being with a man like Jonathan, who was the proverbial rolling stone, moving from one thing to the next. She'd seen what a man like that had been like in her own family. When her father came home, it would be quiet at first, but slowly, the pressure would build as his wanderlust took hold. Like water set to boil on the stove, the fights would start, growing larger and more frequent until her father's need to escape would erupt and he'd be gone again.

When her father had gone for good, she'd felt relief, even if their lives had gotten harder in some respects. Money had been scarce, and her mother had worked herself nearly to death until her grandparents had finally relented and brought them into their fold.

She'd vowed never to know such poverty again but also never to fall for a man who wouldn't be responsible and stick around.

She'd misjudged Jonathan seven years earlier when he'd said he wasn't going to school, but his actions had been too reminiscent of her father.

She didn't want to misjudge him again, but his escapades with his company's products and his seemingly never-ending quest to try something new scared her. But it also scared her to think she would never feel with someone else what she felt with Jonathan.

Because of that, she'd give their organic relationship a try, even if it wasn't something she normally did. Maybe you had to break the rules sometimes, she thought.

—⁓—

Jonathan hesitated at the front door of his family's home, certain of the kind of reception he would get and yet unwilling to let his father drive him away from the place he loved. And, of course, Dudley and his laptop, just as Connie had surmised.

He turned the knob and opened the door. Hesitantly, he stepped inside, and Dudley's happy barks and what sounded like a human laugh greeted him, only he couldn't recall the last time he'd heard his father laugh. Or seen him smile for that matter, but as he walked through the house and toward the noise, he found his father feeding bits of bacon to Dudley.

"Sit, boy," his father said. When Dudley complied and glanced up at him lovingly, his father patted him on the head, smiled, and offered him another piece of bacon. "That's a good boy."

To say Jonathan was shocked would be an understatement. He'd never seen his father so relaxed and, dare he say, happy. His father's eyes looked a little swollen, as if maybe he'd been crying, although that was impossible. His father was a bitter, emotionless shell of a man.

"Father," Jonathan said in greeting.

His dad didn't look his way as he offered Dudley another treat and said, "I was wondering how long you'd stand there, looking like something the cat just dragged in."

And there was the nasty man he remembered. Before he could respond, his father said, "Is this little pup yours?"

"He is," Jonathan said and approached the end of the

table opposite his father. As he did so, Dudley raced
to his side and sat at his feet, seemingly declaring his
loyalty. With a little bark, Dudley demanded his attention, and Jonathan bent, rubbed the dog's head, and said,
"Who's a good boy?"

The dog happily yipped and licked his hand as if
in apology for his apparent defection, hoping that
Jonathan understood the irresistible temptation of the
bacon. Smiling, Jonathan rose and faced his father.
"Owen and I were surprised you were here but didn't
come to the wedding."

His father shrugged. "I didn't want to be noticed."

Jonathan raised his hands and spread his fingers in
emphasis. "Big fail. Next time, don't turn on the lights, or
better yet, be human and celebrate your son's happiness."

The elder Pierce barked out a laugh and waved a
bony, age-spotted hand. "Happiness? So you think this
marriage is for real? I didn't think Owen was that good
a liar."

Jonathan wanted to retort that his brother had so far
been able to deceive their father into thinking the marriage was only about getting the Sinclair properties, but
he held back. Owen was walking a precarious line with
neither Maggie nor their father knowing the full truth. In
time, he knew his brother would make things right. He
couldn't jeopardize that, no matter how much he wanted
to prove his father wrong.

"So you came here to gloat? To savor putting the
final nail in the Sinclair coffin?" Jonathan asked.

A sudden change came over his father as sadness
crept onto his features. "I had my reasons," he said but
didn't elaborate. Instead, he deflected just as Jonathan

had done seconds earlier. "What are you doing here? This is not your home anymore."

Stick the knife in and give it a twist, why don't you? he thought, but he contained his hurt. It would please his father to know that he'd struck a vulnerable spot. With a careless shrug, he said, "It's just a place to hang my hat. I'll be out of here as soon as I change and round up my things."

He didn't wait for a reply, but it chased him out of the room. "I told you years ago that this wasn't a place for you to drift to off and on while you tried to find yourself. Since that hasn't changed, you're not welcome here."

His father hadn't changed, he thought as he climbed the stairs, feeling way older than his years. He had hoped that his dad would one day see who he really was and all that he'd accomplished in the nearly eight years since he'd been disowned. It was time to move on to the next phase of his life and make a home for himself that wasn't bogged down by past hurts and disappointments.

Chapter 14

THEY'D HEARD THE SQUEAL OF WHEELS AS JONATHAN had raced out of his driveway on Sunday morning. Clearly, things hadn't gone all that well with his father on Jonathan's return to the Pierce mansion. She'd waited to text him a short message to find out if he'd gotten home okay. His brief reply confirmed it and nothing else. Nothing to indicate just what the next step would be in their "organically" developing relationship.

She tried driving him from her mind for the rest of the morning as she, Emma, Maggie's dad, and Mrs. Patrick recovered from the wedding festivities. By early Sunday afternoon, she was packed and ready to go back to her condo in Jersey City. She thought about visiting her mom in nearby Union City, but her mother had always been able to read her like a book. She'd take one look at Connie's face and know that something was up.

More than just one something, she thought. There was her job and what she planned on doing about the disappearing partnership possibilities. Jonathan. A surprisingly warm, fuzzy feeling swept through her at the thought that he might be back in her life. It was quickly replaced with a giant knot of worry at how long it might be before he got bored and moved on.

By Tuesday morning, she was wondering if he'd reconsidered and, worse, didn't want to reach out to him first and make herself vulnerable. She'd settled on casual relationships with men for a long time, since her focus had been on her career. That had made her forget the anticipation and uncertainty that came with starting a real relationship.

Setting her coffee cup on her desk, she sat to tackle the matters needing her attention, and luckily, there was nothing pressing except a response from a headhunter who had reached out to her a year earlier. The recruiter had had a client looking for someone just like her for their legal department, but she'd passed on the opportunity because she'd thought she was going somewhere at her firm. Now she had to reconsider her plan.

She quickly answered the recruiter's email and sent off a copy of the résumé she'd updated when she'd gotten home on Sunday. Hopefully, he'd have some positions that met her level of expertise and her salary requirements. She was paying off not only her own condo, but also part of the mortgage payments on her family's house in Union City.

Turning to the first file on her desk, she reviewed the correspondence from their foreign counsel. She was about to draft a response when her phone rang. She recognized Jonathan's number, answered, and walked to close her office door for some privacy.

"G'mornin'," he said in a sleepy drawl that had her imagining him whispering those words in her ear while they lay wrapped together, savoring a peaceful morning.

"Mornin'," she replied, hating how husky her own voice sounded.

"I'm sorry I didn't phone yesterday, but we had some issues at work, and it was past midnight when I got home."

"Sorry to hear that. Anything you want to share?"

"Lawyers. Why does everything go south when lawyers are involved?" he said, deep frustration mingling with humor.

"I totally know the feeling," she said, since she had run into many attorneys who didn't know how to play well with others. "Can I help with anything?"

"Not really, but I could use your help with something else this weekend," he said.

She could tell it cost him a little to ask, as if he was also having that mix of anticipation and uncertainty she'd been feeling. "I'm free this weekend," she said without hesitation, wanting to move past the doubt so they would really explore what was happening between them.

His sigh of relief drifted across the phone line. "Awesome. Pick you up on Friday? Around six?"

Since everything was under control on her desk, she said, "That sounds fine. What do you need help with?"

"Finding a house."

Jonathan opened the door to the suite that he'd reserved at the Sea Kiss Inn. He stepped aside to let Connie enter and wasn't disappointed by her sigh of pleasure.

"This is lovely," she said as she did a little pirouette to examine the main room of the suite that was decorated with Victorian-era antiques. On one table by the couch, a fragrant bouquet of roses sat in a crystal vase. At either side of the room, doors opened to the two bedrooms in the suite that each had their own bathrooms.

She narrowed her gaze and glanced from one door to the other. "Two bedrooms?" she asked with a surprised look.

He should have guessed that Connie, who worried about his being unpredictable, might read all the wrong things into that choice. He faced her, cradled her cheek, and said, "Making love to you last weekend was amazing, but I didn't want to assume or rush you."

A hint of a smile tugged up one corner of her lips. "Because you're all about being organic," she joked.

He grinned and whispered a kiss across her blossoming smile. "Get settled. I made an eight o'clock reservation for us at The Dunes."

"The Dunes? That's my favorite place, but I thought they didn't take reservations."

He grinned and said, "I know the right people. The owner was a short-order cook at a bar where I worked, and we stayed friends." He didn't add that when Hurricane Sandy had done serious damage to the restaurant located close to the Sea Kiss River inlet, he'd helped out his friend when delays in insurance claims and public funds had threatened to forever close the business.

Connie seemed to realize that there was more to the story that he wasn't saying. "I'll have to pry the rest from you over dinner," she said.

"Go get ready. I'm a growing boy, and I'm starving."

She did as he asked, wheeling her overnight bag to the room at the far side of the suite. He grabbed his duffel and took it to the front bedroom that had a balcony that overlooked Main Street and also had a fabulous view of the ocean. The early fall sun was pouring in through the windows but would be setting soon. He tossed his duffel at the side of the bed, walked over to the french doors along the balcony, and threw them open to take in the sunset.

A second later, he heard the rap against the doorframe and glanced back to find Connie waiting by the jamb. He held out his hand in invitation, and she strolled over and joined him on the balcony.

"Beautiful, isn't it?" he said and wrapped his arms around her waist to draw her close as she stood before him.

She relaxed against him, her head tucked just under his chin. Her arms rested on his as the sun faded to the west and bathed the street and ocean with its last golden rays. Dusk settled a cape of reds and purples over the town, and as it did so, Connie turned in his arms and ran her hands up to his shoulders.

She didn't say a word as she reached up and raked her fingers through the longish strands of his hair. With a smile, she rose up on tiptoes and gifted him with a gentle kiss filled with promise. As she shifted away slightly, she skimmed her hand along his cheek, and at his questioning gaze, she said, "Thank you for being so thoughtful. The rooms. The restaurant."

"The lovely sunset I planned just for you," he kidded.

She rolled her eyes and swatted his arm playfully. "You're good but not that good. Let's go eat."

Hand in hand, they strolled down to the lobby and exited onto Main Street. Many of the shops along the avenue were open late to take advantage of tourists staying for the gorgeous weekend. In another couple of weeks, it would start getting too cold for most of the beach lovers, and the businesses would buckle down for the sometimes-lonely winter months.

They ambled away from the center of town and turned toward the inlet and the restaurants and inns that faced

the river. As they headed toward the restaurant, a number
of locals passed by them, and not one of them failed to
greet Jonathan with a smile or a respectful dip of their
head. Jonathan responded by offering everyone a smile.

———

Connie couldn't help but notice how popular Jonathan
seemed to be. But she was pleased that quite a number
of the people they passed likewise greeted her with a
friendly smile. She had worked with some of them on
a committee to help rebuild after Hurricane Sandy. A
number of other people had been pro bono clients she'd
helped with assorted legal issues related to the storm.

As yet another person walked by and smiled at
Jonathan, she leaned close and said, "Did I miss you
being elected mayor or something?"

With his typical without-a-care shrug, he said, "Just
friends. You seem to know a lot of people in town too."

Again, she had the sense there was more to his explanation, but Jonathan wasn't one to toot his own horn,
and in reality, neither was she. Before long, they'd
arrived at the restaurant. People lingered on the sidewalk
in front of the Victorian-style building and all along the
first-floor veranda where luckier patrons had been able
to snag a space to enjoy drinks before dinner.

Jonathan skipped up the steps with her following, and
as he neared the hostess podium, the attractive young
woman working there smiled and walked around to hug
him. "It's good to see you again, Jon," she said.

Connie wrestled down the little green monster.
Luckily, since a second later, Jonathan said, "This is
Meghan, my buddy's wife. Meghan, this is Connie."

The woman glanced at her as if to say *That Connie?*, which made her wonder just how long Jonathan had known the restaurant's owners. But there was little time to ponder it as Meghan said, "I've got your table waiting. Let me get someone to take you up."

With a wave at a young waitress who scurried over, Meghan handed the twentysomething woman two menus and told her the table number. The young lady quickly led them up the stairs to the third floor of the restaurant and then out to a balcony and a corner table. The location of the restaurant and its height gave them an unimpeded view of Sea Kiss Beach, the river inlet, and, across the way, the piers and lights of the neighboring Jersey Shore towns to the south.

"This is totally beautiful," Connie said as Jonathan held out the chair for her and she sat. He took the spot next to her, facing the beach and inlet.

"We couldn't ask for a better view or a nicer night." He tacked on, "Or better company."

She thought he couldn't be more right. The early fall day lacked any humidity, and the temperature had been in the high seventies earlier. It had cooled somewhat as night fell, but it was still comfortable. Beneath the clatter of cutlery and glasses and the soft chatter of the nearby patrons, there was the calming susurrus of the ocean. The longer she sat there perusing the menu, the more she relaxed.

She felt that way often in Sea Kiss, which explained why she liked to visit as much as she could. Maybe one day, she could even afford a little place here for herself as a weekend getaway. Maybe if she got her career back on track. Maybe even if this thing with Jonathan turned out to be more. More of what, she couldn't say, because Jonathan was still an unknown variable.

The waitress came over to take their drink orders. Jonathan glanced at her and said, "Would you like some wine? A cocktail?"

Not that alcohol had played all that big a role in what had happened the night of Maggie's wedding, but she wanted to keep a clear head this weekend. "No, thanks. A diet cola would be fine."

"The draft IPA for me, thanks. Did you decide on what you want?" he said.

With a nod, Connie ordered her meal and Jonathan did the same, but after the waitress left, he said, "Are you sure you don't want a salad or appetizer?"

She shook her head and motioned to her body. "I hate salad, which explains all these curves, so I cut down where I can."

He eyed her appreciatively, inched closer, and whispered against the shell of her ear, "I love every inch of those curves."

Heat flashed through her with his words.

He glanced at her from the corner of his eye and added, "And I love that you blush. I love seeing that color all over your creamy skin."

When he sat back in his chair and met her gaze, a sexy smile filled with promise on his lips, she grabbed her glass of ice water and chugged down a few healthy gulps to try and cool the heat he had created. Luckily, the waitress returned with Jonathan's beer and a tasty appetizer the chef-owner had specially created for them.

Small chunks of lobster, barely dressed with a homemade mayonnaise, sat on a delicate leaf of soft, creamy butter lettuce. Connie ate a forkful of the lobster, and the light, lemony taste of the mayo was a perfect complement to the tender shellfish.

"Delicious," she said and ate slowly to savor the elegant sample.

Jonathan devoured it in a few forkfuls but murmured his approval. "I always knew Mac was wasted at flipping burgers."

"You said you met him when you worked at a bar?"

A slight grimace crossed his features, and as he spoke, the tension in his voice was apparent. "At the Sandbar, after I decided not to go to school. I worked there for a few months before I went to SoCal. When I came back to Sea Kiss, Mac was just opening the restaurant. I helped out until I sold that first big idea and decided to start my company."

She got the reason for his discomfiture. Bringing up his decision not to go back to school had been the deal breaker for their relationship at the time. She'd been unwilling to consider anything other than her vision for their future. She still wasn't sure if she could handle his impulsiveness, but she was willing to try.

"You took a risk, and it paid off. Not everyone is brave enough to do that."

He eyed her directly, seemingly uncertain, but then smiled with that enticing, crooked grin. "I think you might actually mean that, Reyes."

She chuckled and retorted, "Does it shock you that I might have changed, Mr. Pierce?"

He leaned close once again, brushed a kiss along her cheek, and said, "Actually, it pleases me a lot."

She tried not to let his comment satisfy her too much,

but as warmth spread across her skin, she realized she'd failed, but she'd own it. Especially as he sat back and his gaze traveled over her face tenderly, as stirring as a physical touch.

She finished her tasting of the delicious lobster just in time for the waitress to set their main courses before them. Hunger took over, forging a companionable silence as they ate. But as she got closer to finishing her meal, she said, "So you want to go house hunting tomorrow?"

He nodded. "And shopping for a new research and development center. We need more space for the company and agreed to look in the Sea Kiss area, since I plan on staying here."

She examined him carefully, but he was clearly sincere about his intentions. She opted not to press him for the moment. "Any ideas what you're looking for?"

"I spotted a building near the train tracks that seems perfect."

"The old guitar company building?" she asked.

He grinned. "Yeah, that one. There's just something about it that's pulling me in."

She understood. The building had charm even if it could use a serious rehab project. "What about the house?" she said as she finished the last of the short rib she'd ordered.

He put his knife and fork down on his empty plate. "On the beach, if possible. At least four or five bedrooms, maybe more. Open concept. Garage and driveway. Nice yard. Big kitchen so I can cook."

It sounded a lot like his family's home, but she kept that to herself. She also wondered why he needed so many rooms, unless of course he was planning for kids, something she couldn't quite picture. Or maybe she didn't want to picture it, because the thought of his having kids with someone else caused a funny ache in her heart. Instead, she said, "So you like to cook?"

"I do and not just Bolognese sauce. Once I find a place, I'll whip you up something epic."

"Epic, huh?" she kidded.

With a boyish grin, he said, "Totally epic. Gnarly even."

She got caught up in his optimism and the promise of the possible future she had pondered earlier. "I'd like that."

A busboy swung by to pick up their empty plates and was immediately followed by the waitress. "Can I get you anything for dessert? Coffee or an after-dinner drink?"

He looked toward her. "Anything?"

"I'll pass for now," she said, clearly surprising him, but he said nothing as the waitress walked away to get their check.

Once the young woman was gone, he leaned close and said, "If I remember correctly, you used to have a wicked sweet tooth."

She dipped her head toward him and said, "I still do, but I thought we could hit up the ice-cream parlor on the way back to the inn."

"No argument here. That place is my fave."

They seemed to have a lot of common faves, from Sea Kiss to the old building to the ice-cream parlor, but was that enough of a foundation for the future?

After the check was settled, he rose and offered her his hand again. She took hold, and he twined his fingers with hers. Comfort filled her with that simple gesture. They walked down and out of the restaurant and strolled back toward the center of town. They ambled past Main Street to the next block, where the old-fashioned counter-style ice-cream parlor reigned next to a number of smaller businesses. Even with the later hour, there was a line of people out the door, but it moved quickly thanks to the efficient staff behind the counter. In a few weeks, the place would close for the winter season.

As in the restaurant, Jonathan was greeted warmly by the servers and the cashier.

"You have made a lot of friends in your travels," Connie said with a lick of her caramel waffle cone ice cream.

Her comment, instead of being taken as a compliment, seemed to shake him. She laid a hand on his arm, urging him to stop and face her. "I didn't mean anything bad by that, Jon."

He shrugged and avoided her gaze, but she cupped his jaw and applied gentle pressure until he met her questioning gaze. "I guess I've let all my dad's negative comments eat at me for too long," he said.

She swiped her thumb across his lips that were chilled from the ice cream he'd just eaten. Smiling, she followed her caress with a kiss, warming his lips with hers, tasting the slight sweetness from his treat. Trying to lighten the mood again, she whispered against his lips, "Didn't take you for a vanilla kind of guy."

He groaned, cupped the back of her head, and kept her near, deepening the kiss. Licking all around her mouth and pulling her closer until the chill of his cone registered against the skin of her upper arm.

With a chuckle against his lips, she said, "I think you're melting."

He shot a glance at the cone and the ice cream smeared against her arm and dribbling down across his fingers. A dimpled grin spread across his lips before he bent and licked away the spot of ice cream on her bicep, shooting a wave of heat through her body.

She mimicked his gesture, took hold of his wrist, and held his hand steady as she licked the melted confection from his fingers. "Sweet," she said.

He swooped in for a brief but intense kiss and retreated to say, "Sweeter."

She wanted to toss aside her ice cream and haul him back to the inn to show him just how sweet it could be between them, but passion had never been an issue with them, just everything else. Because of that, she grabbed hold of his hand and swung it playfully as she said, "There's a nice breeze tonight. I bet it's even nicer on the boardwalk."

He breathed out a laugh and said, "Not too obvious, Reyes."

Despite that, he strolled with her to the boardwalk while they ate their ice creams. The breeze was stronger but not unpleasant. They sauntered southward toward the jetty and the lighthouse, then leaned against the railing surrounding the lighthouse to silently watch the ships far out at sea and the sweep of the light across the whitecaps the wind had kicked up.

As the breeze grew ever stronger, it chilled her, and she shivered in his arms.

"Ready to go back to the inn?" he asked.

Chapter 15

JONATHAN HELD HIS BREATH AS HE WAITED FOR HER answer. *Ridiculous*, he told himself. Where else was she supposed to go? Not to mention there were two rooms.

"Yes, that would be nice," she said.

With a nod, he wrapped an arm around her shoulders to offer some protection against the wind, and she tucked herself into his side. The soft fullness of her breast pressed against his chest while her rounded hip bumped his as they walked. It felt right in so many ways, but he didn't want to read more into it. Whatever this was going on between them was just too fresh and too uncertain.

He didn't make any assumptions about their quickened pace. It was chillier thanks to the stronger breeze and maybe even the ice cream they'd eaten, which had stolen some of their body heat. Within minutes, they were turning up Main Street and back toward the inn a block away from the ocean.

He used his key to unlock the front door and enter the lobby. Soft lights were on to welcome guests, and they treaded softly up the stairs so as not to disturb anyone who had already settled down for the night. When they entered the suite, a light on one of the end tables cast a warm, welcoming glow. A bowl of fresh fruit and a dish with chocolates sat on the coffee table beside a bottle of champagne in an ice bucket and crystal flutes.

"Did you do this?" she asked, taking in the sight of the treats.

"I wish I could take credit for this, but I can't. Doesn't mean we can't enjoy it." He walked over to the champagne, grabbed the bottle, deftly opened it. He poured bubbly into the glasses and handed one to her.

She eyed the glass and kidded, "Trying to get me drunk, Mr. Pierce?"

He shook his head vehemently. "No way, Reyes. I want you totally aware of everything we do."

"And what will we do?" she said as she strolled toward the couch, glass in hand, and sat.

"Whatever you'd like," he said, which earned a moue from her.

"Because you don't want to assume or rush me? Because you want me to be in control of what happens?" she challenged, confusing him with the hint of pique in her voice.

He joined her on the couch and took a sip of the chilled champagne. He examined her as he said, "Too much pressure, Reyes?"

She surprised him with a nod. "If I get involved with you—"

"*When*, not if," he corrected.

She directed a laser-sharp look at him. "When. I want a partnership where you and I"—she motioned between the two of them—"do this together."

He couldn't resist her when she got too serious. But he also couldn't resist shattering that composure. "I prefer together. Doing it alone is never as much fun."

A sharp chuckle burst from her. "You're so bad."

He scooted across the couch until his knee brushed

her thigh. "You may deny it, but I think that you like that."

She shook her head but avoided his gaze.

He dipped his head so she couldn't avoid him and said, "Come on, admit it."

She pushed his chest playfully, urging him away as she said, "If I admitted it, you'd be even worse."

With a laugh, he said, "I'll take that, Reyes." He reached over to the chocolates on the table, picked one up, and offered it to her. She took a bite of the creamy truffle, and he finished off the rest of the treat. He took another sip of his champagne, and she did the same, finishing off her glass.

He went to refill the glass, but she held her hand over the flute to stop him. With a nod, he returned the bottle to the ice bucket and gave his attention to her, trying to read the signals there. Trying to figure out where to take this night.

~⁓~

Connie searched his features, hesitant about what he wanted. Unsure of what she wanted. Their physical attraction had always been intense, but beneath that was an allure of a different kind. His humor and intelligence. His kindness. His strength. Beneath that undemanding and easygoing persona, he had a backbone of steel. He'd had to develop one to survive his father.

She wanted to experience that strength. That kindness.

She leaned in and skated a kiss across his lips, tracing the hard line of them, nipping at his full lower lip, and urging him to open to her.

He accepted the slide of her tongue, met it with his.

He tasted of champagne, chocolate, and Jonathan, an intriguing mix that had her meeting his kiss over and over. Had her straining to be against his hard body until he bracketed her waist with his hands and urged her onto his lap. He inched his hands to her back and splayed them there, dragging her tight to his chest.

Her breasts brushed that wall of muscle and tingled from the contact. At her center, the hard ridge of his erection pressed into her as she straddled his legs. Her insides clenched with want, but she fought against that desire, afraid of losing herself to that need again.

He must have sensed her conflict, because he slowly tempered his kisses and gentled his hold. She leaned her forehead against his and sucked in a rough breath, whispering, "You make me want to forget everything."

He tunneled his fingers into her hair and massaged her scalp. "The passion is still there, Reyes, but I understand. It's not any easier for me."

"What do we do about it?" she asked and rested her hands on his shoulders, soothing the strong line of them because she couldn't resist touching him.

"I want you. I think you know that. But I want more than just this, and I think you do too." He ran his hands up and down her back, his touch gentle. As he met her gaze, his crystal-blue eyes were filled with determination but also understanding.

"I do," she admitted, and with his help guiding her off his lap, they sat facing each other again on the couch.

"We should call it a night then. We're going to be running around a lot tomorrow." He rose from the couch and held out his hand. She slipped her hand into his, and he walked her to her bedroom door, waiting there for a second before brushing a quick kiss across her lips. "Night, Connie."

"Night, Jon," she said, but she couldn't resist adding, "Dream of me."

A sad smile crept onto his lips, and he cupped her cheek. "I always do."

———

Mary Sanders, the real estate agent, was obviously frustrated. They had visited more than half a dozen houses in Sea Kiss and the adjacent towns. Each residence had more than met Jonathan's criteria. Each one was beautiful in its own way, but not one of them had been acceptable. Connie suspected that it was because not one of them was the Pierce beach house.

With little success in the hunt for a home, Mary turned her attention to the search for the new location for the research and development center for Jonathan's business. At his request, they started at the old guitar manufacturing building across the tracks from the Sea Kiss train station, just blocks away from the heart of the town.

There was something stately about the look of the place with its stucco walls, detailed woodwork on the window frames and doors, and the clock tower with the hands permanently frozen at 3:35. Inside, the plaster walls needed work and paint, as vandals had gotten in and spray-painted their tags in some areas. The first floor must have been a display area of some kind at one point, since there was a large open space in the middle flanked by a half dozen or so nice-sized offices.

Jonathan was silent as they walked through the

building, his gaze darting from one area to another until he finally said, "We could open up the back wall into the parking lot to allow us to bring in some models for display." Whirling, he swept his hand across one row of offices and said, "And those could be used as classrooms for the coding workshops I want to hold for anyone who wants to take the classes."

They walked up the stairs to tour the three other floors, avoiding the elevator in the corner that needed to be totally rehabbed. The two middle floors were in fairly good shape, but the upper story had signs of water damage, as did the clock tower. Despite that, Jonathan had a gleam in his eye and a smile on his face during the entire tour.

Connie appreciated his enthusiasm and vision as he talked about restoring the location to its former glory as well as making the building an efficient and comfortable workspace for his staff. Mary was pleased that, unlike their earlier house search, Jonathan might actually be thinking about buying the place despite the work that it needed.

As they returned to the bottom floor, Jonathan said, "How much are they asking?"

The real estate agent rattled off a number. "Two point two million. It's more about the land than anything else. And I have to warn you, the town council is thinking about rezoning this area to residential."

Connie shook her head, befuddled by the statement, and gestured to the location. "We're in the middle of a warehouse district and right next to the train tracks. Who would want to put up residential here?"

Mary shrugged. "A few towns over, they built condo

units directly next to the tracks. The tax base from those units is a reliable source of income for the town."

"And if I buy this place, I will not only be paying taxes on it, but it'll also bring prestige, jobs, and opportunities to the town," Jonathan countered. "Offer one point five for this place as is. They must know the building inspection will reveal that major work is needed to deal with the water damage and that elevator."

With another shrug, Mary said, "It's a little low, but it's been on the market for some time. I'll draw up the papers."

After they walked out and the real estate agent returned to her car, Connie stood by Jonathan as he placed his hands on his hips and considered the building once more. He glanced at her sideways and said, "What do you think?"

"A little late to ask, isn't it?" she said, but at his smirk, she continued. "It has good bones, but it'll take work. The rezoning thing bothers me. That could get tricky."

He nodded. "I agree, but you practice in Jersey, right?"

"I do. I've worked with the town council on some things," she said as they meandered to Jonathan's Jeep and hopped in.

"Then you can help me with the purchase and zoning if you don't mind taking me on as a client," he said. He watched the traffic and executed a U-turn to drive them back toward the inn. He handled the 4x4 competently, his hands graceful but strong on the wheel. Inside her, heat rose at the recollection of those hands guiding her as they made love. Of the gentle way he'd held her last night while banking the passion between them.

"They say it's not good to mix business and pleasure," she said, risking a glance at him from the corner of her eye.

His head whipped toward her for only a second before he returned his attention to the road, a wry grin on his face. "I wouldn't want to make you choose between the two."

"But friends help friends. We are friends, right?" she said, wanting to give a name to what was happening between them.

"We are that and more," he said and grinned that irresistible grin.

Chapter 16

JONATHAN HAD BEEN LOOKING FORWARD TO THE "AND more" part of their relationship ever since their return to the inn after the house hunting. But as much as he wanted her, he was determined to prove to Connie that their relationship could be one based on fun, friendship, and respect, not just passion. Not that passion wasn't important, but when that lusty fire burned out, there had to be other embers that kept the relationship alive. Not that he expected the five-alarm fire they ignited to extinguish anytime soon.

As they strolled hand in hand into their suite, he applied gentle pressure and urged her into his arms. "Thank you for helping me with the house search."

She laid her hands on his chest and stroked his pectorals. "You didn't like any of the places we saw, but there were a few nice houses."

He shrugged, and she shifted her hands up to run them across the broad line of his shoulders. "You know how sometimes you walk into a place and you know you were meant to be there?" he said.

At her nod, he continued, "None of them felt like home. We'll just have to keep looking."

"You will find one that feels like home," she echoed, but there was a note of doubt in her voice.

He bent and peered at her directly, trying to discern

the reason, and it became clear to him. "You don't think I will."

"I think your heart is tied to your family's beach house. I think you have to let go of that place to find your own home," she said and cradled his jaw, as if to soothe any sting from her words.

He couldn't take exception with what she'd said. Turning his face, he kissed her palm, then smoothed back a lock of her hair from her face as he said, "You're not wrong. So much of my life is there, both good and bad. My mother and father. Owen. You."

"I hope I'm one of the *good* things," she teased.

"You are, so maybe I just need to make new memories with you in another place."

"Like here? Tonight?" she said sexily from beneath half-lowered lids.

"I've been telling myself not to rush you, but you make it so hard," he said with a shake of his head and a chuckle.

Connie reached between their bodies and ran her hand along the bulge in his jeans. "I can make it even harder if you'd like."

His body shook, and beneath her caress, his erection blasted to life. "I'd like. A lot."

She laid her hands on his chest again and urged him back toward the couch. As the backs of his knees hit the edge, he sat. She was immediately on him, undoing the button on his jeans and dragging the zipper down over his growing erection. He sprang free, covered only by the thin cotton of his briefs. She pulled those away as well and fisted her hand around him, watching his face as she stroked him.

"Tell me how you want it, Jon. Soft?" she asked and barely floated her hand over him. "Or hard?" she teased, increasing the pressure of her hand around him.

He covered her hand with his and showed her just what he wanted, groaning with pleasure at her touch and her playful lick.

"I want to see you," he said and reached for the buttons on the simple, white camp shirt she wore. He fumbled as he undid them and parted the fabric to reveal the lacy demi bra beneath.

"You're so beautiful," he said and danced his fingertips along the swell of her breasts.

"I want to see you too," she said.

She grabbed hold of his waistband and helped him wiggle free of his jeans and deck shoes. A second later, he ripped off his T-shirt, baring himself to her. After he did so, she ran her hands up his thick, muscular thighs and back to his erection, which she encircled and stroked once again. She bent and took him into her mouth, dancing her tongue all along him as she made love to him with her mouth.

He closed his eyes against the sight of her loving him, afraid he'd lose it too fast, wanting to hang on to the pleasure she was giving him with her sure caresses and kisses. He shifted his hips upward and fisted his hands at his sides, denying himself what he wanted most: to touch her. Taste her.

He was on the edge, barely holding on, when she kissed her way up his body while stroking him. As she whispered a kiss along his lips, she leaned close and said, "Open your eyes, Jon. I want to see you go over."

Fuck, I'll lose it, he thought, but he did as she asked,

meeting her gaze, which was molten gold with desire, sneaking only a quick glance down to see her hand on him.

"Connie," he said and covered her hand with his, trying to fight his release.

"Come for me, Jon. I want you to come for me," she said, and with another few strokes, his climax took him over.

"Sorry, Connie. Sorry," he said, but she silenced him with a tender kiss and a gentler caress.

"Wait here," she said with another kiss and rushed off to her room.

As if I could move, he thought. His legs were still trembling with the aftershocks of his release while his heart pounded a staccato rhythm in his chest. He had barely calmed when she hurried back in, an unbelted robe barely covering her nakedness, and tenderly took care of him. Impossibly, passion rose again from that simple touch.

She sat beside him on the couch, her legs tucked under her, the robe leaving a wide swath of her creamy skin visible. Her gold-green eyes were dark with her desire and full of invitation.

Invitation that not even a saint could resist, and he was no saint.

Connie had known that taking things slow was something that would be virtually impossible for them. Especially when Jonathan had gone out of his way to show restraint and caring. It was like catnip to a cat. Speed to a race-car driver. Irresistible.

She stroked the back of her hand across the soft hairs

on his chest and rested it over his racing heart. She met his gaze, the crystal blue now a sapphire as deep as the ocean at night. A muscle ticked along the side of his jaw from his restraint, so she took hold of his hand and brought it up to cradle her breast.

"I want you, Jon. I want what we have together," she said, the tones of her voice low and husky with need.

He held the weight of her breast in his hand and leisurely swept his thumb across the hardening tip. The caress dragged a soft sigh from her, and Jonathan repeated the gesture, a little harder, a little more urgently.

She leaned back against the arm of the couch, letting the robe fall open, drawing her legs out from beneath her, and running one hand along Jonathan's arm to invite him to join her.

He rotated the tip of her breast between his thumb and forefinger, sending a tug of need to her center. Surging forward, he took the nipple into his mouth, licking and sucking it while trailing his hand down her body. He parted her, unerringly finding the sensitive nub beneath her curls, caressing it with the press and stroke of his fingers until her body was vibrating with need.

"Jon," she pleaded, wanting to finish what she'd started.

He surprised her by shooting to his feet and lifting her into his arms. As the world whirled from the action, she grabbed onto his shoulders, laughing in delight. He smiled and kissed her, drinking in that joy. He walked with her to his room, where he gently laid her on the bed and spared only a heartbeat to take protection from the nightstand and ease it on.

She spread her legs, welcoming him to join with her, and he accepted that summons, driving into her.

He swallowed her cries of pleasure with his kisses as, with each stroke of his hips, he took her ever higher. His powerful body was hard against hers and yet gentle, his mouth mobile as it drifted down to her breasts and he kissed them. Sucked them into his mouth in the way that he knew she liked.

She closed her eyes against the pleasure. It was almost too much. She could lose herself in him. In the passion he brought her. In the lightness of his humor and the tenderness of his caring.

"God, oh God," she said as that awareness washed over her and she gave herself over to it and to him. Her body shook with her release. Her heart trembled with joy and fear of the truth she could no longer deny.

She loved him. Against all reason and common sense, she still loved Jonathan Pierce, and she didn't know what to do about it.

Chapter 17

JONATHAN DIDN'T KNOW IF SHE SLEPT AFTER THEY made love. He didn't. His mind raced with the enormity of all that had happened in the last few weeks. How much his life had changed in that short time.

He'd decided to find a home for a variety of reasons. A brother who might need him. A dog who did need him. A friend was watching Dudley until Sunday afternoon. A woman who didn't need anyone, much less a man like him. A man who, up until a few weeks ago, was always on the go in one way or another. Running off to test a new invention. Spending weeks on the road while chasing after a new partner or acquisition for his company.

A man running away from his past and the emotions he kept buried. The loss of his mother and maybe even Maggie's mom. His father's constant disapproval and being disowned when he'd failed to return to college. Connie's disapproval so many years earlier.

But she's here in my arms now, he thought and tightened his hold on her, drawing her attention.

She rubbed her hand across his chest and murmured, "Relax. I've heard the gears in your head turning for what seems like hours."

He glanced at her as she looked up at him. "Which means you've been awake as long as I have. Want to share what kept you up?"

"Probably the same thing that's keeping you from sleep, but I'm not sure now is the time to talk about it," she admitted and swept a kiss along the underside of his jaw. It was a kiss meant to soothe and not to rouse passion.

With a masculine grunt, he shrugged and eventually said, "Probably not."

Seemingly to lighten the mood, she said with a little laugh, "It wouldn't be organic to push it."

A chuckle erupted from him, and he rolled to trap her against the mattress. Nuzzling his nose against her cheek, he said, "Sometimes we can be too smart for own good. Too thoughtful."

She narrowed her eyes, puzzled. "Because any two normal, red-blooded people wouldn't be lying in bed together deliciously naked and not making love?" she said.

"For sure," he replied and proceeded to show her a much nicer way to spend the rest of the night.

―⁓―

The morning sun streamed in from a side window, forcing Connie awake. Her body felt boneless, her muscles like jelly after a delicious night of making love. She reached out for Jonathan but jolted upright as she realized she was alone in bed. The snick of the lock in the room outside had her slipping out of bed and pulling on her robe. She belted it tight as she walked out to the main room of the suite.

Jonathan was there, freshly showered and dressed. He placed coffee cups and two takeout dishes on the table in front of the sofa. He grinned as he saw her and said, "You were sleeping so peacefully, I didn't have the heart to wake you."

She walked over and kissed him, her hand resting at his waist. She pinched him and said, "And because you know I'm not a morning person."

"Totally not a morning person," he echoed. "But I hope coffee and pork roll sandwiches will tame the morning beast."

"They will," she murmured against his lips and then sat to enjoy the breakfast he had brought up for her.

He joined her on the couch and swiftly unwrapped the sandwiches. As they ate, he said, "I'm sorry we have to leave early today, but my neighbor can only watch Dudley until the early afternoon."

"Not to mention you miss the little guy," she said around a mouthful of pork roll, egg, cheese, and crusty roll.

"Yeah, I do. I'm going to have find a place that will let us bring Dudley when we come back down to look at more houses."

She tried not to read too much into his thinking she'd be a regular part of his house hunting. "The Lighthouse Inn is nearby, and I think it's animal friendly."

"I'll check into that for next week. Are you free?" He held his breath and gave his breakfast sandwich undue attention while he waited for her answer.

"Unless something comes up at work, I should be free. And when you get the contract for the guitar building, send it over, and I'll take a look at it."

"I'd appreciate that, Reyes."

"I'll also reach out to some of the town council and see what they're thinking about the rezoning. But what if they're dead set on making it residential?" she asked.

"Then I guess we turn the building into condos and keep on looking," he said.

She didn't doubt that he would do just that. He was that flexible, and while some might view that as a favorable trait, it scared her to think about whether he'd be like that with her. Whether he'd move on without a thought, just like her father had so many times in her life.

"Let's hope it doesn't come to that," she said, but he saw through her acquiescence.

"I'm not afraid to fight for something I want, Connie."

As she met his gaze, she realized he wasn't talking about the building, and it alleviated some of her fear, but not all. It would take a lot more on his part to convince her he was here for the long haul if that's what she wanted.

Restlessness rambled through her as she walked through the door of her Jersey City condo. Jonathan had dropped her off and gone home to deal with Dudley, eager to make sure his baby was fine, like any new papa. It made her wonder what he'd be like as a real dad, which was part of the reason for her restlessness. She was missing family and friends now that she was alone, something that normally didn't bother her.

Her mother and grandparents would be having their Sunday supper, and she was always welcome. But her eagle-eyed mother would quickly recognize that something was up with her, and the CIA had nothing on her mom when it came to interrogations. She didn't feel like explaining what was going on with not only Jonathan, but also with her career.

Normally, she'd turn to Maggie when she was feeling like this, but with her friend and Owen in the newly-wed stage of their marriage, she didn't want to intrude. Besides, her law firm's office was in the annex connected to the Chrysler Building, where Maggie worked. She could always see her friend during the week.

She had missed seeing Emma that weekend in Sea Kiss. Emma lived on the outskirts of town not far from where Jonathan wanted to set up his new research and development center. Longing to hear Emma's friendly voice, she speed-dialed her, but when her friend answered, it was hard to hear her over the noise in the background.

"I'm sorry. It sounds like you're busy," Connie shouted into the phone.

"I'm with Carlo and his family. Are you still in Sea Kiss?" Emma asked.

"We came home early. I should let you go," she said, since it clearly sounded like her friend was in the middle of some kind of party.

"Hold on," Emma said, and it was accompanied by a muffled burst of chatter, as if Emma was holding her hand over the mike on the phone. "Carlo says you should come over. I think you should too."

Connie had been to one of the da Costa family parties over the Christmas holidays, and it had been fun, but she didn't want to intrude. "I'll talk to you later."

"You'll talk to me when you get here if you don't want to piss off me and Carlo."

Before Connie could reply, the call ended. She stared at her phone, wondering if she should go or ignore her friends. The little voice in her head said, *Go. It's only twenty minutes away.* Her sensible side said to take the afternoon to think about the weekend and work and everything else that was making her worry.

Fuck being sensible, she thought and grabbed her car keys.

—⁓—

The Ironbound section of Newark where Carlo's family lived was an enclave of mostly Portuguese, Brazilian, and Galician Spanish immigrants. Sandwiched between the airport and the Passaic River, it had managed to survive the economic ups and downs of losing businesses in the area. The da Costa family home was just a few blocks off Ferry Street, the heart of the Ironbound section and the location for their business, the Caminho Bakery. The home, like many in the area, was modest but well kempt. A carefully tended garden boasted flowers and a massive fig tree ripe with the last of the season's fruit.

Connie was lucky to find a parking spot just a few doors down from the house. After parking, she walked to the front gate and stopped to run her hand over the intricate tile azulejos of the Lady of Fatima by the stoop. Muted chatter filtered from the backyard, and she walked up the steps and around the side of the house to the garden behind the home. Carlo and Emma, along with assorted members of Carlo's family, sat around two picnic tables resting in the shade of a large maple tree.

Carlo spotted Connie as she entered the yard and quickly rose to hug her and walk her to an empty spot next to Emma before sitting on the other side of her friend.

"Hey, Connie," Emma said and embraced her.

"Hey yourself," she replied, but she barely had time

to say another thing as Carlo's two older brothers and their wives hurried over to the table with platters of food. They laid the dishes on the tables, and there was a flurry of activity as people started serving the different offerings family style, while Carlo's younger brother, Paolo, and his friend Victor continued cooking at an immense barbecue grill.

In less than a minute, she had a dish swimming with clams and shrimp in a white wine sauce, as well as grilled sardines sitting in front of her. It was enough food for a meal, but she knew from her prior experience that the da Costa family was just getting started with both the food and the conversation.

"It's always so much," Emma groused in mock complaint as Carlo's older brother Ricardo scooped a large sardine onto her dish.

"You're too skinny, Emma. Eat up! Carlo needs more meat on his woman," Ricardo retorted with a waggle of thick, black brows. It earned him a playful elbow from Carlo, not that it dissuaded Ricardo.

"You too, Carlo. My little brother is getting too skinny," he said.

Connie eyed Carlo and thought that no one could ever accuse the handsome man of being either too skinny or little. At six foot two, he was well muscled and powerful looking. But she supposed that to his much taller and more rounded brothers, he was a runt. His older brothers clearly indulged in their bakery's products a trifle too often. His younger brother was built much like Carlo and just as handsome.

"Ignore them, Carlo. You're just right," she said in defense of her friend.

"You can say that again," Emma whispered beneath her breath.

Carlo either didn't hear or didn't want to respond, since he seemed embarrassed by his brother's comment.

As she dug into her food, Emma said, "How did it go this weekend?"

Connie shrugged. "No luck with the houses, but Jon fell in love with a building for the business."

"I guess there weren't any nice houses," Emma said while Carlo leaned forward to listen to the conversation.

"They were all *really* nice, but Jon said none of them felt like home." She didn't add that she worried he'd never find one until he let go of his attachment to his family's home.

"Sometimes it's not the place. Maybe Jon just needs the right person to share it with," Carlo said and eyed her with too much interest.

Much as Carlo had elbowed his brother before, Emma nudged him in the ribs and glared at him in warning. Since Carlo was not a stupid man, he kept his silence as another round of food was served. But it wasn't long before Emma said, "So you had a nice time with Jon?"

Since she knew her friend wasn't going to give up without some kind of answer, Connie said, "I did. Jon is different but the same. He seems to want to settle down, but then he's talking about changing what he's doing."

"Like?" Emma pressed, needing more of an explanation.

"Like buying a building for his business. Mary, the real estate agent, said that they might be changing the zoning, but he didn't care. He said he'd just turn the building into condos. And then what? Will he find somewhere else for the facility? Maybe he'll go out to the West Coast. It's where so much of the tech sector is located. Who knows what his plan is?" Of course, she could have asked, but she'd been afraid of the answer he might give.

"And you're all about the plan," Emma added.

Connie nodded. As her gaze connected with Carlo, who, like her, always seemed to have everything in order, she said to him, "It's like a recipe, right? You know what you have to do to make it come out tasty, and you follow those steps."

Carlo smiled and gave a regal nod of his head. "Life *is* like a recipe, but you know what I've discovered over the years?"

Both Emma and Connie looked over at him as he paused.

"Sometimes the best recipes are those you experiment with, changing up one ingredient or another. Embracing something new to have an unexpected but totally tasty result."

"Unexpected doesn't always work out well," Emma sputtered, because Carlo's wisdom didn't only apply to her and Jonathan, Connie knew.

"You'll never know until you try, Emma," he said. The words were drenched with sadness.

To try and alleviate the dark mood, Connie grabbed a sausage from a plate that Ricardo's wife held out in front of her and plopped it on her plate. She cut off a piece and cheerfully said, "This looks wonderful. What is it, Carlo?"

A mischievous smile warned she wasn't about to like

his answer. "*Morcela*," he said, and at her puzzled look, he translated. "Blood sausage. Eat up."

She met Emma's amused gaze and said, "The things I do for a friend."

Chapter 18

DUDLEY IS BETTER THAN ANY ALARM CLOCK, JONATHAN thought as the little terrier jumped up on the bed and excitedly licked his face. Not that he normally used an alarm clock. He'd always had a natural biorhythm that had him up just past the crack of dawn and let him stay awake long past midnight. If he was tired during the day, he'd catch a power nap and then go back to work. Since he listened to his body, he'd rarely used a watch for most of his life. It was only now, when his partners and business demanded that he attend meetings or other events, that he relented and used his phone to keep track of the time. Too often, he got caught up in his work and forgot that others needed his attention.

Luckily, no one needed his attention today except Dudley. And Connie.

It had been barely twenty-four hours since he'd dropped her off at her condo, and he was already missing her. Missing the way she tucked herself into his side, her soft curves molding to his body. Missing the tickle of her hair just beneath his jaw and the fresh smell of her skin. The sound of her laugh and her sigh of satisfaction after making love.

Dudley jumped up onto his chest, sloppily licked his chin again, and let out a few determined barks, cutting short his musings.

"Okay, boy. I know you have to take care of

business." He patted the dog on the head, tossed on jeans and a T-shirt, and walked Dudley the few blocks to Union Square and the dog park. He turned the little terrier loose to play with the other canines there but kept a close watch, since many of the dogs were quite a bit larger than Dudley. Luckily, the dogs played without incident, chasing each other around for several minutes. Seemingly tired of the game, Dudley returned to his side, and Jonathan took a ball out of his pocket and tossed it up in the air. The pup quickly snared it and returned it to Jonathan's hand. Jonathan tossed the ball a few feet away, and Dudley raced after it, returning it for another pat on the head and toss. For the next fifteen minutes, they played a game of fetch.

"Good boy," he said and rewarded the dog with a treat from his jeans pocket. Dudley eagerly lapped up the treat and grinned, then barked at him for another treat. When Jonathan hesitated, he jumped up on Jonathan's lap and licked his jaw, almost pleading. Laughing, Jonathan relented and gave him another treat. Satisfied, Dudley hopped back down. Jonathan thought that he was going to have to make sure he wasn't giving Dudley too many treats. There were even TV shows these days about obese pets. At this rate, Dudley was going to get roly-poly if Jonathan didn't watch out.

He snapped on the leash again and walked Dudley back toward his loft, stopping at a local deli to pick up a bagel and coffee, because he didn't want to waste time making anything when he got home. Besides thoughts of Connie, his mind had been whirring with ideas for expanding the use of the batteries they'd developed into home and industrial power storage, as well as designing a new organic fuel cell to eliminate the use of expensive and environmentally damaging heavy metals.

When he got home, he fed Dudley, made sure he had enough water, and then sat at the large oak trestle table he used as a desk and not for dining. He usually gobbled down his fast-food dinners while sitting on the couch in front of the television. He cleared a space free of the research papers and notes he'd collected the last couple of weeks and plopped his coffee and bagel next to his laptop. Using a secure VPN, he tapped into the files and notes on his company's network and went to work.

Except for a bathroom break for himself and Dudley, he kept at it, mindless of the hours spent running through equations, formulas, and designs. It was only when his stomach growled loudly that he realized that it was well past time for dinner. He considered calling Connie to ask her to join him, but as he'd told her, he didn't want to rush her. Not to mention he wasn't above a bit of ego and didn't want to seem too needy.

That rationale didn't keep him from thinking about her as he did another walk around the block with Dudley and then returned home. He fixed a dish for Dudley and then went online and placed an order for Chinese. As he tackled his emails for the day, he rubbed the pup's belly and waited for his food to be delivered. Most of the emails were routine requests, but he saw that the real estate agent had gotten back to him with a contract for the purchase of the guitar building. His finger hovered over the forward button for long seconds as he recalled Connie's comments about business, pleasure, and friendship.

After this weekend, he had no doubt about the

pleasure part of being with Connie or even possibly about the business part. He was sure they could keep those two issues separate. The friendship thing, however, was an unknown. He liked her and not in a friend with benefits way.

He hit the forward button before he could reconsider and left the message blank, because thinking of what to say to her would take way too long and probably sound stilted anyway. Counting to ten to contain his impatience, he phoned her as soon as he hit ten.

Each ring had him holding his breath until she finally picked up. "Hello, Jon. I was hoping you'd call, not that I was sitting around waiting for it," she said.

He thought he detected a muffled curse across the line. "I just wanted to make sure you got the email with the contract, but that's not the only reason I was calling," he said, annoyed that, all of a sudden, they both seemed as tongue-tied as teenagers on a first date.

"I did get it, thanks. I'll look at it in the morning. I've got an urgent project I've got to get finished tonight."

"I guess that means you can't do dinner," he said, thinking that he could always refrigerate the Chinese food he'd ordered if she said yes.

"I'm sorry, but it's a sandwich at my desk for me tonight," she said.

He thought he heard the shuffle of papers. "I'll let you go. I'll wait for your call on the contract." Maybe by then, he'd have found a way to eliminate his reluctance around her. Normally, he just forged ahead for whatever he wanted, so he wasn't used to being so tentative. He sure as shit wasn't used to waiting, but for Connie, he'd learn some patience.

She must have sensed something in his voice. "I promise I won't be long."

He smiled and wished for a moment that he had video-called her. He was big on tech, so he wanted to smack himself that he hadn't thought of it. "I'll be waiting. Thanks again."

"Anytime," she replied and disconnected.

He sat there for long moments after, replaying the call, trying to figure out what she was thinking and where he stood with her. Funny really, considering they'd fucked each other's brains out at least twice in the last two weeks. And maybe that was part of the problem.

"I'm an idiot, Dudley," he said, worried that he had rushed things, but then again, she had rushed things as well.

In sympathy, the terrier jumped up onto his lap, laid his paws on Jonathan's chest, and licked his face as if to say, "No, you're not."

Jonathan smiled and rubbed the dog's head. "Thanks, buddy," he said but thought, *Next time, things will be different.*

As his intercom buzzed to warn that his food had arrived, he shut down thoughts of Connie. It was time to get focused again and get back to work.

Focus, Connie. Focus, she told herself as the words on the page blurred together from a combination of exhaustion and, truth be told, boredom. She'd seen contracts like this one time and time again during her tenure as a new associate and normally didn't do work like this anymore due to her years of experience, but Goodwyn had assigned her the project at the last minute and demanded it be done by the morning. It was a power play, but until she made a decision about whether to stay or go, she had to dance to his tune. It grated on her, but she had no choice.

She hated the feeling of being powerless. She'd experienced that too often in her young life. Had seen her mother struggle in a similar fashion for so many years. She'd vowed that she would never let herself be in that situation again, and yet, here she was.

Shaking her head, she mustered her flagging energy and sharpened her focus to read through the last few pages of the contract and make the changes she thought were necessary. She'd get in early in the morning and do another review, since even one word or comma could make a world of difference.

Grabbing her phone, she called for a car to take her home. It was hours past the last ferry ride to Jersey City. Luckily, at this hour, the traffic through the Lincoln Tunnel would be light, making for a short trip home. But not short enough to avoid thoughts of Jonathan and their rather awkward call earlier.

Her uneasiness hadn't been about reviewing the contract. It had been all about the weekend they'd spent together and where they would go from there. Could they do the whole "let's do dinner" thing and date as if they hadn't been intimate? Incredibly intimate like old-time lovers who were thoroughly comfortable with each other.

Which they were. They'd spent an entire summer as lovers. Even back then, it had been spontaneous and wild and satisfying. That hadn't changed, and Jonathan wasn't entirely to blame. In fact, if she was honest, she'd been the one to push the envelope, because she found him just too irresistible.

But I have to resist, she thought, her stomach doing a little turn as they entered the tunnel. She hated tunnels. Hated the thought of being underneath all that water with limited ways out. It was why she'd chosen a condo close to one of the ferry stops in Jersey City. She held her breath as they sped through the tunnel, grateful for the lack of traffic that kept them moving. She'd been stuck in traffic many times with stomach-churning results.

As the sedan pulled out into the fresh air, she released her breath. With a sense of freedom restored, thoughts of Jonathan returned. Jonathan, who was so free of spirit. Full of light and life. Funny and unpredictable.

Unpredictable, unpredictable, unpredictable, she repeated over and over. It was her biggest bone of contention with him. Since the day he'd walked out that summer night, she'd known that Jonathan wasn't one to stay. And he'd reminded her the other day during lunch that he was a rolling stone. She'd thought he hadn't changed, and yet in the weeks leading up to the wedding and after, there had been a glimmer of something different in him. Something more substantial and steady. Something that said maybe she wasn't crazy to be seeing him again.

When the sedan arrived at her condo building, she thanked the driver and stepped out. She turned and glanced back across to Manhattan, where Jonathan was. For now, since he wanted to move to Sea Kiss. *And when he does, where does that leave me?* she thought as a breeze off the river brought a fall chill that made her shiver.

She'd always imagined herself as a partner in a big New York City law firm, which seemed at odds with Jonathan's plan. Two words she'd never thought to use together: *Jonathan's plan*. If Jonathan could actually make a commitment to live and work in Sea Kiss, maybe it was time for her to consider that her plan could change. *Maybe*, she thought, whirled on one heel, and strolled into her building.

Chapter 19

CONNIE HAD DELIVERED HER COMMENTS ON THE contract for the purchase of the new building just as she'd promised. Jonathan had detected a hint of weariness in her as she'd called to discuss the changes she'd recommended and their plan for contacting the town council. He'd written that off to the late nights she'd apparently had to work in the past week. It was also why he hadn't been all that upset when she'd put off having dinner with him. Or at least that's what he told himself midweek. With the weekend approaching and his search for a new house progressing, he video-called her on Thursday night after texting her to see if she was up and at home.

"Hey, Jon," she answered and shot him a tired smile. There were faint smudges beneath eyes that had none of their usual bright light.

"Hey yourself, Reyes. How are you doing?" he asked despite worrying what the answer would be.

She sighed, looked away, and dragged her fingers through her hair in apparent frustration. "I'm still a little crazy here. It seems like every time I turn around, Goodwyn has another 'project' for me," she said, air quoting the one word.

Since she'd told him about what was happening at her office, he had no doubt that Goodwyn was trying to make her unhappy so she'd quit and save him the battle with his partners about whether Connie should move up in the firm. "I'm sorry he's making your life miserable." He wanted to tell her to tell her boss to fuck off, but Connie had never liked being told what to do.

"Yeah, me too, but I'm handling it. I'm not worried," she said, but he was worried. Connie didn't like having her plans upset, and this was a major game changer. Just like getting back together with him.

"I'm here if you need me, Connie," he said, hoping she could put aside their past and her fears about him to believe that.

An uncertain smile passed across her face before she hesitantly said, "I know. Are you going down to Sea Kiss this weekend?"

"I'd been kind of hoping *we* could go down the shore this weekend," he said, but at her grimace, he realized that wasn't going to happen.

"I'm sorry. I have to work this weekend."

He hesitated, curbing his own disappointment to be supportive. "I get it. I've had my share of weekends at work. Maybe I can swing by your place on my way back to the city on Sunday night."

The smile that came to her face reached up into her eyes and brightened her features. "I'd like that. I'll call and let you know what time I'll be home. We can have dinner at my place."

"I'll see you Sunday," he said and grinned, pleased with the outcome, even though he'd miss her this weekend. Especially as he did the house hunting. He'd really been hoping she could help, in large part because in the back of his brain, he'd started picturing the two of them living together in whatever house they chose. A pipe dream possibly, but he'd had many similar dreams turn into reality. Why not this one?

—⁓—

Connie dragged herself through the door, her clothes filthy with dust and her body aching from the latest project Goodwyn had assigned her: a review of the files in their basement storage area. Under the firm's retention policy, they only held on to materials for five years, and every five years, someone had to undertake that odious task. Usually, the work would be assigned to a new associate who would also be given a list of the files with instructions on which ones should be reviewed prior to destruction.

Hating the thought of it dragging into another weekend, she'd worked like a demon to go through what seemed like an inordinately large amount of files, even lifting boxes herself when the file clerks assigned to help her hadn't been fast enough. Hence the dust and assorted muscle aches. But she'd finished, and while she didn't have time to prepare dinner, she knew just where to order from while she took a quick shower and prepped for Jonathan's visit in less than forty-five minutes.

She scrubbed, dressed, and even preened a little, wanting to look her best for him when he arrived, uncertain of what the plan would be for after dinner. Would he stay the night or head back to his place in Manhattan? More importantly, did she want him to stay the night, or did she need a little space because the relationship was moving too fast too soon? After all, he'd had her help him look for his new home. That wasn't the kind of thing people did after only two dates. If you could even call their wedding-night hookup a date.

The *ding* of the intercom warned that either food or Jonathan had arrived. Luckily, it was the food, which gave her time to put it into serving dishes and into the oven to keep warm while she set the table. She opened a bottle of red wine to let it breathe, and the intercom dinged again just as she finished laying out the plates and wineglasses.

Her palms sweaty and her heart picking up its pace, she advised the security guard to let Jonathan up and waited by the door, trying to disguise her pleasure at his arrival. At his knock, she opened the door with measured restraint, swept a kiss across his cheek, and said, "Hey."

He eyed her funny and said, "Hey yourself, Reyes. I brought some pastries from Del Ponte's." It was her favorite bakery in Sea Kiss and had some of the best cannolis and cream puffs she'd ever had.

She accepted the box he thrust at her. "Thank you. Would you like some wine?"

"I'd like something else first," he said, took hold of her hand, and drew her near. At her questioning glance, he said, "A real kiss and not one like my grandma would give me."

With a shake of her head, she lifted on tiptoes and brushed another kiss across his lips, but as she would have drawn away, he cradled her head and prolonged the kiss. Over and over, he coaxed her mouth with his, urging her closer until the press of the box against her midsection dragged up the restraint she'd lost.

"Dinner is ready," she said in a shaky voice and stepped back, her insides trembling. She laid a hand on her midsection and motioned in the direction of the far side of the room and the dining table. The building was barely a year old, and the condos boasted an open concept design with the kitchen, living, and dining areas run together. The far wall of that space was all windows that faced east and provided a spill of sunlight all morning as well as gorgeous views of Manhattan.

"Nice digs, Reyes," he said, glancing around her home. He stuck his hands in his jeans pockets, as if to keep from reaching for her again, and followed her across the room to the table. He waited there as she tucked the bakery box into the fridge and then went to the oven.

"I hope you don't mind, but I ordered in. I didn't have time to cook," she said.

"No problema," he said and poured the wine. He waited patiently at the table while she spooned food onto the plates and brought them over. She returned to the island to grab a bowl and basket and placed an avocado salad and bread on the table.

She motioned to the chair at the head of the table and took a spot adjacent to it. With a shaky hand, she reached for her wine, needing a little Dutch courage. She held up the glass for a toast but couldn't think of a thing to say. Luckily, he rescued the moment by tapping his glass to hers and offering up, "To a lovely dinner. Thank you."

She repeated the toast and took a big sip, hoping to quell the anxious flutters she always had around him. Silly, considering all that had happened between them. She wasn't a shy schoolgirl, even though he made her feel like that at times. That he seemed to recognize that only made things harder, not easier.

"Relax, Reyes. Just go with the flow and enjoy this incredibly tasty Cuban food and wonderful company."

She couldn't hold back her chuckle and decided to join in with the lighter mood. "We just call it food," she teased.

He narrowed his gaze. "Huh? Food?"

"Yeah, Cubans. We just call Cuban food 'food.' Get it?" she kidded.

With a laugh, he nodded and said, "Get it. No Chinese food in China either. Just food." He dug into his rice and beans, murmuring an appreciative "Good" after he swallowed.

She followed suit, and it was as good as he said. The rice was perfectly fluffy and a great combo with the earthiness of the beans. The roast pork, while not as good as her mother's Christmas Eve roast, was deliciously flavored with garlic, cumin, and assorted citrus juices. There was silence as they ate, probably since the moment she tasted the food, hunger had kicked in. It was only as they both finished their first helping and Jonathan served up the avocado salad that she started a conversation again.

"How did the house hunting go?" she asked and dug into the creamy, buttery avocado.

A half-hearted shrug anticipated his answer. "Not so good. There wasn't really anything I liked. The good news is that we got a reasonable counteroffer on the guitar building. My partners and I are discussing it before I head out of town next week."

The proverbial rolling stone, she thought as she asked, "Anywhere interesting?"

"Rochester. There's a new company there that's got

some radical cameras we're considering to improve our self-driving and collision-avoidance capabilities." A prolonged pause was followed by, "Want to come with?"

A rolling stone who maybe gathered some Connie moss, she thought with pleasure and disappointment. "I'd like to, but my schedule is packed, and Maggie is reopening the Savannah Courtyard restaurant in her family's store this coming week. Didn't you get the invite?"

"Yeah, I did, but I'd already set up this meeting and couldn't reschedule. I really wanted to attend. I remember going there as a kid with my mom and Owen," he said, a hint of wistfulness in his voice.

She laid her hand over his. "Maybe the two of us can go when you get back. Or we can wait a few weeks for the Winter Wonderland to open up in early November."

He grinned, and his sky-blue eyes glittered with pleasure. "That would be epic."

As the awkwardness faded, she got up to clear the dishes and bring out dessert, but as she laid a plate before him, he said, "How about we eat this over on your couch? Sit and enjoy the view while we're at it."

She always loved seeing dusk fall over the city and the awakening of the lights in the buildings, like fireflies on a summer night. "I'd love that. Would you like an after-dinner drink?"

He waved her off. "I'm driving," he said, her first hint that maybe he hadn't planned on spending the night.

She handed him the plates. "Go sit. I'll get dessert."

He did as she asked but stopped to turn off the lights in the dining room and living room, leaving only the spill of under-cabinet illumination from the kitchen area.

It put the couch in a decidedly romantic darkness, not that she would complain.

She grabbed the box with the pastries, laid out the desserts on a plate, and walked over to sit beside him. As she did so, he laid his arm on her shoulders and tucked her tight to his side. He was silent for a long moment, and after a relaxed sigh, he said, "This is really nice."

It is, she thought, leaning into him and staring out the windows as the first pink, mauve, and gray streaks of color appeared in the dusky sky and the window glass of various city structures captured the waning rays of the westward sun. Little by little, the sky darkened, and thousands of tiny points of light burst into life in the buildings across the river.

"Beautiful," he said.

She whispered her agreement and glanced at him from the corner of her eye to find him staring at her and not the sunset. Heat rushed to her face, and he smiled, obviously aware of the flush of color even in the dim light.

Jonathan raised his hand and skimmed the back of it against the smooth skin of her cheek and the stain of pink there. "*You're* beautiful," he said, leaned in, and brushed a tender kiss across her lips while tunneling his fingers into the thick wealth of her hair.

She shook her head at the compliment but welcomed his kiss, opening her mouth, kissing him over and over until they were both breathless and straining toward each other, but she suddenly pulled away.

"Where are we going with this?" she asked, perusing his face intently. She raked a longish strand of his hair away from his face as if to make sure she wouldn't miss a thing about his response.

It was a question he'd asked himself often in the last few weeks, and while he knew what his answer would be, he wasn't quite so sure about hers. At least not right at this moment, so he delayed and said, "I've always admired how driven you are. How headstrong."

She squinted, trying to read him. "Headstrong's another way of saying stubborn, isn't it?"

He chuckled. "Maybe, but not in a bad way. But as determined as you are, sometimes you have to stop and appreciate all that you've accomplished to not lose sight of what's really important."

"I know what's important," she said, grew tense, and shifted away from him on the couch.

He cradled her cheek, hoping to ease her upset. "You've been pushing ahead as long as I've known you. Best in your high school class. Scholarships to college and law school, not to mention law review."

The blush came again, and she whispered, "I didn't think you had kept track."

He had, but not in a stalker kind of way. Despite their breakup, he'd stayed in touch with Emma, because she had settled in Sea Kiss after finishing college. Every now and then, he'd asked about Connie, wondering how she was. Wondering if she'd found someone else.

"We're not that different, really. If I want something, I go for it, but I take the time to appreciate what I've done along the way. Just like you should celebrate all your accomplishments," he said.

She huffed out a harsh laugh and shook her head.

"And what good does that do now? I'm watching my dream job turn into a nightmare."

"Maybe it just wasn't meant to be. You can keep on pounding away at it like a ram in heat, but that will only give you a massive headache," he teased and ran his fingers across the worry lines on her forehead.

A brittle laugh escaped her, and she wagged her head. "I'm not like you that way. I can't be organic or foot-loose or go with the flow."

Because he knew better than to keep on pounding his head against that wall she'd erected, he said, "Just know that no matter what, I'll be here for you."

She met his gaze, hers questioning, but then she relaxed and tucked herself into his side again. She asked, "So what do we do now?"

He kissed her temple and said, "We sit and enjoy this beautiful night."

Chapter 20

WHEN SHE WAS LITTLE, CONNIE HAD GONE TO Maxwell's, Maggie's family's store on Fifth Avenue, every Christmas with her mother to visit Santa. Maxwell's had always had fabulous window displays, and the Winter Wonderland had been the height of her holiday season, because she knew how hard her mother had worked to be able to afford a small toy and high tea at the restaurant in the store. She'd been sad when the Savannah Courtyard had closed and when, years later, the store had stopped doing the Winter Wonderland.

It was, therefore, a happy moment to see Maggie reopen the restaurant as part of her plans to turn around the struggling chain of retail stores. In just a few weeks in early November, the Winter Wonderland would like-wise come back to life, and she hoped with all her heart that Maggie could save her family's business.

But as she stood beside Emma, Tracy, Mrs. Patrick, and Maggie's dad, she sensed tension between Maggie and Owen and worried. It had all been going so well with them in the months since their wedding, despite the family feud and the work pressures they both faced.

It was clear that Emma also thought there was a problem. Her friend leaned close and whispered, "Do you feel that chill?"

"I definitely do," Tracy replied and glanced at Connie.

"It's downright arctic," Connie said, but with the

crowd gathered for the festivities, it was impossible
to have a private moment with her friend. She did the
best she could to help with the assorted guests attending the event. The mayor was there along with some
local celebrities and reporters from various newspapers
and television stations. Longtime Maxwell's employees
mingled with special customers who had been invited to
attend the event. All in all, as the hours passed, it seemed
like the Savannah Courtyard's revival was being well
received by everyone. When it was only close friends
and family left, Connie wanted to take Maggie aside, but
her friend looked exhausted.

"Time to go home. You look beat," Owen said.

Maggie nodded. "Yeah, I am tired. Thank you all for
coming," Maggie said.

Everyone chimed in with their compliments. Mrs.
Patrick and Maggie's dad were teary eyed, and Maggie
hugged her father tightly as he said, "Good job, Maggie.
You were so right about reopening the Courtyard."

"Thank you, Dad. That means the world to me."

"Ready when you are, Maggie," Owen said and held
out his hand to Maggie, but she didn't take hold of the
hand he held out to her. Her blue eyes were clouded with
worry, and the tight smile she gave him was bracketed
with fine lines of tension.

So not good, Connie thought but didn't say as Maggie
and Owen walked out.

If Mrs. Patrick and Maggie's dad noticed, they
didn't say anything, but as the three friends walked
out of Maxwell's, they paused to look at the limo pulling away from the curb. It headed down Fifth Avenue
toward Maggie's brownstone across from Gramercy

Park, a home Maggie had mortgaged along with the family home in Sea Kiss to try to keep the Maxwell's stores open.

"I think that reporter rattled their cages with his questions," Emma said, accurately pinpointing the moment when the Ice Age between Maggie and Owen had started.

"Do you think she knew about Owen's dad threatening to disown him?" Tracy asked as they started the walk across town. Emma and Tracy were both headed to Penn Station to catch a train, and Connie hoped to make the last ferry to Jersey City. Fall had settled in fully with cooler temps, and the city was starting to get crowded with early holiday tourists. They huddled together against both the chill and the crowd as they walked up Thirty-Fourth Street.

"I don't think she did, and I don't think he had any idea about the loans Maggie took out on her homes," Emma said.

Connie mulled over her friend's comments, recalling her own warnings to Maggie about starting off her marriage with what amounted to a business contract. She had been afraid that it could only lead to grief, and she hated that she might have been right. But she wanted to remain optimistic. "They'll work it out. I have no doubt they love each other. They were forced into a corner because of that stupid feud."

Silence reigned for a long time as they walked. When they paused to cross the street at Herald Square, Emma faced her and said, "Do you really think Owen's dad would disown him? He's such an important part of the business."

It made her think of Jonathan, who would be home by

the weekend, and how his father had disinherited him so many years earlier. How even now, his father refused to acknowledge a son who was bright, loving, and almost too good to be true.

"I think he would," she said without hesitation.

"Then he's not only bitter, he's stupid," Tracy said vehemently.

Connie couldn't disagree.

A block later, she left her friends at the corner to head to one of the bus stops for the ferry service. She made the last ferry with barely minutes to spare and was winded from her dash down the pier to board. *Winded and a little nauseated*, she thought, placing a hand over her midsection as it did a little turn in warning.

She moved toward an open window and gulped in the fresh air, driving away her queasiness with the clean, cool, and slightly salty scent of the breeze spilling in. With a few measured breaths, the sick feeling slowly passed, and by the end of the fifteen-minute ride, she was back to normal.

Her condo was only a short walk from the ferry terminal, but there was a strong breeze sweeping off the Hudson, chilling her to the bone. She smiled at the security guard in the lobby and headed up to her floor. Inside her apartment, she kicked off her shoes, strolled to her couch, and plopped down to enjoy the view of New York City. The sun had set over an hour earlier, and nighttime New York had come to life.

She sat there for a long time, thinking about how the day had gone both at work and at Maggie's event. Work had luckily been uneventful, a morning of paper pushing before heading to Maxwell's. The event had seemed to be going well until the reporter had blurted out the rapid-fire questions to Maggie and Owen. She had seen their bodies recoil, as if they'd been shot, and the looks that had crossed their faces. Disbelief. Distrust. Emma had been right to pick that as the moment when things had gone south between Maggie and her newly-wed husband.

Almost as if there were some telepathic link between them, her cell phone rang, and Maggie's number flashed on the screen. She swiped and answered with, "Are you okay?"

"I don't think so," Maggie said, her voice strangled and husky from what sounded like tears.

"What happened, Mags?" she asked, although she already had a solid clue.

A pregnant pause filled the air before Maggie said, "I didn't mean to keep the mortgages from him. I really didn't. I forced them to the back of my mind, because I didn't want to think about them anymore."

Connie understood. Maggie had been determined to save her stores, and if she did so, the loans on her Jersey Shore home and New York town house would have been a nonissue. She didn't have time to support her friend's decision, because Maggie jumped in with, "And why didn't he tell me about his dad threatening to disown him? That business means everything to him, and he stood to lose it."

Connie had often worked in the role of concilia-tor as a lawyer, and this was as good a time as any to use those skills. "Just like you stood to lose your homes. Maybe he didn't want to think about it either. Or burden you with it, because he already knew how much you had going on. You've both sacrificed a lot to be together. Don't let this drive a wedge between the two of you."

A hesitant sigh and a big sniffle answered her. "I just can't talk to him again right now. I need a little space and time."

"Just don't let it get to be too big a space and too much time, Mags. You love him," she said.

"I do love him, Connie. I do," Maggie replied.

"Then fight for him, Mags," she said. Her friend mumbled her assent and hung up.

She stared at the phone for a long time, hoping Maggie would be able to set things to rights. Wondering how she'd set her own life to rights, which made her think of Jonathan and their discussion the other night.

He had been right about her. She'd always had laser-like focus on reaching her goal, moving like the speed of light from one moment in her life to the next. Never stopping to appreciate what she had accomplished to reach that goal. Never considering whether to take a detour, except possibly for Jonathan.

He'd been an unexpected stop, a bypass, that she'd considered back in college. She was wondering where he fit into her life again. How they could possibly mesh such disparate lives. His in Sea Kiss, when he wasn't busy traveling around for work. Hers here and in New York, requiring stability and permanence, two words she didn't associate with Jonathan.

With a heavy sigh, she rose from the couch and walked to her room, feeling tired to her bones although it wasn't all that late, barely nine o'clock. Feeling unsettled, an emotion she didn't like. As she undressed and slipped into bed, her phone chimed to signal an incoming message.

Jon, she thought as she read the text message.

Stuck in meeting. Thinking of you. Miss you.

She smiled as a smidgen of that uncertain feeling fled. She texted back, Miss you too, and added a smiley face and heart to the message.

A flood of crazy and fun emojis was his response, brightening her smile and lifting her spirits even higher. Luv u, she texted back without thinking and held her breath as she waited for his reply.

Luv u too. Can't wait to see you.

Chapter 21

JONATHAN SAT IN WHAT SEEMED LIKE THE HUNDREDTH meeting with his partners and the lawyers and representatives of the camera company. While he appreciated that the company was a start-up and needed to get the most out of any deal with them, they'd been belaboring the same small points in the contract. He'd had enough.

He'd talked to his brother a couple of days earlier and knew there was trouble between him and Maggie. Jonathan wanted to get home to be able to support him. But more importantly, he wanted to see Connie. He wanted to go home to her.

Shooting a quick glance at Andy and then over to Roscoe, it was pretty clear to him that they felt the same way he did. He grabbed the pad in front of him and scribbled *I'm done with this*.

He slipped the pad in front of Andy, who peered at it and passed it to Roscoe before his partners slipped it back. Normally, Roscoe was the strong arm during the discussions, but before his partner could react, Jonathan rose and said, "Gentlemen, we value all the time you've given us. We understand and appreciate all your concerns, but you have to consider that your technology is just one part of our new vehicle design. We intend the new Lightning model to be one of a kind. Zero to sixty in 2.2 seconds, which is unheard of for an electric vehicle. Amazing AI to support top-notch camera systems, even LIDAR in the future. All that will make our car an industry leader in autonomous driving and collision avoidance systems. Our next model, the Thunder, will be every soccer mom and dad's dream SUV. We'd love you to be a part of that, not to mention that it will bring incredible attention to your company. But if you don't want to share in that success—"

The CEO of the camera company jumped in with, "We *do* want to be a part of it."

Jonathan looked at his partners, who nodded, almost in unison. "Okay. Then let's get serious and do this."

—⁓—

Connie's days passed in a blur between a combination of long hours at work, worrying about Maggie, and missing Jonathan.

His meeting had dragged on far longer than he'd expected. She'd spent the weekend alone, mostly slogging through every shit file Goodwyn tossed her way. She'd met Maggie for a drink on Monday night, not that she'd finished it, since her taste buds seemed to be off, and the drink, not to mention the spicy food, had had little appeal.

She'd dropped exhausted into bed every night after that, wondering why she was feeling the way she was, both emotionally and physically. If there was one thing that seemed to drive away her malaise, it was a call or text from Jonathan. *Jonathan, who will be home tomorrow*, she thought with a smile as she finished up her review of yet another contract.

She missed the last ferry home on Wednesday night and called for car service, dreading the ride home.

It was raining, and that always meant heavier traffic on the streets and through the tunnel. *The tunnel*, she thought and grimaced as the sedan pulled up in front of her office. She got settled in the backseat and buckled up. She started going through emails as the driver maneuvered across town, but each little turn and dodge around another car caused a funky roll of her stomach. Figuring that it was because she was reading emails, she jammed her phone into her bag and sucked in a few deep breaths, drawing the attention of the driver.

"Are you feeling all right, miss?"

"Fine. Would you mind if I open the window a little?" she asked, and at his nod, she cracked the window open, and cool autumn air washed clean by the rain wafted into the car. The chill freshness revived her, and she leaned her head against the seat back. She watched the passing lights of the streetlamps, the neon of Times Square, and the headlights of nearby cars until the sedan reached one of the approaches for the tunnel.

She tensed, trying to head off the edge of almost panic that filled her in the tunnel. The lights of the city gave way to the sterile illumination in the tunnel, reflecting off glaring white subway tiles. Gasoline-scented fumes replaced the rain-fresh air. Nausea hit her like a fist in the stomach. She hit the button to shut the window and started counting, knowing just what number she had to reach to tell her they were near the end of the tunnel. But there was no keeping to her measured count as her stomach roiled like she was on a wild roller coaster ride.

It was so bad, she opened the window wide and

leaned toward the air streaming in. Soon, the hint of rain tinged the air again, and seconds later, they were out of the tunnel and veering toward the road to the turnpike. There was nothing but cement barriers on either side, but coming up in a few feet was an exit.

"Pull off," she instructed, and at the driver's questioning glance, she repeated it more forcefully. "Please pull off."

He did as she asked and drove away from the exit until there was a place he could stop on the shoulder to an on ramp for the highway.

She immediately got out of the car, bent over, and vomited the sandwich she had eaten earlier all over a strip of grass beside the sidewalk. As she finished, the driver stepped up to her, handing her tissues and a bottle of water. She thanked him, cleaned up, and got back in the car for the rest of the drive home.

Her stomach had settled somewhat, but her skin was clammy, and the tiredness that had dogged her for the last two weeks dragged her eyes closed for the remainder of the ride.

The slow stop of the car woke her, and she thanked the driver again as she exited and entered her building. She forced a smile and waved at her security guard. Fought another round of sickness as the elevator surged up to her floor. She barely made it to her bathroom, where dry heaves had her body jerking in misery before her stomach settled. She dropped to the floor, exhaustion claiming her. The cool of the tiles below her and on the wall slowly restored her. She forced herself to her feet, splashed cold water on her face, and cleaned up. She stumbled to her room, stripping off her clothes as she did so before dropping into bed, fast asleep before her head even hit the pillow.

———⁓⁓⁓———

It had been nearly two weeks since his brother had fought with Maggie. As Jonathan sat across the table from him over a late-night dinner, it was obvious the dispute had taken a toll on Owen. Dark smudges sat beneath his charcoal-colored eyes, and lines of tension bracketed his mouth.

"Did you make things right with Maggie?" Jonathan asked, wondering if his brother had come totally clean with his newlywed wife about the situation with their father. His brother's hesitation confirmed that he hadn't.

"If there's one thing this fight should prove to you, it's that you need to tell her the whole story, Owen. Before she finds out from someone else," he stressed, wanting it to work out, because his brother and Maggie were perfect for each other. Since Maggie and Connie were like sisters, he could see the four of them building a life together as a family.

His brother combed a hand through the thick strands of his dark hair. "It's not that easy, Jon. She won't understand."

"She will if you're honest with her. Tell her about the lie you told our father. Tell her that you married her because you love her and not because of that stupid deal you made with each other." He'd tried to convince his brother from the get-go to be up front with Maggie. To admit to her that their father thought the marriage was just a scam so he could reclaim the properties that he thought Maggie's family had cheated him out of. But it was obvious Owen was reluctant.

"When the time is right, I'll tell her. I don't think now is the right time."

As the waiter brought over the steaks they'd ordered, Jonathan kept silent. Owen could be as stubborn and determined as anything, and he'd shut down. No matter that Jonathan wanted to say there was never a right time for such a revelation. That sometimes you just had to suck it up and do it, no matter how hard it might be.

Which made him think of the text message he'd gotten days earlier. That simple and unexpected response from Connie and his equally simple but incredibly complicated response: Luv you too.

He loved her. He'd always loved her, and maybe he should take a cue from what he'd told his brother and tell her face-to-face. Ask her to explore the possibility of a life together, despite how different their current lives might be. It would be a lot to ask, but as he'd thought moments earlier, sometimes you just had to suck it up and do it.

Chapter 22

THE ROLL OF THE BOAT WAS FAMILIAR, BUT THAT DIDN'T keep Connie from finding herself leaning over the edge of the ferry, tossing up the cup of *café con leche* and Cuban toast that was her go-to breakfast.

One of her ferry buddies stood at her side, rubbing her back in a soothing gesture. "Easy, Connie. Take a deep breath," the young woman beside her said and rubbed her back.

Connie straightened and inhaled deeply. The fresh air streaming across the deck helped settle her stomach. She accepted the bottled water from her friend and took a long sip. The water slipped down her throat, alleviating the rawness from her sickness.

"I don't know what hit me," she said.

Her friend, Anna, examined her features. "It's a little rough today, but maybe you should go to the doctor. You were looking a little green yesterday too."

She had been feeling punk over the last few days, and it was only getting worse, not better. "There's a stomach flu going around the office. Maybe I just caught the bug."

"Maybe," Anna said, but Connie heard the doubt in her friend's voice.

"I'll run to the doc-in-a-box at lunch. It's right near the office," she said and sipped the water again, feeling restored by the breeze and the cool water.

Anna nodded but was stopped from saying anything else as one of the crew members announced that they'd be arriving at their stop in a few minutes. Arm in arm, they strolled to seats, then waited for the bump that warned them that they had docked. After the announcement confirming it, they disembarked onto the deck and walked to the buses to Midtown.

"I think I'll take a cab today," Connie said, worried that the bus ride might make her sick again. She hugged Anna and waited until her friend had gotten on a bus. With a wave goodbye, she opted to walk to her office building. It might take a good twenty minutes or more, but she needed the time to think.

Maggie and Owen seemed to be patching things up after their argument two weeks earlier. Jonathan was home. He'd texted her early to say Good morning and ask if she was free for the weekend. Her response had been an immediate Yes. If Goodwyn intended to stick her with another garbage project this weekend, she'd have two words for him, and they wouldn't be *happy birthday*. Especially since the headhunter to whom she'd spoken weeks earlier had a number of positions that might be good for her. She just had to pull the trigger and tell him she was interested.

But am I? she wondered as she walked uptown toward Forty-Second Street. Despite everything that was going on with Goodwyn, she hadn't quite given up on staying with the firm. Maybe she was as Jonathan had said, headstrong and determined, but she didn't want to be driven out by a shit like Goodwyn. And then there was what was happening with Jonathan. With his supposedly settling down in Sea Kiss of all places. She loved Sea Kiss, loved spending time there, but living there full time? She was a city girl. Union City. Jersey City. New York City. City girl in a quaint Jersey Shore town? Maybe. A totally unexpected maybe, it occurred to her. It seemed like her life was filled with a lot of maybes lately.

By the time she reached Bryant Park, the turmoil in her stomach had settled down and she was actually hungry. She stopped at a local deli for tea and a toasted bagel with cream cheese, because the thought of coffee or eggs had her stomach twisting again. Weird, since they were two of her favorite foods.

She sipped the tea as she walked, and by the time she reached the Chrysler Building, she was feeling fine. The bagel went down and stayed down, and that made her reconsider going to the doc-in-a-box for lunch. The files on her desk flew off as the morning passed and she finished the work on each of them.

Since she was feeling better, she took time for a quick lunch with Maggie, who seemed to have made amends with Owen. Her friend was optimistic they could put things to rights in their marriage. But that led to talk of Jonathan.

"What's going on with you two?" Maggie asked as she ate the sandwich they'd picked up at a local deli and brought back to Maggie's office. They were seated at the small couch at the far side of the room, their lunches spread on the antique table in front of them.

"I'm not really sure." Connie shrugged and nibbled her sandwich thoughtfully, hesitant to say, because the idea that it was becoming more with Jonathan was still so uncertain.

"You care for him," Maggie said, and it wasn't a question.

Since she couldn't deny it, Connie said, "I care for him. I never stopped caring for him, but so what? He says he wants to settle down, only I'm not really sure he's serious."

With a nod, Maggie said, "He's always been a wanderer, but I sense that he's ready for a change."

She had sensed it too, but was it long term? It was a question she'd asked herself time and time again, especially since he hadn't been able to make up his mind about any of the fabulous houses they'd seen during their house hunting. And then there was the guitar company building and his flippant comment about turning it into condos if the zoning decision didn't go his way.

But even if she gave him the benefit of the doubt about both those things and acknowledged that he had changed, their journeys were still on divergent paths.

"He wants to live in Sea Kiss. My life is here."

"Only you're not happy here, are you?" her friend said, ever astute.

She couldn't deny it, so she shrugged and said, "I'm not going to let one man stand in the way of what I want." She instantly added, "Whether it's Jon or Goodwyn."

That seemed to surprise Maggie, who peered at her intently. "They're not even in the same league, and you know it. You're just scared of what Jon is making you feel and think. Don't let that fear keep you from the best thing in your life."

Another thing she couldn't deny. She was afraid of her feelings for him. That he was making her think about taking a different route in her life. Something she didn't know if she was prepared to do right now.

"You're not wrong, Mags. But I really need to think about what I want and what's happening with Jon."

"Will you see him now that he's back?" Maggie asked.

She nodded. "We're going down to Sea Kiss this weekend."

Maggie reached over and laid her hand over Connie's, squeezed reassuringly. "Enjoy the time together, Connie. Don't overthink it. Don't logic yourself out of something that could be wonderful if you let it."

"I'll try, Mags," she said, only it was truly a case of it being easier said than done.

As Connie opened the window of the Jeep just a crack, Jonathan risked a glance at her from the corner of his eye. A greenish tinge colored her skin, and her body was rigid with tension.

"You okay? Do you want me to pull over?" he asked and started looking around for where they could stop on the parkway. They were nearly at Sea Kiss, but he didn't think that she could make it that far.

"I'll be okay. The fresh air is helping," she said and inhaled deeply.

He brushed the back of his hand across her cheek. Her skin was chilly, but he couldn't tell if it was from the air streaming in through the slight opening in the window or her sickness. He pressed on, finished the last leg on the parkway, and exited for the final few miles to the inn where he'd rented the entire top floor so he would have a place to stay while he finalized his plans for their new building and maybe found a home for himself and Dudley. *For Connie too*, he thought as he glanced at her again.

Her color seemed restored, and she met his gaze, smiled brightly. "I'm okay. It's just a touch of a stomach bug or something."

With a nod, he turned his attention to finishing the journey to the inn. As he got closer to the ocean, Dudley, who had been napping peacefully in the backseat, hopped up between them and yipped excitedly. Jonathan rubbed his puppy's head and said, "Yeah, boy. We're almost home."

"It is home for you, isn't it?" Connie asked, but there was something in her tone that made him worry. It didn't keep him from being honest.

"I feel attached to this place. I don't know why, but I do."

"Your family has roots here," she said.

Nearly two centuries of roots reaching deep into the heart of Sea Kiss. Memories of spending summers here with his brother and mother. His mother, who for some reason had been on his mind a lot lately. Maybe because he was thinking about settling down with Connie. It made him wonder how any woman could just walk away from their family and never look back. How Connie's father could have done the same thing, and how both those desertions had affected them.

"It does, but it's not just the place that makes it home," he said and glanced in her direction, wanting her to understand that she might be a part of the reason why he felt this way. She'd been an important part of those summer memories.

"It's not just the place," she said, but she seemed uneasy in her agreement and fell silent.

He didn't press, and it wasn't more than five minutes later that they pulled up to the Lighthouse Inn, so named because it sat directly opposite the inlet and the lighthouse that warned sailors about the nearby jetties. He grabbed his duffel and her small rolling suitcase. She took Dudley's leash, not that it seemed necessary, since he obediently walked at her side and then sat to wait patiently while the innkeeper handed Jonathan the large brass key for the suite.

Three flights later, they were in the large penthouse suite at the front of the building, but there was only one bedroom, unlike the last suite he'd rented.

"Do you mind?" he asked, worried that she might object. Stupid, considering the ring he'd purchased earlier that day and had tucked into his duffel to await just the right time to pop the question.

She walked up to him and brushed a kiss across his cheek. "Not at all."

She looked tired, and her color was still off with a hint of pallor beneath her normally creamy, olive-colored skin. He caressed her face, brushing his thumb across the high ridge of her cheekbone. "How about you get comfortable and I get us some takeout? We can stay in, watch some movies."

She smiled and said, "I like that idea. Thanks."

With a nod and a quick kiss, he left and took Dudley with him for the short walk to Main Street. With her stomach acting as funky as it was, he wanted to get something neutral to help settle it and knew just the place. The corner luncheonette had originally been a pharmacy with a counter area for sodas, ice cream, and light meals. The pharmacy was long gone, but the restaurant had expanded to feed the overflow from the counter service. During the summer months, they had a small al fresco area that handled the spillover of tourists clamoring for a good home-cooked meal.

Remembering what her favorite had been when they used to sneak away together for late-night summer meals, he ordered her a meatloaf platter and got himself a burger and fries. He also ordered a plain hamburger patty to add to Dudley's dry food and went back outside to where Dudley waited patiently for him, his leash tied around a street sign pole. As he walked over, Dudley hopped up and down happily, welcoming his arrival.

He bent and rubbed the dog's ears, earning a doggie kiss and what he was sure was a smile. Untying the leash, he walked over to another shop to peer into the window at the Victoriana merchandise there and then strolled back to the restaurant. A very small crowd of determined tourists bucking an early fall chill was in line by an outside window to order ice cream while others mingled in front, biding their time until a table became free. It wasn't long until one of the servers from inside popped out with a bag with his order.

"Saw you waiting, so I thought I'd bring it out for you," the teen said as he passed it to him.

"Thanks, Rick. I appreciate it," he said and slipped the young man a nice tip.

Bag in hand, he hurried back to the room. Connie had changed into a T-shirt and sweats and was lying on the couch. She'd cleared off the coffee table, and the television was already on.

"There's an Adam Sandler marathon. *Waterboy* just started," she said with a playful grin, and he noticed that healthy color had returned to her cheeks. Her eyes were bright despite the slight shadows of fatigue beneath.

"Good food, funny movies, and a beautiful woman. A perfect night," he said as he spread the food out on the table, then walked to the minibar he'd stocked last weekend with beer and soda.

"You remembered my favorite. Now I don't have to open a can of whoop ass on you," she teased as she took the lid off the platter he'd placed in front of her.

"Gnarly! An awesome woman who can quote lines from my favorite movies."

"And my fave," she reminded him.

He broke up the burger patty to feed it to Dudley, who hurried across the room to happily eat. Jonathan sat next to Connie, who had curled up on the couch with her plate in her lap and was devouring her meatloaf and mashed potatoes. As she did an appreciative murmur, he took a big bite of his burger and echoed her pleasure. "Epic."

"For sure," she said.

Hunger made quick and silent work of the meal. He collected the takeout dishes and threw them out, then they snuggled together on the couch to watch the movie. Dudley returned to his spot in Connie's lap, where she stroked his head lazily, and the puppy mewled in pleasure before quieting. She rested against Jonathan's chest, and he wrapped his arms around her, content to savor the peacefulness of the simple moment.

It wasn't long before her smooth, regular breaths and the relaxation of her muscles told him she had fallen asleep. She probably needed the rest to recover from whatever bug she was fighting.

Carefully easing her to the couch, he dragged a blanket over her as Dudley hopped down to the floor. He was going to move her to the bed when a little whine from Dudley warned that Jonathan had to take care of him first. He snapped the leash on the little terrier, slipped on a lightweight jacket, and they rushed out for a quick walk.

The night outside was gorgeous even with the slight chill of the mid-October day. Tourists and residents alike lingered on the street, but not as many as in the height of the summer. He liked the seasonal changes in the activity in town and on the beach, especially the peacefulness of deep winter. Not to mention the bigger waves during the winter months. He was looking forward to a day out in the water followed by warming up in front of a roaring fire with Connie cuddled next to him.

Connie, he thought with a heavy sigh. *Connie, Connie, Connie.*

Complicated, complicated, complicated, he thought as he waited for Dudley to relieve himself.

But as complicated as it could be, he had no doubt that he wanted to be with her. That he wanted to build a life with her. He expected that she'd have lots of reasons for why that didn't make sense, but he intended to convince her otherwise.

Dudley barked, almost in command, and Jonathan glanced down to find his pup patiently waiting by the curb, since he'd finished faster than usual. With a grimace, he cleaned up after the terrier and deposited it in a nearby trash can. Dudley took off impatiently, yanking on his leash, something he rarely did.

"Easy, boy. She's not going anywhere," he said, but he picked up his pace, as eager to get back to Connie as his dog seemingly was.

She was still asleep on the couch, and a soft snore escaped her, dragging a smile to his face. He inched his arms beneath her and gently lifted. She cuddled against his chest with a murmur of approval, brightening his grin. In the bedroom, he laid her down on the bed and managed to get her under the covers without her waking.

He stripped and got in bed. As he slipped beneath the covers, Connie sighed and moved toward him. She nestled against his side and released another pleased sound. Wrapping an arm around her, he drew her close and kissed her temple. Whispered, "I love you, Reyes."

Mostly asleep, she replied with a sigh. "Love you."

As Dudley hopped up onto the bed, grinned, and turned around a few times before settling into a spot at their feet, peace and contentment filled Jonathan. He couldn't remember if he'd ever felt like this, but he was going to make sure it wouldn't be the last time he did.

—⁓—

Connie had tried to be patient. She really had. So had Mary, the real estate agent, after showing Jonathan yet another perfect home barely a few doors down from the Pierce and Sinclair beach houses. Jonathan hadn't had any particular excuse for why he wasn't interested in the house. It just hadn't felt like home.

With no other houses on the list, the real estate agent had forced a smile to her face and promised to find him other possibilities for the following weekend. Connie suspected that no matter how many homes the woman found, none would be good enough for Jonathan.

She didn't know why that caused a little pit of worry in her stomach. One that grew as Mary raised the issue of the old guitar company and the rezoning.

"I've set up a meeting with some of the councilmen," Connie said.

Jonathan joined in with, "Don't worry about it, Mary. We'll get it worked out."

Mary rolled her eyes but said nothing else. Closing the portfolio that held her copies of the listings for the homes they'd viewed, she said, "I'll keep on looking and give you a call once I have anything else."

"Thank you," he said and turned to Connie. "You look a little beat. Would you like to head back to the inn?"

She *was* beat. Luckily, she hadn't felt any nausea while they'd driven around to the various homes, but that didn't mean she was feeling fine.

"A nap sounds like heaven right now," she said and twined her fingers with his.

With a lopsided grin, he nodded and tugged her in the direction of the inn. They walked in silence, strolling slowly, peacefully, in the bright sun of the fall day. In no time, they returned to their room at the inn, where Dudley was waiting for them. As soon as they walked in, he dashed to Connie, who kneeled and rubbed the little terrier's head until he rolled over for his belly rub.

"You silly goose," she said but playfully complied, chuckling at the dog's antics.

When she rose, smiling, happiness filling her soul, Jonathan cradled her cheek and whispered, "I love you, Connie."

There was something in his gaze, in the tone of his voice, that sent a skitter of worry through her. That feeling was justified as Jonathan suddenly dropped to one knee, reached into his pocket, and took out a small velvet box. Grinning, his blue eyes glittering with happiness, he held it up to her and said, "I'm not normally one to do things the traditional way, but—"

"Don't," she said and raised her hand to stop him. "Please don't do this now."

Disbelief skipped across his features, and he rose deliberately, almost woodenly, his gaze trained on her face. "I don't get it. If we love each other—"

"I love you, Jon. I really do. But neither of us is ready for this." She looked away from him, shook her head, and raked her fingers through her hair, hating that she'd sucked the joy from him. Hating herself for not being able to immediately say yes.

With gentle pressure on her jaw, he urged her to look at him again. "I *am* ready for this, Connie. I've never been more ready."

"No, you're not, Jon. How many homes have we looked at in the last few weeks? How many, and you can't choose even one?" she urged, covering his hand as it cradled her cheek and stroking it lovingly.

"It's not because I don't want to find one," he said and pulled away from her. He stalked a few feet away before whirling to face her. "I want a home. I want a home with you."

She walked to stand in front of him. "Do you? Then why can't you pick a house? Why?"

Chapter 23

WHY? JONATHAN HAD ASKED HIMSELF THE SAME THING after the last two house-hunting sessions, but for the life of him, he didn't have an answer.

"I don't know why. All I know is that I want to be with you."

Connie's gaze skipped over his features lovingly. She cupped his jaw and traced the line of it with her thumb. "It's not just you, Jon. I hate that I don't know what's going on with my career. I feel like my life is too unsettled right now, and I can't make a rational decision about leaving it all to be here with you in Sea Kiss. I never pictured myself working anywhere except New York City. Because of that, it wouldn't be fair to you to say yes."

"Fair to me?" he said and tapped his chest. "Do you think it's fair to push me away time and time again?" To run away from him time and time again, just like his mother had run away so many years earlier.

A sad look passed across her face. She closed the distance between them and embraced him. She whispered, "I don't want to push you away, but I don't want to take the next step when neither of us is ready for it."

He placed his forehead against hers, his heart breaking. With a shaky breath, he said, "Where do we go from here, Reyes?"

She stepped away and cradled his cheek again. "We

both need some time to think about everything. To think about what we want in our lives."

He wanted to say that he already knew. That he wanted her in his life and that was all he needed, but he understood that she wasn't ready. That she thought *he* wasn't ready. "I'll drive you home," he said.

"It's okay. I'll go to Emma's. I can take the train home," she said.

He didn't press. He'd give her whatever space and time she needed if, at the end of the day, it meant she'd come back to him.

It didn't take her long to pack her bag, and despite her protests, he drove her the short distance to Emma's quaint cottage on the edge of Sea Kiss. After he pulled up in front, he sat there, staring forward, unable to watch as Connie got out of the car. But she surprised him by brushing a tender kiss across his cheek as he sat there.

"This isn't goodbye, Jon," she said before she hopped out and hurried up the walk to Emma's front door.

He finally looked and watched as Emma opened the door and peered at her friend and then at him and back to Connie. She wrapped her arms around Connie and drew her inside, but not before shooting him a sad smile.

He sat there for long moments after Emma's door closed, wondering what to do next. Trying to understand why, despite the love they had for each other, they were apart again and what she had meant by that cryptic comment. No matter her words, it had felt like goodbye all over again. Like she was leaving him. Again.

As an inventor, the why of things had always intrigued him. He loved to solve the puzzle until all the pieces fell into place. Pieces like why no house he'd looked at had been right. Why Connie was so dead set on a job at a place where she wasn't respected and wasn't happy. Why neither of them could find some middle ground so they could be together.

Pulling away from Emma's home, he vowed to solve that puzzle, because nothing was more important to him than having all the pieces come together so he could be with the woman he loved.

—◦◦◦—

Emma had been there for Connie for the remainder of the weekend, but she had also known when to give her some space. It was Emma's gift to know just what to do and when. On Saturday night, she had comforted but hadn't pressed for details. On a rare Sunday without any bridal events, Emma had devoted herself to Connie. An amazing brunch with homemade crepes topped with fresh fruit had led to an afternoon of watching movies and a nap. Afterward, they'd done a leisurely walk into town for dinner. Despite the cold in the night air, dessert had been ice cream from the corner luncheonette followed by more movies until Connie had excused herself to go to bed early, feeling exhausted both physically and emotionally.

Everywhere she went in Sea Kiss reminded her of Jonathan, but she suspected that even back in New York City, her thoughts would have been with him. She did love him. She hadn't lied to him about that, nor had she lied to him about feeling as if things were too out of control to decide what to do. She didn't want to jump into a relationship with him in Sea Kiss because her life in New York City was falling apart.

Not to mention that despite what had happened with her parents, she did believe marriage was a forever kind of thing and not to be taken lightly. When she committed to Jonathan, *if* she committed to Jonathan, she meant for it to stick. She wanted for them to have a stable home. One where when Jonathan walked out the door, he came back because he wanted to be there more than he wanted to be somewhere else.

As the alarm on her phone blared on Monday morning, she swiped it off and lay in bed, feeling as if the room were swaying back and forth, fighting yet another bout of nausea for long minutes. A soft knock came on the door along with Emma's muffled, "Are you up?"

"Come in," she called out, her voice hoarse.

Emma entered, still in her pajamas. It was early for her to be up for work, since her job was only fifteen minutes or so away.

As Emma sat on the edge of the bed, Connie's stomach did another whirl of displeasure, forcing her to take another deep breath to combat the queasiness.

"It's not easy being green," Emma teased, earning her a glare.

"It's not funny, and why are you up so early?" Connie said, uneasy with the knowing look her friend shot her.

"Big wedding to plan. I need to put in a few extra hours today. What time are you leaving?"

The thought of work only added to the upset in her stomach. For the first time in forever, she was going to do something she'd rarely done at Brewster, Goodwyn, and Smith.

"Would you mind if I stayed with you for a few days? I need to be away from everything, plus there's something I promised a friend I would do." The friend being Jonathan and the something being her discussion with the town council members about the rezoning, but she wouldn't mention that to Emma. She would read just way too much into that when all Connie wanted to do was be done with it so she could have some space to think about what to do with her life.

"You're welcome to stay as long as you like," Emma said, then bent and hugged her hard.

"Thank you," she said and held her friend tight, grateful for the support she always provided. Hoping she could one day return the favor.

"See you tonight," Emma said, leaving Connie to lie in bed, contemplating what she would do that day.

First thing was to call the office. Her initial dread at that was replaced by a surprising sense of freedom once she'd told the office manager of her plans.

There had been a hint of shock there, probably because in her four years with the firm, she'd rarely missed a day of work or taken any kind of real vacation. She'd been too worried that taking time for herself would send the wrong message. She wasn't sure what message she was sending by taking the days now, but the fact that it felt so liberating only reinforced the decision she had made to look elsewhere for a position.

She indulged herself by going back to sleep for another few hours. She woke feeling more refreshed and took a long, hot shower before dressing for a day of just doing nothing. Or at least only a few things, she told herself as she skipped downstairs and strolled to the tidy little kitchen. As she made herself some tea and toast and sat to watch the morning news, she examined

Emma's home. She'd been there dozens of times before, but today for some reason, it really resonated with her that her friend had turned the cottage into a very restful and welcoming place. A refuge.

The light pastel colors of the walls in the various rooms were offset by welcoming pops of vibrant color on pillows, paintings, or furniture fabrics. As she glanced out one of the many windows that filled the rooms with light, the beds of fall flowers in Emma's garden were in full bloom. There were pumpkins and hay bales here and there in the landscaping in anticipation of Halloween, and the playfulness of the look brought joy.

She understood better now why Emma loved living here and could picture her and Carlo starting their family in this happy home. But could she picture herself in a place like this? Or like one of the homes she and Jonathan had looked at over the last few weeks? Maybe was the immediate answer that came again. Another surprise, because if someone had asked her just months earlier, it would have been a resounding no. Which just confirmed to her that there was too much uncertainty in her to make a decision as important as a lifetime commitment to Jonathan.

After she finished breakfast and cleaned, she went back to the guest bedroom and hauled her computer from her bag. She returned to the kitchen and set herself up on the table. Powering up her laptop, she did a quick look at her office emails and found nothing pressing. Free of that worry, she turned her attention to what she would say to the town council in two days. How she would say it. Originally, the plan had been for a videoconference, but since she was in town, she dialed the office of the councilman who had organized the meeting. Luckily, he was available and had no issues with turning it into a face-to-face discussion. The council members had been planning to meet for the videoconference, so they were going to all be in the municipal building anyway.

Satisfied with that resolution, she opened the file with her notes. Over the last two weeks, she'd gathered a lot of facts and figures about Sea Kiss, its residents, and their needs to add to what she knew from helping a number of residents after Hurricane Sandy. She understood the economic requirements of the town and its businesses and thought she could make a compelling argument as to why Jonathan's new research and development center would be better than condos. Little by little, she created a presentation with all that data, but as she finished with the first draft hours later, she sensed she was missing the last little details that would close the deal in Jonathan's favor.

She set aside the computer, needing a break and time to mull over what was absent from her preparations. Emma wouldn't be home for a few more hours, and she wanted to make her friend dinner to thank her for everything she'd done. After rummaging through the refrigerator and kitchen cabinets, she had an idea of what groceries she'd need to make chicken and rice, one of Emma's favorite Cuban dishes.

Grabbing her jacket, she slipped it on and headed out of the cottage and back toward Main Street. In no time, she had stopped by the butcher and had him cut up a whole chicken for her. At a small Mexican-owned store a block or two off Main, she picked up some plantains, chorizo sausage, saffron, and a perfectly ripe avocado.

She doubled back to Main Street to purchase some Italian pastries for dessert.

As she was returning to Emma's, she passed the library, and it occurred to her that she might be able to find out more about the guitar company and its history if the library had archives of local newspapers or old official documents. She walked to the entrance, but unfortunately, the library had closed just minutes earlier. Noting the schedule, she made plans to return the next day to do more research.

Barely ten minutes later, she was back at Emma's and prepping the ingredients for dinner. Her grandmother had teased Connie's mother that chicken and rice was a lazy Cuban woman's meal because it was so easy to make and to keep in case guests were late to arrive. Regardless, it had always been a favorite dish in her home for a variety of reasons, including that it was usually inexpensive to make and made for good leftovers as well.

As she browned the chicken, it brought back memories of cooking with her mother. Happy memories of the two of them spending time together. Although she had talked to her mother on the phone often in the last month or so, she'd avoided visiting, because her mother would see past any facade that Connie erected and know that something major was going on with her daughter. But maybe it was time to talk to her mother about her father and all that had happened. Maybe that would help her put things into perspective so she could settle all the current uncertainty in her life.

Jonathan hadn't been able to stay in Sea Kiss after dropping off Connie. He'd gone back to the inn and packed his overnight bag and Dudley into his Jeep. As they'd driven away, Dudley had whined pitifully and given him the mother of all hangdog expressions. That was until he'd looked in the rearview mirror and seen the sadness in his own gaze, which was far worse than Dudley's.

He replayed the proposal in his head the whole way back to New York, trying to figure out what he could have done differently to get a different outcome. It was what he did when faced with any kind of problem, only no matter how many times he did it, the result was still the same. Maybe because the two major elements in the equation were still the same, and none of the other variables could really change their basic nature.

Although he had changed from the unsettled young man he'd been when Connie had first said goodbye to him that long-ago summer. He was more determined and responsible. More sure of himself than he had been, despite his daddy issues.

And what about your mommy issues? the little voice in his head challenged.

He hadn't really thought about her all that much until Owen's wedding and his talk with Connie that night. In the two months since then, his mother had been on the edges of his mind as he wondered how any woman could just abandon her two sons.

Or how Connie could have just up and left you? Twice? that nasty little voice goaded.

Connie and his mother were nothing alike, he told himself. Connie had her reasons for needing space from him, and he was strong enough now to understand them. To understand her need for stability because of her family life and how it had shaped the woman she'd become. He was determined to prove to her that he could be the man she could rely on in her life. A man who wouldn't just leave like her father had. Like his mother had.

He and Connie were peas in a pod, and maybe that was what had drawn them together but what likewise kept them apart. Just as he knew she had to put the past away so they could have a future together, maybe it was long past time that he did the same, he thought as he wheeled his Jeep into the parking garage around the corner from his loft in Chelsea.

He grabbed his bag and snapped the leash on Dudley, who eagerly jumped from the car onto the sidewalk. As anxious as he was to get to his loft and do what he should have a long time ago, he took the time to walk Dudley and let him do his thing. Then he hurried home, tossing his bag to the ground and setting Dudley free before he rushed over to a file cabinet by his oak trestle table. He opened the top drawer and pulled out the inch-thick folder he'd tucked away in the back of the cabinet.

His hands shook as he placed it on the table. He stared at the folder for long moments, recalling the day nearly four years earlier when the private detective had handed it to him, months after he'd sold his first patent for millions. One of the first checks he'd written from that money had been for the private detective, but when the man had presented him with the results of the investigation, Jonathan hadn't been able to open the folder. He hadn't been able to face knowing where his mother was and maybe even why she'd left him and Owen.

He wasn't sure he was ready now. He walked to a dry bar at the edge of the dining and living room areas of the loft and poured himself a stiff drink of whiskey. He returned to the table and stared at the folder. The only thing on the face of the file was the name of the investigation company, emblazoned in gold lettering. Nothing to give away the subject of their investigations. The agency believed in being discreet and had assured him that his mother was none the wiser about the inquiries they had made on Jonathan's behalf.

He placed the glass of whiskey on the table and sat. With a deep breath, he took hold of the edge of the file and slowly opened it.

His breath left him in a rush as blue eyes so much like his own stared back at him from the photo pinned to the first page of the file. His throat constricted with emotion, and he fought to take another breath. Grabbing the whiskey with one hand, he slugged back a bracing portion as he removed the photo from the file and examined it.

Besides the damning color of her eyes that confirmed he was hers, he noted the similarities in their shape and that of her nose and cheeks. The slight dent in her chin and dimples. Both he and Owen had gotten those features from her, and while his brother had their father's dark eyes and hair color, Jon clearly had his mother's light-brown shade.

With another shot of liquid courage, he placed the photo above the file, where her face would stay in sight as he read through the investigator's report. The cover page provided her current details: *Genevieve Gordon. Age 56*.

She had aged well and was still a beautiful woman.

There were only a few laugh lines around her mouth that didn't quite gel with the sadness visible in her gaze.

He continued reading. *Current residence: Coronado Island, California. Occupation: Artist.* In his mind's eye, he recalled the landscapes on the walls of his family's beach home. Lively and expert scenes depicting Jersey Shore life with the initials GG painted into one corner. His mother's work. That prompted another memory of his father ranting and raving about her "Left Coast values" years after she'd gone. Someone like his father could never understand an artist like his mother.

Or like me, he thought as he continued reading.

His parents had met when his mother had come east to study with a famous landscape artist. As her California family had been relatively well-off, that had put Genevieve on the fringes of the social set that included the Sinclair and Pierce families. His father had met her a few short months before Maggie Sinclair's parents had married. Within a year of meeting Genevieve, his father had proposed, and Owen had followed a scant three years later. Two and change years after that, he'd followed, and from what he could see in the report, the marriage had been stable, but not necessarily happy, for about another four years. Then it had all gone to hell.

The investigator had managed to obtain a copy of the divorce decree but not the settlement itself. After the divorce, Genevieve had moved back to California and her parent's home in Coronado, where she still lived and worked out of a small studio in the back of the family home. Photos showed a nice-sized, Spanish-style structure across the street from the municipal golf course and just blocks away from the Hotel Coronado, a yacht club, and the beaches.

Pricey real estate, he thought, and although it had been her family home, it would take a lot of money for upkeep and taxes. He wondered if his father was responsible for paying for it. But the next part of the report was filled with long lists detailing Genevieve's various gallery showings as well as retail locations where her art could be purchased. Clearly, she was a commercially successful artist, although he noted that all of the showings and locations were on the West Coast.

Left Coast values, he remembered again and wondered if his father's anger and bitterness were responsible for her avoiding the East Coast. Or maybe it was the possibility of running into her former husband and sons that kept her three thousand miles away.

That's about to change, he thought and was about to close the file when the family tree in the next section caught his eye. He ran a finger across the list of names dating back to the 1700s and a Spanish settler who was his ancestor, something he hadn't known. But then again, he didn't know anything about the Gordon side of the family. As he moved farther down the list, he jerked to a stop at the name below Genevieve's: Thomas Pierce.

A brother? I have a brother? he thought and peered at the date of birth. Thomas had been born seven years after him, during the divorce proceedings. That would make him about nineteen.

He remembered himself at nineteen. He had been trying to find himself after his first year at college. After falling in love with Connie. It had been hard for him, especially when his father had disowned him, but he'd had Owen. He'd always had Owen.

Who had Thomas had? he wondered. *What was he like?*

He slammed the file shut, experiencing so many emotions. So much hurt and anger, but also hopefulness. Until you drew your last breath, it was still possible to change. If you cared to, that was. Certainly, his father wasn't open to it, given their last discussion at the Pierce home. But he wasn't his father.

Grabbing his computer, he went to the website for the Hotel Coronado and was pleased to find that the hotel permitted pets. He smiled and called out, "Looks like you're going to take your first plane ride, Dudley."

Chapter 24

CONNIE PERUSED THE FACES OF THE FIVE TOWN COUNCIL members as they sat next to her at the conference room table. She'd caught several of them nodding as she'd recited some of the facts and figures she had provided during her presentation. The nodding was a good sign, she had learned in law school. A very good sign, but she knew that what swayed people most was emotion, and she had saved that for last.

"Having the Pierce company's research and development center in Sea Kiss will provide both prestige and a steadier stream of income for the area's inns and businesses. It will provide opportunities for the area's children to learn coding and be able to compete for STEM positions, gifting them with greater possibilities for their future."

More nods came with her words, and two of the members bent their heads close to whisper to each other. Members with young children, she knew from the research she'd done in preparation for the meeting. Pleased, she pressed on.

"But just as you have to consider Sea Kiss's future, it's important to remember the town's rich history, which includes the Chitarra Guitar Company building," she said, then reached into her briefcase and removed another set of materials. She rose, handed the photos to the council members, and remained standing, intending to weave them a story they couldn't refuse.

"Imagine a young man in Sicily. An apprentice to a master builder of violins, guitars, and mandolins. A young man with dreams who knew his future was in the United States. He boards a ship with the money he's saved and makes it to Ellis Island. He finds himself in New York City, but he's not a city boy. He loves the sea after his long ocean trip and wants to be closer to it. So he works his way down the Jersey Shore until he comes to Sea Kiss."

She motioned to the first photo of a young man standing next to a building that was little more than a shack right next to the railroad tracks. Right where the guitar company building would later rise.

"That man's name was Vincenzo Scordato, and in the 1930s and '40s, Vincenzo was one of the pioneers in advancing the electric guitar. After Les Paul developed the solid body electric guitar, in Mahwah by the way, Vincenzo engineered his own models. In time, those early models became some of the most coveted guitars used by the top names in rhythm and blues and rock and roll. Through Vincenzo and his company, Sea Kiss is a part of that musical history."

She paused to let that sink in, especially as the members thumbed through the photos she had included of some of music's most famous musicians playing Chitarra electric guitars. As they began to chatter among themselves, she took a few breaths and launched into her finale the same way she might a closing argument before a jury.

"Pioneer. Inventor. Dreamer. Those words describe Vincenzo, but they also apply to Jonathan Pierce. Jon is a man who appreciates the past but thinks toward the future. If he's allowed to, Jon will not only preserve

Vincenzo's legacy, but also safeguard the future of Sea Kiss by providing jobs and opportunities that condos for summer folk won't ever do."

She waited, letting them consider her words, and as her gaze connected with that of the councilman who had arranged the meeting, it was obvious he saw that future. With a nod, he seemed to be giving her permission to finish. She dipped her head in understanding and said, "I want to thank you for taking the time to listen to me and now, if you have any questions…"

A hand went up and then another. For nearly an hour, she patiently answered their questions and clarified any doubts that the members had about the facts and figures she had presented and also with regard to the plans that Jonathan had for providing coding classes and internships for local students and adults. When she was done, several of the members exchanged glances before her contact on the council rose and gestured her toward the door.

She gathered her things and exited with the councilman following. As they strolled down the hall, the older man said, "That was quite a presentation, Counselor. Jonathan Pierce is a lucky man in more ways than one."

His words brought her up short. She looked at him, puzzled, until he said, "I've seen the two of you together around town. Am I wrong to assume there's more to it than the purchase of the guitar company building?"

She shook her head and said, "It's complicated."

"I'm sorry to hear that. I was rather hoping that you'd be spending more time here in Sea Kiss. In fact, after that presentation you made, I'm sure I wouldn't be alone in thinking you might be a good candidate to replace the township attorney who's retiring in a few months."

"The township attorney?" she asked, surprised.

"I know that position is probably nothing like your big, fancy job in New York, but I know you care about the people in Sea Kiss. That was obvious not only from that speech, but also from the way you helped so many of our citizens after the hurricane. Not to mention the countless hours you spent on the rebuilding committee with Ms. Sinclair and Owen Pierce."

"I like helping people, and there were too many good people who needed my help," she said and started walking again toward the exit.

The councilman matched his pace to hers, strolling beside her. "Did I mention it's a part-time job? That would leave you time for your own clients."

Her own clients. Ones like those that she'd had to battle Goodwyn to take on. People like those she'd helped after Hurricane Sandy.

"I appreciate your confidence in me—"

"Such a polite way of saying you're not interested," the older man said.

She stopped again and examined him. "I think it's another case of it being complicated, but I will keep it in mind."

He reached into his pocket, pulled out a business card, and handed it to her. "In case you sort out all those complications and decide some fresh sea air is just what you need."

Hesitating, she glanced at it for the space of a few heartbeats and then reached out and took it. "Thank you, Mr. Eaton. I promise that I will keep the position in mind."

With a nod and a smile, he said, "Good. I suspect we'll be giving you a call soon to tell you we've tabled the rezoning discussion."

She laid a hand on his suit sleeve. "If you do table it, I'd appreciate it if you'd contact Mr. Pierce directly. I'm sure he'd love to hear the news first."

Eaton narrowed his eyes and looked at her. "And it would make things less complicated for you, I suppose."

She smiled. "You suppose right."

———

Jonathan had sauntered past the home two or three times. If he'd done that in New York City, it would have brought unwarranted attention from passersby. On this stretch of sun-drenched street in Coronado, he hadn't seen a person pass by in the fifteen minutes he'd been walking back and forth. *Maybe when you had gorgeous weather virtually every day, there was no reason to step out and enjoy another glorious day*, he thought.

He wished he smoked. It would have given him something to do as he paced past the home another time, building the courage to walk up to the door. In his mind, he imagined knocking on the ornate, hand-carved wooden door and seeing it open.

Will she look like she did in the headshot that the investigator snagged from her website? He'd pored over the website and the report for hours before he'd boarded the flight to San Diego and after he'd checked into the hotel. The words on the internet and in the file had done little to tell him anything about the woman who was his mother.

But the pictures…her paintings and sketches had

told him so much more. They were vibrant, and while realistic, there was a dreaminess in them that called to him on some level. *Maybe we are alike in some ways*, he thought and stopped dead at the foot of the walk leading to the front door. And maybe they were nothing alike, because he couldn't ever imagine leaving behind his brother and never seeing him again. His father? That was a whole 'nother case, since he couldn't care less if he ever saw the old bastard again. Or at least that's what he told himself.

He should have brought Dudley with him, only the pooch was busy being pampered by groomers at the hotel. He'd felt not so alone with the little terrier, especially since Connie had said goodbye again. *Or did she?* he thought, recalling her last words to him. "This isn't goodbye," she'd said, but she'd still walked away, just like his mother had walked away nearly twenty years earlier.

He wasn't done with Connie by a long shot, but it was time to put an end to the questions he'd had for so long about his mother. And now about a brother he hadn't even known he had.

He propelled himself up the walk and to the door. Wondered if he should have called ahead to see if she was home, but he hadn't wanted her to know he was coming. He hadn't wanted her to be able to avoid him.

The sounds of some kind of classical music wafted out from behind the impressive wooden door. Soothing sounds at odds with the bold colors and life in her paintings.

He looked for a doorbell, but there was none. Just the big wrought-iron knocker on the door. He grabbed it. The metal was slightly rough against his fingertips. He raised the heavy metal ring and then knocked on the door three times. Waited.

He thought he heard someone say, "Coming." A soft, very feminine voice.

A second later, the door swung open, and he was staring into blue eyes just like in the photo. His eyes. His mother's eyes.

There was a hint of puzzlement in her gaze for a moment, but then her eyes opened wide and a surprised "oh" escaped her before she laid a trembling hand on her mouth. There were hints of paint on her fingers, and she wore a smock smeared with a kaleidoscope of colors. He had interrupted her work.

"Genevieve? Or should I say Mother? Do you mind if I come in?"

She hesitated, but with a shaky hand, she drew the door open wider and stepped aside to let him enter. As she did so, she grabbed a small towel she had tucked into her smock waistband and wiped her hands clean. "I'm not quite sure what to say," she said.

"'Hello, Jonathan' might be a good start."

They had walked into a spacious area that was a living room at one end and a kitchen on the other. There was a door at the end of the kitchen, and through it, he could see the spill of light and the hint of an easel leg. *Her studio*, he thought.

"Do you mind?" he said and gestured in the direction of that door.

"No. I'll make us some coffee," she said as he strolled away from her and walked through the door into her space.

The clank of glass and metal followed him into the studio that was a conservatory added to the home. A half-finished canvas sat on the easel. A seascape, but not anything like the others he'd seen. This one was dark, the ocean turbulent and rough. No calm sea to welcome sailors but one to drag them down into deadly depths.

The smell of coffee hit him a second before she came in through the door carrying a tray with a carafe, cups, a little white cow, and sweeteners. She walked to the far end of the room and a wrought-iron table painted in white. She set the tray on the surface of the table and then sat on one of the chairs. As she waited for him, she folded her hands primly in her lap like an obedient child waiting for instruction.

So proper. The home so traditional. Nothing at all like the spirit in the paintings.

He sauntered over and sat, the metal hard beneath his ass. It kind of fit the mood he was in at his mother's too-calm reaction. "So is this how it happens? We sit down like civilized folk and have some coffee? Chat about old times? Maybe you get around to telling me why you left me and Owen and never looked back? What about Thomas? Is he here? When do I get to meet my long-lost brother?"

She reacted to that finally. Tears shimmered in her eyes a second before she looked away, hiding her gaze from him.

Pity and anger warred inside him. Pity won out. He cupped her cheek tenderly and urged her to face him. "Momma," he said, sounding like the scared little child who had cried for his mother for days after she'd left.

"I'm sorry, Jonathan. I never wanted for it to be like

this. I never wanted to leave my boys," she said as the tears finally escaped and ran down her cheeks.

My boys. How he remembered her calling them that when they were children. Laughing with them as they played on the beach in Sea Kiss. Memories lashed at him of those good times. Of building sand castles and even of her helping him finger paint. Making chocolate chip cookies and sitting at the kitchen table together, having warm cookies with ice-cold milk.

"Do you still bake?" he asked, not sure of how to continue their discussion.

She nodded and dashed the tears away from her face. "I do. I wasn't sure you'd remember. You were so young..."

"I remember a lot, Momma. I remember," he said, but then charged on. "Why did you leave?"

She took hold of his hand at her cheek and tucked it into hers. Looked away as she said, "It's complicated, Jonathan."

"Please, Momma. I need to know," he said and silently added, *So I can get on with my life.*

Head still shaking, she said, "I knew when I married your father that I would never truly have his heart. He loved someone else, but I was a dreamer, and I thought that I could change him."

She sucked in a deep inhale, held it, and then more words rushed out of her mouth. "It wasn't bad at first. You might even say it was good. I never lacked for anything, and he was as loving as he could be. When you boys came..." A bright smile came to her eyes and more tears. "You were the light of my life. It made everything else tolerable, especially after Elizabeth Sinclair died."

He didn't remember that. He'd been way too young, although he had vague memories of Maggie's mom and his father smiling on the beach. "He was in love with her?" he asked.

His mother shrugged. "I had suspected as much... The way he got after she died confirmed it for me. He was angry and so, so sad. Impossible to live with, but I dealt with it because of you and Owen, until he started in on my boys. That's when I decided to divorce him."

"But you left us behind with him. You left us with that bitter, angry, miserable bastard," he said, his initial pity eaten away by anger that had been simmering inside him for so long. "Do you know how he treated us? How he belittled everything we did?"

She slammed her hand on the table and skewered him with her gaze. "You had a roof over your heads and food. You went to all the right schools—"

"And that's why you left us? Didn't it occur to you that we might have traded all that for a mother's love?"

She broke again and buried her hands in her face, crying harder. Repeating the same thing over and over. "You just don't understand. You can't understand."

He wanted to understand. Wanted to know why she had left, because he suspected there was more to it than her wanting them to have all the right things. He gently took hold of her hands and drew them down. "Help me to understand. Tell me why you left."

Help me be whole again, he thought. He waited patiently as she wiped away tears and then poured them both coffees, obviously needing something to do in order to maintain her composure. She took hers black and cradled the mug in her hands while he prepped his coffee, slowly adding sugar and cream to give her a chance to collect herself.

Once he took his first sip, she started talking, the tone of her voice low, hesitation making her every word leak out of her mouth like molasses in winter. *Bitter like molasses too*, he thought.

"When I filed for divorce, he was furious. He couldn't understand why I would want to leave him. Why I couldn't live another day with him and why I wanted to take my boys with me. We fought and fought over it. Lawyers racked up lots of big bills," she said with a harsh laugh before continuing.

"We even tried to reconcile at one point, but it didn't work out. Months later, I realized I was pregnant again. We were still fighting over the divorce terms, but when Thomas was born, that all changed."

Her hands shook as she raised the mug to her lips and took a sip of the coffee. "Your brother Thomas. We knew as soon as he was born there was something very wrong with him. The doctors said that if he lived, he would require extensive care. That became your father's ace in the hole."

"He used that to get the divorce settlement he wanted," he said, putting the pieces of the puzzle together just like he'd hoped when he planned this trip.

"He wanted you and Owen to stay with him. He thought I'd be a bad influence. I was too much of a dreamer. Too creative. I wouldn't be good for his sons, especially you. He could see even back then the two of us were a lot alike. Owen was always more like him. More responsible and mature. But you…"

She smiled, and her face lit up with joy, the blue of

her eyes bright as the ocean in Sea Kiss. "You were always asking questions. Wanting to know why. Taking apart your toys and putting them back together. You were so special, and he saw that. He wanted to rein that in. Make you more like him and Owen."

"So the deal was us for Thomas, is that right?" he asked, although he knew the answer even before she confirmed it with a nod.

"As long as I stayed away from you and Owen, your dad would provide alimony and pay for all Thomas's needs, and there were so many needs. He had severe mental and physical issues that required multiple hospitalizations and full-time care. What your father provided helped me keep Thomas alive and as healthy as he could be."

The lives of two sons for one, he thought. He wondered how anyone could make such a choice. How anyone could *force* someone to make such a choice. "Is he... Is Thomas here?"

With a barely there shake of her head, she said, "Two years ago, he started needing more care than I could provide at home. I wanted to keep him here, but the doctors said that he would be better off somewhere he could get the medical attention he needed."

Jonathan digested that statement, and it went down his throat like acid. "Can I meet him? Would he know... Does he understand when, you know, you talk to him?"

She nodded with a little more force. "He knows when I'm there. When I talk to him. Sometimes he smiles. If you're staying—"

He jerked his thumb in the direction of the front door. "I'm at the Hotel Coronado."

With a determined dip of her head, she said, "I can make arrangements for us to see him tomorrow if that's good with you."

"That's good with me."

He nodded and rose, intending to return to the hotel when his mother said, "I was done for the day. Maybe you can stay and we can talk some more. I've read a lot about you in the papers. It made me so proud."

She seemed sincere and almost…hopeful. As if you could wipe away twenty years of distance, of absence, of secrets, with talk. Maybe you could, but he wasn't ready for it today. There was too much to process, even for someone like him, who could grasp the most complex of problems almost instantly. This was way more complicated than any of his equations or inventions. More delicate than the most fragile of his experiments.

"Thanks for the invitation, but I need a little time to sort things out," he said. Just like Connie needed space and time. "I'll call later to firm up tomorrow."

"I understand, Jonathan. We'll speak later," she said as she followed him out of her studio and to the front door.

He waited there, unsure of what to do. A hug? A kiss? What did you do after almost twenty years of separation? But before he could act, she took the decision from him. She wrapped her arms around him and buried her head against his chest. With a sniffle, she said, "You smell like Sea Kiss. Like summers on the beach. I never forgot those summers together."

Awkwardly, cautiously, he returned the embrace. Bent his head to hers and whispered, "I never forgot either."

Chapter 25

WHEN THE CALL HAD COME FROM OWEN SAYING THAT he'd fucked up, Connie's one and only thought had been to go to Maggie and make sure her friend was okay. It had been Owen's one and only thought as well. Not that Maggie would do anything crazy, because she wasn't normally one to do anything like that, although some might consider that marrying the son of your father's worst enemy was crazy. But if they'd known the very businesslike way that Owen and Maggie had gone about getting married, they would have thought otherwise.

Connie, on the other hand, had worried about it being that way. She had thought there might be more to it than either of them was saying, and now she knew why: Owen had lied to both Maggie and his father about the reason for the marriage.

Now, as she held Maggie and let her cry it out, she dealt with the aftermath of that lie and with the fact that Connie believed Owen really loved Maggie despite his subterfuge. "It'll be okay, Mags. Trust me. It'll be okay," Connie crooned and stroked Maggie's back.

"I know," Maggie said, but there was no conviction in her words.

Connie hoped that with a little time, the wounds would heal and her friend could forgive. Could get on with her life and with her marriage.

Half an hour later, after Maggie's tears had been

spent, Connie packed her friend into a cab and got her home. She poured her a glass of wine or two and, much later, tucked her into bed.

Connie stayed the night and woke up feeling slightly nauseated again, after the last few days in Sea Kiss when she'd been finally feeling well. She wrote it off as the stress of the day before with both Maggie's upset and another run-in with Goodwyn. Luckily, her headhunter had lined up a few interviews for her later in the week. Plus, there was that offer of sorts from the Sea Kiss councilman that had lingered in her brain far longer than it should have.

First, she had to deal with Maggie and her request that Connie draw up divorce papers. She was reacting in anger, and as both Maggie's friend and her attorney, Connie needed to convince her to think things through. To give herself some time before acting rashly.

By the time she showered and dressed, Maggie had already gone to work. Not her friend's normal practice, but then again, nothing was normal in Maggie's world after yesterday. She understood. Ever since Jonathan had walked back into her life, nothing had been the same. Which made her wonder about Jonathan and whether he had known about Owen's deception.

Even though it was just after eight in the morning, Jonathan was usually an early riser, so she called him. The phone rang a few times before Jonathan answered with a groggy, "Connie? Are you okay?"

"I am. I'm sorry. I thought you'd be up already," she said and fought back pleasure that his first thought had been concern for her.

"I'm in California. I had something to take care of," he replied, slightly more alert.

"Shit, I'm sorry. It's barely—"

"Five something, but that's cool. What's up?" he said, apparently unaware of what had happened the night before.

"Have you talked to Owen?" she asked, hesitant to reveal too much and yet also wondering just how much Jonathan had known in the first place.

"No, I haven't," he said, and after a long pause, she heard a muffled curse before he continued. "Maggie found out, didn't she?"

Upset skyrocketed with his words. "You knew?"

A tired sigh drifted across the line. "I did, but I tried to convince him a thousand times to tell her. He loves her, Connie. He always has, only he couldn't think of any other way to be with her and keep our father from ruining his life."

Amazingly, she believed him. Jonathan had never been a liar, and she had always understood that the Pierce boys had a complicated and mostly unhealthy relationship with their father. Her understanding, however, didn't keep her from holding back.

"Your father is a fuck."

He sighed again, a heavy sound filled with regret and sadness. "You don't know the half of it, Reyes."

An uncomfortable silence followed until she finally said, "I've got to go. I've got to keep Maggie from making the worst mistake of her life."

"Marrying Owen?" he said.

"No, divorcing him," she replied and hung up before Jonathan had a chance to respond.

Jonathan stared at the smartphone that still displayed the avatar of Connie's smiling face. He placed the phone back on the nightstand, and at the motion, Dudley wiggled closer to him in bed and licked his hand. Still on East Coast time, his poor pooch probably needed to be walked. The walk would do both of them a world of good.

"Hey, boy," he said, rubbing the dog's head. His hair was softer after the grooming, and the trim made it seem even curlier. Dudley had almost pranced before him when he'd picked him up at the pet spa. This dog had the most winning personality. "I just need a minute."

He rose, washed, and yanked on a T-shirt and sweats. He slipped his feet into a pair of flip-flops, since he planned on taking Dudley to a dog beach that one of the groomers had mentioned to him the day before when he'd picked up Dudley after visiting his mother.

My mother, he thought as he clipped the leash on Dudley, and the dog yipped happily and gave him a puppy grin. The simplicity of those canine emotions eased his troubled spirits somewhat. He had already been worrying about what to tell his older brother and when. Now Owen was dealing with the fallout from his deception with Maggie.

I can't add another thing to his troubles, he thought as he led Dudley out of their beachside room and up to street level. The dog beach was several blocks away.

He walked without purpose, letting Dudley linger here and there as the pup searched for his perfect doggy spot. When Dudley finished, he cleaned up after him, tossed away the garbage, and then continued the walk, needing time to think about all that had happened in just the last few days. Dudley was content to humor him, trotting beside him on the walk, glancing up every now and then as if to make sure he was okay.

So many things to process. Connie. His mother. Owen's troubles and his newfound brother Thomas. A brother who he would meet later that day for the first time, but he hoped it wouldn't be the last time he saw him. Saw Thomas.

Memories, both new and old, assaulted his brain. Good times. Bad times. Very bad times. They bound him to the past, but they also tied up his future and not for the better.

Connie was right that there was something wrong with him not being able to pick one of those beautiful houses to be his new home. Maybe it was because every time he pictured himself living in Sea Kiss, it was in his family's home. A home that deserved more than him and Owen popping down every now and then. Even the Sinclair home had Mrs. Patrick there to give it life, as well as regular visits from Maggie and her friends.

In his mind's eye, he pictured the home the way it had been when he had been a young boy. The glorious colors in the flowers that had spilled from their beds onto the walk. The bright paint on the house before it had been replaced with sorrowful darkness. It occurred to him that it had happened shortly after Maggie's mother had died. Elizabeth Sinclair, the woman his father had really loved and for whom he'd gone into mourning.

They reached the dog beach, and he unclipped Dudley's leash and raced with him to the water's edge. The dog splashed through the water, his happy barks filling the early morning air. The sun was just coming up to the east over Coronado, bathing the homes and hotels with bright golden light. A very different sunrise than on the East Coast, but no less beautiful.

He let Dudley romp in the wash for a few minutes, then picked up a piece of driftwood and played fetch with the lively terrier, and little by little, the dog's happy antics drew some of his darker thoughts away. They had him smiling and thinking about going home and playing on the beach in Sea Kiss with his dog. Walking there with Connie beside him.

She hadn't said goodbye, he reminded himself. She was waiting for him to deal with his past. Waiting for herself to settle her own past and maybe her future. She had so many plans, his Connie. Sadly, none of those plans had ever included him. Or at least he didn't think so. But he'd seen a change in her lately, he thought, much like he hoped she'd seen a change in him. A change that said that maybe they had a future together.

He tossed the driftwood one last time, and after Dudley returned it, Jonathan walked back up the sand toward the street. Dudley dawdled in the surf, but after a low whistle, the dog obediently chased after him, following him to the sidewalk. He clipped the leash on Dudley, and together, they hurried back to the hotel. Back in their room, he dried down Dudley and then showered. The simple routine gave him peace, especially as the pup bared his belly for a rub and then licked his face happily. The routine also gave him purpose.

It was with that sense of purpose that he dressed, hauled out his laptop, and checked his office messages. Nothing pressing. He checked his smartphone. No call from Owen. His brother had always been one to hold in his emotions. It had been Owen's stalwart, steady presence that had been Jonathan's rock when their mother had left. Now it was his turn to be that rock for his brother, but not through a phone call. He had to finish this with his mother and Thomas and then head home.

He was needed there. It felt good to be needed. He only wished that there was a better reason for him to go home.

Chapter 26

Jonathan sucked in a deep breath, preparing himself for the moment he'd envisioned since reading the investigator's report.

"It'll be fine," his mother said and rubbed her hand back and forth across his shoulders in a soothing gesture. A rush of memories filled him as he recalled her calming him in much the same way when he'd been a young boy suffering his father's disapproval.

He glanced at her from the corner of his eye and nodded. "I'm ready," he said, although inside, he was anything but ready.

"Let me go in first. He knows me, and it'll help keep him calm," his mother said.

He nodded, and Genevieve stepped past him and opened the door to the room. The assorted beeps and chimes of medical equipment hit him before the antiseptic hospital smell.

As the door opened wider, he caught sight of the frail figure in the bed. He was motionless until his mother approached the bed. The twitch of a foot and a rough grunt came from his brother. Thomas's eyes opened wider, and shock hit Jonathan at the blue of them, so like his own, but he had Owen's dark hair. Their father's dark hair.

He stepped closer, and Thomas's head shifted slightly in his direction.

His mother had been speaking to his brother, almost crooning. Words he'd been unable to hear, but as he stepped closer, he finally heard, "This is your brother, Thomas. His name is Jonathan."

Another grunt came with a jerky motion of his brother's hand. "Yes, that's him, Thomas," his mother said, obviously understanding, although he didn't know how.

He moved a bit closer, so that his chest brushed against Genevieve's back, and placed his hands over his brother's. Thomas's hand was chilled. Smooth like a baby's. "Hi, Thomas. I'm your brother Jonathan."

The blue eyes brightened, and past the *whoosh* of the respirator that kept his brother breathing, he heard another strangled sound.

"He's happy to see you," his mother said.

"I'm happy to finally meet you, Thomas. I'm sorry it took so long to get here."

A hint of a smile came to Thomas's lips, and the monitors beeped more rapidly as if to confirm his joy.

Jonathan didn't know what else to say or ask, so he started telling his brother about himself. About what he did and his company. About Connie and how he hoped she'd be in his life again soon.

His brother listened, his eyes drifting closed every now and then before popping open. His mother patiently stood there, listening as well. Taking in his words as if she were a thirsty man in the desert. Maybe because after so many years apart, his presence was like rain on parched soil.

At one point, his brother's eyes closed, and the beep of the monitors slowed and became regular. Too regular. Thomas had fallen asleep.

"It's time we go. He can't really handle too much excitement, and this was a lot for him today," his mother said.

Jonathan nodded, and they left the room. On the steps of the facility, they paused and looked at each other. "Thank you for bringing me," he said.

"He liked seeing you. I could tell," Genevieve replied and kicked at something imaginary on the cement of the step.

"I'd like to come back, only...I need to get home. Owen needs me."

"I understand. Don't take too long to visit again, Jonathan."

--~~--

Connie had tried her best to convince Maggie not to serve Owen with the divorce papers. It hadn't done any good. Days later, they'd sat in the conference room in Connie's law firm, waiting for Owen and his lawyers to show up. They hadn't.

It was a good thing she hadn't had to sit there for long, as another wave of sickness, more powerful than the others over the last few weeks, had hit her. She'd barely made it to the restroom, where she'd tossed the minimal amount of food she'd been able to eat that day.

Nothing seemed to sit well with her, and it was long past time she acknowledged that it wasn't a stomach flu, she thought as she leaned against the counter in her bathroom at home the next morning.

It was more, way more, she thought as she stared at the test with the pink lines that said she was pregnant. She tossed the test into her bathroom garbage can and grabbed the second test she'd done as a precaution. One of the fancier kits that was supposed to be more accurate. Its little screen not only had "Pregnant" across its face, but an indication that said "3+ weeks."

Three plus weeks, she thought and laid her hand over her still-flat stomach, trying to think back to the last time she'd had her period. It had been over two months since the night of Maggie and Owen's wedding. Had it been that long since she'd had her period? She had been irregular at times, especially when she got stressed out. She'd been stressed out a lot lately.

And now this, she thought. *Shit*. She laid her hands on the rim of the sink and lowered her head, wondering how her life had gotten so complicated. She had made plans and worked so hard to stick to them, only God had laughed and laughed hard.

She threw out the second pregnancy test and straightened. Stared hard at her reflection in the mirror, wondering what she would do now. What would she do with her life and the baby growing inside her?

Is that what her mom had felt like so many years earlier? *Like mother, like daughter?* she thought and realized it was long past time she call her mother. Long past time that she talked to her about the past and tried to understand. Tried to put it all together so she could decide what to do with her life and with Jonathan.

She pushed away from the sink and hurried to her bedroom, where she grabbed her briefcase and coat. She had work today, just like she'd had work for the last four years, only today it was different. *She* was different in a major way.

Connie planned to call her mother once she got to the

office. Her mom would be at work also, but hopefully, she'd be free tonight so she could talk to Connie about what she had felt like when she'd realized she was pregnant. How she'd let her dreams disappear and struggled as a single mom after her father had left.

Once Connie had talked to her mom, she'd have to decide what to do. She had to make her plans, because that's what she did. It was what she always did, and being pregnant wasn't going to change that.

———

A half inch of condensed milk sat in the bottom of the espresso cup, waiting for her mother to fill the rest with potent Cuban coffee. She knew pregnant women were supposed to avoid caffeine, but Connie had sacrificed her morning coffee, and this cup was more milk and sugar than coffee. Besides, her mother would totally know something was going on if she passed it up. It was always a favorite for her along with the guava and cream cheese *pastelito* her mom placed in front of her on a plate.

"My favorite," she said and offered her mom a smile, but her mother, Lilli, wasn't fooled.

"It's about time you stopped avoiding me, Consuelo," Lilli said.

Her full name was never good. If her mom dragged out the rest, she was done, Connie thought.

"I've been busy at work," she lied, avoiding her mother's gaze and focusing on the cup of coffee and stirring it. Watching it go from the dark, nearly black of the coffee to the beige that said the sinfully sweet milk had mixed in.

"I suspect it's more than that. *Mija*, whatever you

need, I'm here," Lilli said, reaching out to still Connie's stirring hand with her own.

Connie's stomach did a flip, but not from illness. From fear. She didn't know where to start or where to end.

Tears slipped down her face, and her mother gently squeezed her hand. "*Mija*. There is nothing you can tell me that will make me love you any less than I do."

"I'm pregnant, Mami," she blurted out and met her mother's surprised gaze. She plowed on. "I don't know how it happened." At her mother's raised eyebrow, she added, "I mean, I know how, but not when. We used protection. We were careful."

"Things happen, Connie. If I know you, you've already decided what to do."

She shook her head. "I don't know what to do. About the pregnancy. About my job," she almost wailed.

A chuckle escaped Lilli. "Funny how you don't mention the man. I guess that means you've made your mind up about him."

Connie laughed hesitantly and shook her head as she wiped away the tears. She wrapped her fingers around the small demitasse cup and took a sip of the sweet but still bitter coffee. It was a lot like the pregnancy, both sweet with possibilities and bitter with all that she might have to give up.

"I love him," she said and then repeated it with more strength. "I love him, but I'm not sure if he's the right man for me. I'm not sure he's the kind who will stay, just like Papi."

Lilli's hands trembled on the cup she raised. "Your papi… I knew he wasn't meant to stay, but I tried to get him to change. To be the kind of man we both needed, but some people just can't change. I wish I had realized it sooner to avoid all the fighting and upset. It would have spared both of us a great deal of pain."

Connie nodded. What little she remembered of the time her father had been in her life had not been good. What followed had been as rough until her grandparents had relented and decided to help out their daughter.

"Why did you keep me? You were going to go to college and become a nurse."

"I did all those things, only a little later than I thought I would," Lilli said and finally sipped the coffee. When she set the cup down, she continued. "It wasn't easy to be a single mom and all alone. I know those early years were hard on you. It's why I understood how driven you were. Why you were determined to not be like me."

"You're a good mom. I always knew I could count on you, but yeah, I never wanted to be single and unwed, and here I am, just like you." Connie grabbed the pastry and broke off a piece, needing something to do with her hands.

Lilli's harsh laugh drew her attention. "*Mija*, you're nothing like me when I found out I was pregnant. You've got a good job—"

"Which I'm thinking of leaving."

"Because of the pregnancy?" her mother asked, arching a brow in surprise.

With a determined shake of her head, she said, "No. Because Goodwyn is a prick and doesn't appreciate what a good lawyer I am."

"And if I know you, you've already got another job lined up," her mother said with pride and a smile.

"I have a few possibilities. One interesting one in fact. Township attorney in Sea Kiss." The offer that the council member had made had implanted itself like an earworm and had refused to let go.

Her mom eyeballed her directly, scrutinizing her features. "As weird as it sounds, I can see a city girl like you there. I mean, look at this 'city,'" Lilli said using air quotes. "*Fulano de tal* at the bakery knows what the other *fulano* down at the grocery store is doing. He knows who's sick in the neighborhood and who's expecting. Who's hungry and out of money so they can slip them an extra *bocadito* for their kid. This city is like a small town but without so many trees," her mother said with a bright laugh.

Connie couldn't argue with that assessment. "It is kind of a small town. I just never pictured myself working anywhere but New York City."

Her mother thought over that statement but then continued. "What about your man? The father? Is he a city boy too?"

Taking a bite of the *pastelito*, Connie chewed on it thoughtfully as she considered Jonathan. Thought about Jonathan and his indecision on the home. Thought about the way he changed directions the way the tides shifted on the shore in Sea Kiss. But as mutable as the ocean was, there was also something constant about it. Steady in the way it returned to shore time and time again. Life giving in so many ways.

Like Jonathan had brought life back to her. Life she hadn't even know she'd been missing until he'd roused her passion and helped her come alive. Held her when she'd needed support. Listened to her when she'd needed an ear to vent. Given her space when she'd needed it.

"He's…interesting. He can be at home in so many places," she said.

"But he's only truly at home with you. I don't need to meet him to know that. I can see it on your face, *Mija*."

"He confuses me, Mami. I never know what to expect with him," she admitted.

Lilli clapped her hands together and laughed out loud. "*Que bueno*. I always thought you could use someone to shake you up. Make you see there's more to life than your job."

Connie couldn't help but chuckle. "Yeah, he's made me see there's more, Mami. So much more, but I'm not sure he's really ready to settle down."

"This man is the one from that summer, isn't he? The one who left school?" her mother asked.

Connie nodded and reluctantly said, "He is."

"The same one who was always in the newspapers?" her mother pressed and stared at her over the rim of her espresso cup.

Again, she had to confirm it, although she felt guilty doing so, as if she was betraying Jonathan with that admission. "It is."

With a dip of her head, her mother said, "And I guess you worry that he's just like your papi?"

It *was* what she'd been thinking, and yet hearing her mother say it made her want to defend Jonathan. "Maybe," she said, hating that that word seemed to be defining her life lately.

Lilli reached out and laid a hand over Connie's. "You know what I see, *Mija*? Your papi was always coming and going because he didn't really want to be with us, no matter how much I hoped it would be different."

"He wasn't happy being tied down."

Nodding, her mother said, "He wasn't, but this man, Jonathan, it seems to me that his reason for coming and going is to build a life. To be able to provide for himself and maybe a family."

She wanted to believe that. She truly did. "But if that's what he wants, why can't he choose a house? Why ask me to marry him when he knows I'm trying to decide what to do with my career?"

A long silence was followed by the clink of china as her mother took another sip of her coffee and then placed her cup down. With another subtle incline of her head, Lilli said, "You'll never know until you ask him."

Chapter 27

OWEN WAS HURTING BADLY, BUT HE HADN'T GIVEN UP on getting Maggie back. That much was clear as Jonathan stared at his brother across the width of his oak trestle table. Jonathan had actually cleared it of all his papers so they could have dinner together and talk after his return from California. Owen hadn't asked why he'd gone, and why should he? He was used to his brother running from one place to another for his company. Another trip was just par for the course. *At least until he got settled*, Jonathan thought.

Owen sat across from him, mindlessly shoveling into his mouth the Chinese food that Jonathan had ordered in. Dark smudges made Owen's charcoal-gray eyes look dead, flat like a shark's emotionless stare. Beneath the remnants of his summer tan was a hint of pallor. Deep lines seemed to have been etched around his eyes and mouth in just the short week or so since his blowup with Maggie.

Dudley must have sensed Owen's upset also. Since Owen had first stepped into the loft, the little terrier had been at his side, rubbing himself against Owen, trying to draw him out of his mood, staying beside him even when his doggy efforts failed.

"What's happening with Father?" Jonathan asked, fearing that his brother would lose the only thing holding him together: his work.

"He hasn't really been around much since... After Maggie overheard, he told me that he'd loved Maggie's mom. That she was the reason for the feud all this time. Not the properties, but losing her to Bryce Sinclair and then to death."

Just like their mother had told Jonathan just two days earlier. Not that he could tell his brother about that and his visit. About their brother Thomas. He wasn't sure Owen could handle yet another upset in his life at the moment.

"What are you going to do?" he said.

"About Maggie?" Owen asked. At Jonathan's nod, he said, "I'm going to convince her to take me back, even if it takes groveling or pleading."

What if she doesn't? he wanted to say, but he bit it back. He not only bit it back, but also took a bullet for his brother, in a figurative sense.

"How's Connie been treating you with all the divorce stuff? Has she been civil, because I know she can be a shark when she wants to be," Jonathan said, shifting the discussion away from Maggie.

"She's been supportive, and speaking of that... Rumor has it she charmed the town council into dropping their notions of rezoning that property you bought," Owen said, eyeing him with a half glance as he ate another forkful of lo mein.

"She did. She can be convincing when she wants to be." Adam Eaton, the head of the town council, had called the day after he had arrived in California to tell him the news. He'd thanked Eaton and wondered why the call hadn't come through Connie until the other man had said that Connie had specifically requested that the call be made directly to him if it was good news.

Which meant that if it was bad news, she would have handled it for him. Just like she'd helped so many people in town over the years. Just like the smaller clients who had come to her for help. It had probably chafed Goodwyn's ass that she'd managed to win those cases when her colleague hadn't even been willing to take them on.

"What are you going to do about Connie?" Owen asked, echoing Jonathan's earlier question.

Jonathan picked up a piece of General Tso's chicken with his chopsticks and popped it into this mouth. He chewed and swallowed as he thought about what to say, then smiled as he said, "I intend to grovel and plead if I have to." But before he could do that, he had some other things to settle.

He'd already made peace with his mother. Now he had to make peace with his father so that his future would be free of the demons of the past.

Whenever something important happened in Connie's life, Maggie would have been the first one she called to share the news. Immediately after, Emma and then Tracy. Her friends had been her support in both good times and bad, but for some reason, the baby news was something she wanted to keep to herself. Something she wanted to hold on to until she could decide what to do about her job and Jonathan, but not about the baby. From the moment that the pregnancy test had yielded its results, she'd had no doubt that she would keep the baby.

At the moment, she had to help Maggie deal with Owen and all that was happening in her life. Which meant a long weekend with Maggie and her friends down in Sea Kiss. It had already been two weeks since Maggie had tossed Owen out. A week since Owen had been served with the divorce papers but had failed to show up for the meeting a few days later. As she'd warned him and his lawyer, they wouldn't wait much longer for Owen's reply. If after this weekend they didn't have the signed papers, she'd be forced to take the next step in the divorce proceedings. She hated the thought of doing that and was still hoping Maggie would reconsider.

The weekend away would be good for Maggie but also for Connie. It would give her time to think about her own life and what to do about it. Hopefully, the Pierce boys would be staying away, but if they didn't, she could deal. She was a big girl, and she could handle it. She'd help Maggie handle it as well, if necessary.

That's what friends did for each other. Just like she'd taken care of Jonathan's problem with the town council. She had hoped that doing so would give her closure with the council, until Adam Eaton had floated that ridiculous offer.

Her as the township attorney. She had almost laughed at the thought at first, except that in the last few weeks, it had started to feel not so far-fetched. And in all the times she'd pictured herself married—usually to Jonathan during those passion-filled nights of their youth—she'd never thought about children. But even if she had, the picture would never have been one of her wheeling a baby carriage down a crowded New York City street. As a city kid, sweltering in the heat of summer sandwiched between brick buildings and hopping across scorching cement walks, she'd always pictured herself at the shore, swimming in the sea and running all around a town where people didn't lock their doors. Enjoying cool ocean breezes and the susurrus of the waves to lull her to sleep and not the murmur of the city's never-ending street life.

Which she and the baby could enjoy if she interviewed for the position Eaton had mentioned. With his backing and her past involvement in Sea Kiss, she thought she stood a good chance of getting the job. That would mean buying a house in the area. Maybe a cute little cottage like Emma had. There was only one thing missing from the picture: Jonathan.

He'd already asked her to marry him, even before finding out he was going to be a father. But his hesitation about buying a house still caused her concern. She knew he had issues and so did she, but she was working through hers. She wondered if he was working through his. Even if he was, it might take time. But with a baby on the way, she didn't know how much longer she could hold off on making a decision on what to do.

Those thoughts were still nagging her as she and her friends finished up dinner at the Sinclair beach house and Maggie excused herself to go for a walk on the beach. Connie rose to go with her, worried about leaving her friend alone, when Emma placed a hand on her arm and shut her down with a look. Not wanting to cause a scene in front of Maggie, she sat back down but glared at Emma. As soon as Maggie was out the door, she turned to her friend, but Tracy piped in with, "Em's right, you know. Maggie needs the time alone to decide what to do. Too many of us being mother hens isn't going to help."

"But Jonathan and Owen are next door," she said. When she and Maggie had arrived earlier in the day, Jonathan's Willys Jeep and Owen's Lightning had been sitting in the driveway of the Pierce mansion. She'd peeked over the edge of the balcony before coming down for dinner, and the cars had still been there. Obviously, the men, just like she and her friends, were intending to stay for the weekend.

"Which could be good and not just for Maggie," Emma said and looked at Connie pointedly.

"I agree. You never were one to back down from a challenge, but with Jon…" Tracy left it hanging there, obviously wanting her to explain.

"It's complicated. Way more complicated than either of you can imagine."

Emma and Tracy shared a look that Connie didn't quite like. A second later, Emma laid a hand over hers as Connie nervously plucked at a napkin lying on the table. "You know you can tell us anything, right? We won't judge."

Tracy reached out from Connie's other side and wrapped an arm around her shoulders. "We won't, and we'll be here for whatever you need, just like you've always been there for us."

The burn of tears rose up and then the wetness as one escaped and trailed down her cheek. "I'm fine. I just need to work some things out," she said, her voice tight with emotion.

"Just know we're here," Tracy repeated while Emma nodded sympathetically.

As much as she wanted to tell her friends about the baby and everything else, she just couldn't. "I know," she said and was about to continue when a shout from outside had them glancing out the french doors. Mrs. Patrick must have also heard the noise, since she came out of her room to see what was happening.

Maggie and Owen were standing on the great lawn, facing each other, the tension in their bodies apparent. Maggie held something in her hand, and Connie immediately knew what it was. "He gave her the divorce papers. Shit, he must have signed them."

"Shit," Emma said. A second later, they were all racing out the door. A crashing sound came from the hedges separating the two homes as Jonathan burst through them. Apparently, he had also realized something was going on, but as they all watched, Maggie tore the papers in half and handed the pieces back to Owen. A second later, they were in each other's arms, laughing and kissing.

"I guess they made up," Tracy said, arching a manicured brow in surprise.

"Thank God," Connie and Emma said at the same time.

As Maggie and Owen turned and realized they had an audience, Jonathan walked over to join them, a smile on his face until he saw her. Then his look grew a little more somber, and he dipped his head in greeting. "Connie," he said, before greeting her friends and Mrs. Patrick, who he gave a huge bear hug that had her giggling like a schoolgirl. Tears came to Connie's eyes again for her friend, who looked so happy walking toward them with Owen, and for her own misery at being away from Jonathan. She had even experienced a moment of jealousy as he'd hugged the seventysomething Mrs. Patrick, which she excused as a by-product of runaway pregnancy hormone mood swings.

As Maggie and Owen stood before them, they shared a loving look.

Owen grinned, faced Emma, and said, "Do you think you could plan a small, intimate wedding for immediate family for next weekend?"

Emma shook her head, obviously thinking that Owen was maybe deranged. "I'm not sure. Do you plan on making it stick this time?"

Connie didn't think it possible, but Owen's smile grew even broader as he said, "Forever this time, Emma. No doubt about it."

———

Jonathan couldn't sleep. He was still out of kilter from the rushed trip to California and back and the emotional upheaval it had caused, not to mention the earlier emotion of that night. His heart was filled with joy that his brother and Maggie had settled their differences and intended to make their marriage work. With their recommitment ceremony planned for the following weekend, he wouldn't have to wait long to tell his brother about his trip to see their mom and the brother neither of them had known about.

But with as much as he'd done, there was so much more he still had to do before pressing his case with Connie again. And there was still his father to deal with.

He grabbed a sweatshirt from the overnight bag he'd brought over from the inn where he had been staying. His brother had insisted Jonathan stay for the weekend, their father's wishes be damned. Jonathan tugged the sweatshirt on against the chill of a late October night. Dudley roused from beside him and followed him through the silent house. Owen had gone to spend the night with Maggie at her beach home.

As soon as he opened the french doors to the patio, Dudley raced out and down to the water, mindless of the night and the slight cold. His pup loved the water so much that he suspected Dudley had been a surfer in another life. He'd have to get him a life vest and take him out on the waves one day.

Dudley was in the wash, jumping and barking, inviting Jonathan to get out of his mood. But as Jonathan sauntered across the boardwalk and down to the sand, Dudley took off in the direction of the Sinclair mansion, chasing a flock of seagulls in the ocean's wash. He looked and noticed the lone figure wrapped in a plaid blanket, sitting on the steps of the boardwalk.

Connie, he thought but didn't turn away, especially as she peered in his direction and offered a tentative smile. He stuffed his hands into his sweatpants pockets to keep from reaching for her and walked over.

She scooted to one side of the step and said, "It's too cold on the sand."

He sat opposite her on the step below. "We've got to stop meeting like this," he teased, trying to keep the mood light.

"Yeah, it's already getting a little too cold for midnight strolls," she said with a chuckle, then rubbed her arms with her hands beneath the protection of the blanket.

"For sure," he said. After a long pause, he plunged on. "How are you doing?"

She worried her lower lip but finally said, "Fine. How about you? How was your trip?"

It was hard to keep the truth from her, but he knew that if he asked, she would keep it to herself. "I went to Coronado to see our mother, but Owen doesn't know about the trip, and I want to keep it that way. There's a lot to tell, and now isn't the right time."

"Is there ever a right time with something that important?" she said, worry lines erupting on her forehead, as if she was talking about more than his trip.

He shrugged. "I don't know if there is. But I don't want to dump anything else on Owen until I can talk to our father. He's kept a lot from us, and I want to know why."

Connie scrutinized his features and asked, "Like what?"

"Like the reason our mother left and a brother we didn't even know we had."

Shock rippled across her features, followed by concern. She slipped her hand from beneath the warmth of the blanket and cupped his cheek. "You have another brother?"

He nodded and fought the emotions roiling inside him as he explained. "Thomas…his name is Thomas. He's nineteen, but he has special needs, both mentally and physically."

"I'm sorry you didn't know about him, Jon. It's not right that your parents kept him from you and Owen."

"Yeah, it sucks. He looks like Owen and me. He's a mix of the two of us. When I talked to him, I think he realized we were related and was happy about it," he said, recalling Thomas's response to his presence.

"Is he with your mom?" she asked and brushed back a lock of his long hair as a land breeze blew it across his face. Even when the breeze died down, she repeated the action, smoothing his hair in a gesture that was both familiar and comforting.

He shook his head. "He's in a home for people requiring extensive care. Genevieve, my mother, tells me my father has never shirked paying for anything Thomas needs."

"So he has a heart, even though it may be way too small," she said, dragging a chuckle from him.

"Way too small is an understatement," he said and went on to tell her about the reasons why his mom left, how his father had forced her to choose between her sons, and he could see Connie growing upset on his behalf.

Luckily, Dudley chose that moment to rush up from the surf to chase the seagulls, half-wet but clearly delighted to see Connie. The terrier jumped up onto her lap, and she wrapped him up with the loose ends of the blanket, earning some doggie kisses as a thank-you.

She laughed at the dog's antics, and Jonathan rubbed Dudley's head and instructed him to sit. Which he did, right in Connie's lap.

"Silly dog," she said, but her words were tinged with laughter and love.

Smart dog, he thought.

"What are you going to do about your mother and father?" she asked, growing serious again. She hugged Dudley tight as the puppy nestled happily against her.

That million-dollar question had been on his brain ever since he'd boarded the plane home. With a shrug, he said, "I plan on seeing my mother and brother again, regularly if I can. As for my father, he needs to make things right with Owen. Owen is the one who has always been there, no matter what my father said or did, and it almost cost him the love of his life."

A sad look passed over her features, and she cradled his jaw and ran her thumb along his cheek. "Your father needs to make things right with you too, Jon."

He nodded and grasped the hand at his cheek. Held it tightly in his as he said, "One step at a time, Connie. Some things just can't be rushed."

As his gaze met hers, it was obvious she understood what he meant. But then she surprised him by leaning over and kissing him. A kiss full of sweetness and caring.

He answered with tenderness and patience, the moment too fragile to rush toward passion. As she broke away from the kiss, her ragged whisper breathed hope into him.

"This is a nice next step," she said. Urging Dudley down from her lap, she slowly rose. The pup whined in protest, and she gave him a final pat on the head to comfort him.

"I'll walk you back," he said, not that he needed to. He couldn't remember the last time there had been any significant crime in Sea Kiss.

"That would be nice," she said, and together, they walked across the short boardwalk, over the dunes, and onto the great lawn. Up through grass wet with the remnants of an earlier rain, Dudley patiently following in their footsteps.

At the french doors leading to the kitchen, she stopped and faced him. "Good night, Jon."

"G'night, Connie. Thanks for listening, and a big

thanks for what you did with the town council. I haven't had a chance to say it, what with everything with my mom and Owen and stuff, but I really appreciate it. My guys are all really excited about working on that facility and all they can do for the area."

She nodded and wrapped the blanket around herself tighter, as if she needed it to hold herself together. "What are friends for, Jon? Besides, Sea Kiss could use some new blood."

He eyed her, aware of what she wasn't saying. "Would that possibly include someone new as the township attorney? I hear that they're looking for one."

With the kind of smile a mother might use on a child wheedling for another hour of playtime, she said, "G'night, Jon. It's late, and I'm really tired."

She didn't wait for his reply before rushing into the house, but he again took hope at the fact that she hadn't denied it outright. He just prayed that all the hope that was building inside him wasn't setting him up for a big fall.

Chapter 28

IN HER ENTIRE LIFE, CONNIE HAD NEVER TAKEN A LEAP without looking. Apparently, there was a first time for everything, she thought as she waited in the anteroom of Goodwyn's office, the anticipation at what she was about to do making her nerve endings tingle.

"Mr. Goodwyn will see you now," his assistant said, rose, and opened the door to his office.

With a deep inhale, she stood, smoothed the skirt whose waistband was already getting a little tight, and marched into his office. As she entered, he was, as usual, shuffling some papers around on his desk, making her wait for his attention. When he looked up, peering at her from above the rim of his bifocals, he gestured to the chair in front of his desk. She demurred and remained standing, surprising him before he carefully schooled his features.

She had been clutching a manila folder to her chest but relaxed her grip and passed it to the older man. He placed it on his desktop, and as he opened it, she began her carefully prepared speech. "I want you to know that I appreciate all that I've learned here at Brewster, Goodwyn, and Smith, as well as the opportunity to work with such a skilled and professional staff."

By then, Goodwyn had opened the folder and read the first piece of paper: her resignation letter. As he did so, his color grew more and more florid until she worried he might have a stroke. Despite that, he said nothing, just eyed her the way someone might glare at dirt on the bottom of their shoe. It didn't dissuade her from continuing.

"I've given you a month's notice to allow for bringing my colleagues up-to-date on any pending matters."

"That won't be necessary," he said brusquely, which was what she'd imagined he might say. It was why she had been taking home her personal belongings in dribs and drabs over the last few days.

"Beneath my resignation is a form letter for the firm to review and, if acceptable, send to those clients with whom I've worked on various matters."

He shot to his feet, but with her heels, they were nearly eye to eye. If he had thought it would physically intimidate her, he was dead wrong.

"As you know, both myself and the firm have an obligation to inform the clients of the change in representation, advise as to who will be taking over the cases, as well as to advise the client that they have the option to remain with the firm or choose to be represented by me or some other attorney or firm."

Goodwyn almost sneered as he said, "You actually think any of those clients will want to leave this firm?"

She arched a brow, splayed her hands on his desk, and leaned toward him, wondering why she'd ever let him intimidate her in the first place. "You mean like the ones you thought were too small to merit your attention? I'll be in my office if you or any of the other partners wish to discuss my resignation or the letter to the clients."

She pivoted on one heel and left him sputtering, "You can't do this."

I can and I just did, she thought, her smile as wide as the Cheshire cat's. Heads popped up over the tops of the cubicles, like prairie dogs disturbed from their burrows, as Goodwyn's continued threats grew louder. She ignored them and glanced at her watch, calculating that she had maybe twenty minutes tops before they'd make their move.

At her desk, she sat and sipped the last of her decaf coffee. She didn't know how she'd survive another seven or so months without the real thing. The doctor had put her at about eight weeks pregnant. That meant that by next Memorial Day, give or take, she'd be a mom.

It took all of ten minutes for one of the other partners, the main man for the litigation area, to come to her office, a security guard in tow. He knocked on the jamb of her door, and she motioned for him to enter. After he did, he closed the door behind him and took one of the seats before her desk. He leaned back in the chair, crossed one leg over the other, and examined her intently.

"I'm truly sorry it's come to this, Connie. We all thought you were going to be a valuable part of this firm for the future," he said, surprising her.

"To tell the truth, Bill, that hasn't been apparent at all in the last few months. On the contrary, not one of you did anything while Goodwyn made my life miserable," she said, her tone calm and dispassionate.

"We all know he's a difficult man, but we can make things right by you," he said.

"With a partnership?" she said, wondering just how far the others would go.

Bill did a little *maybe* shrug. "It's certainly something we can discuss in the future."

She was surprised at what he'd said so far, since litigators tended to be more circumspect with their language, especially in a situation like this one. But his noncommittal shrug and promise of the future were too little too late at this point.

"It's nice to know that a partnership might have been possible, but I've made up my mind about leaving," she said.

"I'm sorry to hear that, Connie. We'll be sending you a check for the month's time you offered in your resignation letter, but we'd prefer it if you left today," he said. After he stood, opened the door, and motioned to the guard standing just outside to come in, he said, "If you don't mind my asking, where are you going?"

"I'm not really sure. All I know is that anywhere is better than here." She shot her hand up like a cop stopping traffic as the security guard moved to enter her office. "No need to call in the reinforcements. I've got nothing to take with me."

When she reached the door, she turned toward Bill and said, "If you need assistance on any of the cases I was handling during the next month, you know where to reach me. After that, I'll send you a bill for services. Please copy me on the letters you send to the clients advising on the change of representation. We wouldn't want anyone to be accused of ethical improprieties." Namely Goodwyn, and she had no qualms about taking him before an ethics panel if he failed to do the right thing.

Head held high, she stopped to wish her tearful

assistant goodbye. On her way to the front door with Bill, the security guard trailing behind them, she was greeted by several other attorneys and a dozen or more staff members who wanted to wish her well. She said her goodbyes to each one, trying to hold back the tears building inside and the fear that she thought she had overcome when she had first made the decision to leave just days earlier. At the receptionist's desk, Bill held his hand out, and she took the lanyard from around her neck and passed him her key card.

"Have a nice life, Bill," she said and exited into the elevator bank. Once inside, she took one deep breath after another, telling herself to hold it together until she got off the floor and down to the lobby. Instead of heading home, she walked through the underground connection to the Chrysler Building, where Maggie's offices were located.

A short elevator ride later, she was standing at the door of Maggie's office. Her friend was on the phone but waved at her to come in, her gaze questioning. As she finished the call, she shot a quick look at her watch. "Half day?"

"Last day," Connie replied.

Maggie came around and sat on the edge of the desk. "For real?" she asked.

Connie told Maggie about what she had just done, and as she finished, she couldn't stop and tacked on, "I'm pregnant."

"Wow." Maggie shifted a chair so she could sit beside her and wrap an arm around her shoulders in sympathy. "Are you okay? Have you been to the doctor?"

"Yes and yes, and before you ask, Jon doesn't know.

I haven't told him yet because…" Her voice trailed off as she mentally considered the long list of reasons why she'd kept her silence, including that he had a whole lot of his own shit going on.

Maggie patted her upper arm, offering comfort. "It's okay, Con. Is that why you quit?"

She shook her head. "There's been a lot going on the last couple of months. I didn't want to trouble you with it."

"Because I was so wrapped up in my own shit that I didn't realize my best fuckin' friend in the whole world needed me. I am so, so sorry."

"It's okay," she whispered, her throat tight with emotion. Feeling suddenly tired, she leaned her head against Maggie's shoulder, and with a sniffle, she said, "It's going to be okay."

"For sure. Why don't we go to my house and get comfy? We can talk, get chip-faced with a pint of caramel waffle cone, order grandma pizza, and watch every season of *Buffy the Vampire Slayer*."

"Except season seven. I hated season seven," she said.

Maggie laughed and hugged her hard. "Everyone hated season seven. Let's go."

Jonathan sauntered around the living room in his father's condo on Central Park East. The condo took up half of a city block and was high enough that the sounds of the street below were almost nonexistent. He walked to the windows along one wall and stared down at the expanse of Central Park that stretched west for a few avenues and nearly fifty blocks northward. The trees had started to lose their leaves, and some were already bare, leaving a patchwork design across the vast city forest.

Prime real estate, his father would say about the condo that had once been home to their family. Now, only his father rattled around in the immense space that hadn't changed all that much since when Jonathan was a child.

He walked over to the dry bar in one corner and poured himself a whiskey. Crossed back over to the couch and took a seat where the old man was sure to see him as he walked in. The last thing he wanted to do was scare him to death since he wasn't expected.

Barely half an hour later, he heard the snick of the lock and the familiar squeak of the door as his father shuffled in and stopped dead as he noticed Jonathan sitting there.

In that awkward moment of silence and staring, a thousand thoughts raced through Jonathan's brain as he took in the sight of his father. Even though his dad was barely past sixty, his thinning hair and the wan hue of his skin made him look far older. He had once been a few inches over six foot, put now he hunched over so much that he had lost several inches in height. His clothing did little to help his appearance. His suit hung loose on him, and the dark color only made his skin seem that much more pale. Although Jonathan had come here to confront him, guilt took hold that his father might not be well enough for a battle.

"Who let you in?" his father asked.

Jonathan held up a key chain. "Owen lent me his emergency set of keys." He tossed them onto the coffee table before him. They landed with a clatter against the polished mahogany.

"You have no right to be here," his father said, but he walked closer until he stood behind one of the wing chairs. He didn't sit but held on to the top of the chair, as if needing support and maybe even a shield.

Jonathan sipped the whiskey and then glanced at his father over the rim of the crystal glass. "And you had no right to keep Owen and me from our mother. From Thomas."

His father's entire body shook, and his face grew even paler. He fumbled his way around the edge of the seat and then plopped down heavily into the chair. "You can't even begin to understand."

"Really?" Jonathan challenged. "You didn't love her. You were in love with Elizabeth Sinclair," he said and waited for a denial that never came.

He continued. "You thought Genevieve would be a bad influence."

His father finally reacted, beating one arm of the chair with his hand. "She was a dreamer. An artist. She was always filling your heads with nonsense. Especially you, Jonathan. I could see how much you were like her."

He couldn't deny that he'd always been a dreamer, but if you didn't have dreams, what did you have? Bitterness and anger like that which had ruined their father?

At Jonathan's hesitation, his father plowed on. "I did it to protect my sons. To make sure they grew up into strong, responsible men, and look at how you turned out. Look at you," he almost shouted and beat on the arm of the chair again.

"Yes, look at me, Father. A man who won't commit to a relationship because he's afraid he's not good enough to be loved. A man who's spent a good part of his life wondering how he could make his father proud," he said.

Before his eyes, his father seemed to shrink into himself, rousing Jonathan's pity. But it wasn't enough to cool the heat of anger that he now realized had been simmering at his core for so long. Like a volcano spewing lava to release pressure, he had to vent the frustration he'd felt for years.

"All I ever wanted was to have your love and that of the mother who just upped and left one day. Knowing why she did so doesn't make it any easier. Knowing I had a brother I never knew about..." He paused to suck in a ragged breath, and his father jumped in at the hesitation.

"It was a mistake. Genevieve and I had already been fighting over the divorce settlement, and when Elizabeth died..." His father dragged in a shaky breath. "I needed something, someone, and Genevieve was there. For a moment, I thought we could reconcile, but it didn't take long for me to feel the anger again. To realize I'd lost the only woman I ever really loved. When Thomas was born the way he was, I knew it was God's punishment for so many things. Coveting my friend's wife. Being dishonest with Genevieve. But if anyone should have been punished, it should have been me and not an innocent child."

His guilt explained part of the reason why he had never hesitated to pay for everything Thomas needed. In his own twisted way, he'd cared, but he shouldn't have used Thomas as a pawn in the divorce proceedings.

"Have you ever even seen him, Father?"

His father's head bobbled up and down clumsily as if he was too weak or tired to move. "I go once a year, and I pray for his forgiveness."

That shocked Jonathan. He'd had no idea that his father had visited, and he wondered if his mother did either, since she hadn't mentioned it. He wondered about something else as well.

"What about our forgiveness, Father? You almost ruined Owen's marriage, and he truly loves Maggie. She's everything he could ever have wanted in a wife."

His father grew teary eyed. With a sniffle, he said, "Maggie is just like her mother. Owen is a lucky man."

"They're getting married again on Saturday. You will be there this time. It's time for you to start making things right," he said.

His father nodded, understanding that it wasn't a request. "And what about you, Jonathan? Rumor has it you're chasing after that Cuban girl again."

He was surprised his father knew, which meant that he might actually care, if only a little. "That Cuban girl is named Connie Reyes, and I love her. I asked her to marry me, but we both have a lot going on."

Jonathan took a big sip of his whiskey and waited for his father's rebuke. One like he'd gotten years earlier when his father had gotten wind of who he was dating.

"She's a smart woman. Strong. She'd be good for you, so don't let her get away," his father said instead. At Jonathan's questioning gaze, he explained. "She handled a lawsuit for us a few years back. Got us out of a nasty situation. And she's a looker too. You'd make nice babies."

He couldn't help but chuckle at his father's rather Neanderthal comment. "Yes, she is beautiful, but I'm not quite sure she's ready to start making babies yet."

"Pfft, these career women. Waste the prime of their lives working," his father harrumphed.

Jonathan felt some of his anger slipping away at the easy camaraderie that seemed to be developing between them. Some, but not all.

"I'm not sure Connie would appreciate that sentiment," he said, feeling the change in the tone of their discussion and maybe even their relationship, although it would take time to heal the wounds of the past. "Can I get you drink?" he said and held up his glass.

His father nodded, and Jonathan rose, walked over to the bar, and prepped another whiskey, taking the time to consider that the night was progressing far differently than he had envisioned. He returned and handed his father the drink. Sat back across from him on the couch.

After taking a sip, his father asked, "What are your plans, Jonathan? Rumor has it you plan on opening another location in Sea Kiss."

He chuckled. "You seem to listen to a lot of gossip, Father."

A hint of a smile chased away years from his father's face. "Owen can be a bit of a busybody."

Shaking his head, Jonathan told him his plans for the new research and development facilities and everything else. The coding classes for anyone who wanted to take them and the internships for the local students.

His father sipped his whiskey and nodded. "That's a sound building and a good location. I actually remember old man Scordato and his son before the company got bought out and they moved production down south."

"You've seen a lot of change in Sea Kiss," Jonathan said.

That prompted his father to regale him with stories of some of those changes and the tales he had heard from his father before him. As he finished one story, he said, "There's even talk that the Pierces and Sinclairs were bootleggers. Made the money to build those homes running rum."

He'd heard the stories and that maybe even old man Scordato had helped them by building barrels. "Are they true?" he asked.

His father shrugged. "The Pierce men have always been determined. Followed their own paths, just like you, Jonathan. I've been a fool not to see that you do the Pierce name proud."

He couldn't have been more poleaxed if his father had actually hit him with a pole.

At his silence and surprise, his father continued. "Sea Kiss needs men like you to keep it going. Taking your business there will be a big help to the entire area."

He nodded. "I hope so, but I need your help to do something else."

"I'll try to help in any way I can. I owe you that much," he said.

With a pleased smile that his father seemed ready to start making things right, Jonathan said, "I don't want to drift from place to place anymore. I need a home, Father."

Chapter 29

A COUPLE OF MONTHS EARLIER, IT HAD BEEN HARD FOR Connie to see Jonathan after so many years apart. This afternoon, as she stood across from him by the arbor that had been set up on the beach, waiting for Maggie and Owen to walk down the aisle together again, was possibly harder.

He was ramrod straight, handsomely dressed in a bespoke suit that hugged his broad shoulders and lean hips. His sun-streaked hair was raked back into a man bun. His face was freshly shaven and with a hint of color that said he might have been out on the water earlier, surfing and getting sun on what was an unusually warm late autumn day.

As the chamber music orchestra began to play the wedding march, she waited for the sight of Maggie and Owen coming over the boardwalk on the dunes before heading past the two dozen or so close family members and friends gathered for this second wedding. But as her friends came into view, she realized that besides Maggie's dad, Owen's father had also shown up for the ceremony.

"Holy shit," Emma whispered.

"I second that," Tracy murmured.

Connie glanced across the way at Jonathan, but there was no surprise there. Just a pleased look on his face that said he might have known about his father's attendance all along. As his gaze met hers, the confident look in his only confirmed her suspicion.

She said nothing as Maggie, Owen, and the two dads walked down to the arbor near the water's edge where the minister and bridal party waited. Given the unusual circumstances of having this second ceremony just months after the first, the minister's message was more about staying committed to marriage than the usual wedding speech. It seemed that in no time, Maggie and Owen were renewing their vows and returning back up the beach for the cocktail party to thank friends and family for attending the ceremony.

The two dads walked arm in arm behind the newlywed couple, earning raised eyebrows from several guests who were aware of the family feud that had been going on for over twenty years. Mustering her courage, Connie walked to the center of the aisle and took Jonathan's arm, imagining how this might have been them if she'd accepted his wedding proposal weeks earlier.

As she stumbled on the soft sand, he gently offered support. "You okay?" he said, his heavenly blue eyes filled with concern.

She nodded. "More than okay."

He smiled and laid his hand over hers as it rested on his arm. Matched his steps to hers as they walked onto the boardwalk and across the great lawn. Since this was supposed to be a less formal gathering, there were only tall tables scattered here and there where guests could stand and have a cocktail or grab an hors d'oeuvre from a passing waiter.

She intended to walk to a table and wait for Emma and Tracy to join her, but Jonathan apparently had other plans. He guided her to where Maggie and Owen stood with the fathers. She hugged her friends and Bryce Sinclair, who had always been kind and supportive. As she came to Robert Pierce, whom she'd met in the past when she'd done some work for his company, she stepped back. "Mr. Pierce," she said with a curt nod.

"Miss Reyes. It's good to see you again. Jonathan has told me a lot about you."

She looked over her shoulder at Jonathan, who shot her a chagrined smile and shrugged.

"All good, I assure you," Robert tacked on.

"So glad to hear that, and may I say it's nice to see you here. I know how much this means to both Maggie and Owen." Her words, while neutral, clearly struck home.

"As long as there's breath, it's never too late to rectify a mistake," Robert said.

His admission surprised her, but she didn't have time to respond as Jonathan said, "If you'll excuse us, Connie and I were just going to get a drink." With a less than subtle nudge against her back, he urged her in the direction of the bar and ordered them champagne.

"A cranberry juice for me," she corrected, earning a puzzled look from Jonathan.

"On the wagon? You always were such a light-weight," he teased.

After the bartender handed them the drinks, Jonathan clinked his glass against hers. "To Maggie and Owen."

She repeated the toast and took a sip. She strolled away from the bar with Jonathan following beside her. Emma, Tracy, and her husband were standing and eating at a nearby table, and she joined them there, but Jonathan did as well. As a server came by with food,

Jonathan swooped some off the tray and placed one of the dishes in front of her.

"Thanks," she said, a little unnerved by his attention, because she hadn't quite decided the how and when of raising the issue of their future. But his attention said that the time spent apart hadn't dimmed his desire to be with her, and she was grateful for that. It would only make what she had to say to him easier.

Another hour passed, spent in mindless conversation with Jonathan and her friends and eating an amazing variety of hors d'oeuvres prepared by Carlo and his staff. Little by little, family and friends drifted off until it was just Maggie and Owen, the dads, Mrs. Patrick, and the group gathered around her table. Tracy and her husband excused themselves to go home while Emma claimed she had to run and give Carlo and his people final directions.

"The plague couldn't have cleared people out faster," Jonathan said once they were all alone.

"I guess they thought we might need some time to ourselves," she said and motioned in the direction of the beach. "Would you join me for a walk?"

"I'd love to," he said and offered her his arm.

They strolled down the lawn, across the boardwalk, and down to the sand. Connie paused to slip off her high heels and left them by the steps. Lately, her back ached after a day of heels, and she longed to sink her toes in the sand and maybe chase away the dull pain.

"You okay?" he asked as he saw her wince.

"Heels are killing me," she admitted and watched as he toed off his dress shoes and socks.

"Nothing better than barefoot," he said, and she silently added, *And pregnant*.

They ambled side by side quietly until the light started to dim with the coming of dusk.

While Jonathan loved nothing more than spending time with her, even in silence, there was so much he wanted to say to her. So much that he hoped would bring them back together. "How have you been?" he said, anxious to hear what had been happening to her during their time apart.

"Busy."

Patience, he told himself. "Goodwyn been busting your chops again?"

She shook her head, smiled, and glanced at him from the corner of her eye. "I can happily say that I no longer work for that prick."

He stopped short and laid a hand on her arm when she continued walking. "You quit? Really?"

She nodded. "Yes, I did. I decided they needed me more than I needed them."

"Epic. So where are you working now?" he asked, almost afraid to hear her answer. But as he glanced at her, he wasn't quite sure what to make of the mischievous grin on her face.

"Actually, I don't have another job. Not yet," she said.

The enormity of that blanked his mind. He let it settle in and said, "Connie Reyes, she of the plans and determination, doesn't have a job? That's too gnarly to believe."

She took hold of his hand and guided him in the direction of the steps to the Pierce home. She sat and patted the spot beside her. At his hesitation, she said, "You really need to sit to hear this."

He did as she asked, and as a sharp breeze suddenly swept off the water, she shivered beside him. He whipped off his jacket and slipped it over her shoulders.

"Thanks," she said and went on with her story before he could ask another question. "I've been thinking about a lot of things lately. I realized that even if I got over this rough patch with Goodwyn, he'd never acknowledge all that I did for the firm. I also realized that if it were up to him, I'd never be able to represent my kind of client."

"Like the people you helped in Sea Kiss," he said, understanding where she was coming from.

"Like them and like all the other companies that just didn't rate in some small minds. I had a headhunter searching for me, and he found some other firms that had a different mentality. They were interested in me, but I received a much more exciting offer."

His heart actually stopped for a moment as he waited for the details, and in that split second, he told himself that no matter where she was going, he would follow if she wanted him to. "Where was the offer? Boston?" he said, aware that she'd spent time there when she'd interned during one summer in law school.

"Sea Kiss," she said, surprising the shit out of him.

"Sea Kiss," he repeated shakily, unable to believe where she might be going with that decision.

"You know the town council was so awed by the presentation I did for you that they asked me to interview for the township attorney's position. I did, and they offered me the job, and I took it. It's only part-time, but that's okay. It will give me time with my private clients. In the last week or so, a number of those clients have left Goodwyn to come with me. Because of that, I was hoping you could help me with some things."

"Anything. Whatever you need," he said eagerly, but he was not ready for what she did next.

She got down on one knee on the sand in front of him. "I've always been kind of traditional, but I know you appreciate drawing outside the lines," she said.

It took him a second to realize what she was doing, and by then, she was saying, "Jonathan Pierce. Would you do me the honor of being my husband?"

He was so honestly tongue-tied that he couldn't speak. So he swept her up in his arms and kissed her, answering her in the only way he could at that moment. She kissed him back, laughter on her lips as she whispered, "I hope that's a yes."

"Sweet lord, of course it's a yes," he said and reached into the pocket of the suit jacket he'd draped over her shoulders and extracted the velvet box. Popped it open to show her the diamond ring inside. "I've been holding on to this for weeks, hoping that there would be a right time to ask, but you beat me to it."

She grinned as he removed the ring from the box and slipped it on her finger. "You know how determined I can be," she said.

"For sure." He reached into an inside pocket of the jacket on her shoulders to take out a folded piece of paper. He handed it to her and said, "That's why I was going to give this to you as well. I didn't want you to have any doubts that I was here to stay."

Her hands shook as she unfolded the document. Shock filled her features as she read it. "It's a deed to your family's beach house. How?"

He shrugged. "I made the old bastard an offer he couldn't refuse. I'm hoping you'll want to live here, but I also wanted to tell you that I would go anywhere you wanted to go. My home is anywhere I can be with you."

When she didn't answer at first and just continued to stare at the deed, he plowed on. "I was hoping we could have our wedding here. Maybe one day, Maggie and Owen's kids will be playing with ours down on the beach while us old folk sit on the sand and watch them."

She carefully folded the deed and handed it to him. "I would love to get married here. Live here or anywhere else with you, because I'm home when I'm with you." She paused for a second and took hold of his hand. Brought it down to rest across the softness of her belly. "As for babies, we might have gotten a head start on Maggie and Owen."

Her words sank in slowly, joyfully. He pressed his hand against her and said, "No way. We're going to have a baby?"

"In about seven months, right around Memorial Day."

He cradled her head in one hand, wrapped his arm around her waist, and drew her even closer. "I love you, Reyes. I have since the day I first set eyes on you."

"I love you, Jon," she said and undid the tie holding his hair back. As it fell free, she raked her hands through it and said, "I love that you're a dreamer and that you have a heart as big as the ocean you love so much. I love that you can make me laugh and that you can make me burn for you."

"I plan on making that happen a lot before the baby gets here," he said with a grin.

"What's stopping you right now?" she kidded and waggled her eyebrows suggestively.

"Excellent! I just love independent women." He surged to his feet and carried her up the stairs and across the boardwalk. There were still sounds of activity from the Sinclair mansion, but no one was supposed to be in his home. Both his dad and Owen had known that he had planned to ask her to marry him after the wedding and that he might need some time alone.

He threw open one of the side doors to the house and then kicked it closed behind them. He hurried with her up the stairs to his room and the immense king-sized bed in the center of the space.

"Do you realize we've never made love here?" she said, peering around his bedroom and wrinkling her nose. "This looks like a sports bar married a tech center. We will definitely have to redo this room."

"For real? Not even married and you're already getting bossy?" he said as he let her slip to the ground in front of the bed, grabbed his suit jacket, and tossed it aside.

"You're totally going to like bossy. Now sit." She pushed him playfully, and he sat on the edge of the bed and hauled her between his open legs. He laid his hand on her belly again, still in wonder at the fact that he was going to be a dad.

"It's still flat," he said.

"Some of my suits are already tight," she groused. "So is this dress," she added with a pout.

"Then let me help you get comfortable," he said and reached around her to draw down the zipper.

The dress fell free, and he balanced her as she

stepped out of the puddle of expensive raw silk. He carefully laid the dress aside and hardened at the sight of all her lush curves in nothing but dusky-rose lace and silk. "I didn't think it was possible, but you're even more beautiful now."

"I feel fat, and my back hurts a lot. My breasts are so sensitive."

"Are they now?" he said and didn't wait for her answer. He leaned forward and sucked at one tip through the silk and lace, drawing a rough moan from her. As he cupped her other breast and her nipple peaked, he tweaked it, and she shuddered in his arms.

"That feels so good," she said.

He undid her bra, baring her to him. He brought his mouth to her breasts again and suckled her. Touched her over and over while she cradled his head and swayed against him as her knees weakened.

—⁓—

Connie's head was whirling from the sensations his loving was creating. Every tug and pull of his mouth, touch of his fingers, sent a blast of need straight to her core. She couldn't last much longer and needed him with her.

With unsteady fingers, she undid his shirt and pulled it off him, tearing the fabric in her haste. He helped her undo his pants, and she couldn't even wait for him to have them off. She jerked down his briefs and freed him. Urged him down with her to the bed and guided him to her center.

He locked his gaze on hers as he slowly eased into her until he was buried deep. Just the feel of him there, the pressure of him inside, had her climax rising faster than she could control. Sensing that, he said, "It's okay, Connie. Let go, love. I'm here to catch you."

She came so hard and fast, the edges of her vision dimmed from the force of it, but he was there, holding her. Kissing the tears from her face and murmuring words of love. His tenderness slowly brought her back from the peak, but it wasn't long before his slow caresses had her rising up again.

He moved in her, seeking his release but taking her up with him again. This time, they both neared the edge together, and as they did, he leaned down and kissed her. Whispered against her lips, "I will love you forever."

"Forever," she said, echoing his promise as they tumbled over together.

Chapter 30

CONNIE FELT NO SHAME AS SHE, JONATHAN, AND DUDLEY walked into the Sinclair home the next morning for the brunch for those who had stayed overnight. Jonathan had leant her an oversized T-shirt and sweats to replace the dress she had worn the day before. Her high heels were probably still on the boardwalk steps, the leather ruined from the morning damp. Considering they were Jimmy Choos, she should have been upset, but she couldn't be after the amazing night she had spent with Jonathan and the good news she had to share with her friends.

Maggie and Owen were sitting at the table with the two dads. Connie was surprised that Robert was still there and that he and Bryce seemed to have buried the hatchet somewhere besides each other's heads. Tracy was there sans husband, and hopefully there was no trouble brewing in that camp. Carlo was at the stove with Emma, helping her prep breakfast, looking so right together as they worked.

Connie grew a little teary that her mother wasn't going to be there, but a second later, Mrs. Patrick and her mother walked in together, chatting like old friends. At her confused look, Maggie said, "When the two of you went off together and didn't come back last night, we figured there might be cause for celebration this morning."

"Thankfully, from the looks of the two of you, we weren't wrong," Tracy said.

Connie held out her hand to display the beautiful diamond ring on her finger. "You weren't wrong. I asked Jon to marry me, and he said yes."

Emma shook her head and pointed between the two of them, as if to confirm that she had heard right. "*You* asked *him*?"

Jonathan grinned and nodded. "Yes, she did. My Connie is not as traditional as we all thought."

"Smart woman," Carlo said and laid a hand on Emma's shoulder in support as she teared up.

Connie looked up at Jonathan, silently asking him to continue. He did a quick little bobble of his head, and still grinning, he said, "There's more. Come Memorial Day or thereabouts, we'll be having a very special celebration at *our* house next door."

"You bought the beach house? Father, you sold it to him?" Owen asked, happily surprised.

"He made me a very generous offer. I intend to set up a trust fund for your children with the money, so you better get going. Bryce and I are eager to be grandparents," his father explained.

"You'll get your wish sooner than you thought, Father. Connie and I are having a baby," Jonathan said and wrapped his arm around her waist to splay his hand across her belly.

The room erupted into all kinds of congratulatory celebration. Dudley hopped and yipped happily, sensing the happiness in the room. The women rushed forward to hug her and Jonathan while the men slapped him on the back as if he'd just won the lottery.

And maybe he had. Maybe *they* had, she thought as he slipped his arms around her and drew her close as everyone sat back down around the table, except Emma and Carlo, who went back to prepping the brunch fare.

"Not so fast, you two," Connie said, drawing Emma's and Carlo's attention. "Even if I have to walk down the aisle six months pregnant, I want the two of you to plan the wedding."

"The most epic of all weddings," Jonathan tacked on.

Emma and Carlo shared a look. Tears shimmered in Emma's eyes again as she said, "We will give you the most excellent wedding possible for two amazing people."

"But it won't take months and months. How does a Christmas wedding sound?" Carlo said.

Jonathan hugged her lovingly. "It sounds better than any gift I could ever get under the tree."

Epilogue

CONNIE HELD HER BREATH AS SHE GAZED OUT AT THE rows of chairs filling the open area of the Pierce beach house. All the furniture had been moved out to accommodate guests. Besides, she and Jonathan had decided the house needed a total makeover to bring it back to life. The only things that would remain were the wonderful landscapes that his mother had done and had been hanging in the home for so long.

His mother, Genevieve, whom Connie had met when she, Jonathan, Maggie, and Owen had flown out to meet her and Thomas. It had been an emotional time for all but a good first step in rebuilding the Pierce family.

Now, just over two weeks later, Genevieve had flown in for the wedding and was sitting in the front row, but not next to Robert Pierce. There was still too much hurt there that Connie hoped would heal in time. *Maybe with the arrival of the baby*, she thought and rubbed her hand across the organza overlay of the blush gown.

"*Mija*, don't worry," her mother said from beside her.

"I want everything to go right," she said and glanced back at Maggie and Tracy as they stood beside Owen, Jonathan's business partner Andy, and Carlo, who Jonathan had asked to be his groomsmen. Emma was off to the side with Carlo, looking slightly harried, and Connie suspected it was about more than just the wedding plans. Her friends had managed to put together everything for the wedding in just over a month, well in advance of Christmas.

As Carlo hurried away to deal with something, Connie excused herself and walked over to Emma. She hugged her and said, "Don't worry. Everything is going to be fine."

"I know. I just need to make sure everything's under control," Emma replied, her voice cracking with emotion.

Connie drew her in tighter and laid her cheek against Emma's. She stroked one hand down her back to soothe her. "Hey, Auntie Em," she teased.

"Dear God, please do not call me that, although with all of you married, I do feel like I'm lost in some other world," her friend confessed.

"Nothing will change, Em. If anything, you're going to get to see more of me for sure since we'll be neighbors."

"There is that," her friend grudgingly admitted.

"And you know Maggie will be coming down more often too. And I suspect Tracy will be needing us." She shot a look back at her friend who had come alone to the wedding.

Emma glanced toward her friend. As hard as Tracy had been trying to hide it, not all was right in her world. "Yes, she'll need us, and we'll be there, right?"

Connie nodded. The front door opened a second later, letting a sharp gust of cold air blast into the foyer where they were waiting before heading down the aisle. Carlo came in brushing snowflakes off the dark fabric of his dark-gray suit.

"Great. Snow. What else will go wrong today?" Emma groused and rolled her eyes.

"The drivers said not to worry. It's only flurries," Carlo said, referring to the trolley operators who would be ferrying the guests from the Pierce home to the old guitar building for the wedding reception. The main floor had been totally renovated just in time for the early December ceremony. By Memorial Day, they hoped to have the building open and ready for business.

"Everything will be totally fine today, because I'm getting married, Em. Getting married! Can you believe it?" she said to alleviate her friend's worry.

"It's been a long time coming," Emma said and then grabbed Carlo's hand and dragged him to the front of the group of people waiting for the trip down the aisle. "Let's get this show on the road," she said and motioned to the cello player at the front of the room to start playing the first of the wedding marches.

Jonathan had caught a glimpse of his wife-to-be as she'd walked across the foyer to chat with someone on the opposite side of the space. Some might say it was bad luck for the groom to see the bride before the wedding, but if it had been up to him, she'd have never left his side after waiting so long for her to be his.

As the cello player pulled his bow across the strings and began to play, Jonathan rocked back and forth nervously, eager for the arrival of his wife. And his baby. It was almost impossible to believe that he was going to soon have both in his life. And in the place he'd felt was home for so long, he thought, looking down at Dudley, who sat at his feet and whined in excitement. He had a jaunty look to him with a bow tie around his neck, and as the pup looked up at him, Jonathan swore there was a smile on his face.

He smiled and glanced around at the house that was already getting new life. Happy colors had replaced the eggplant purple and gray. Brightly colored mums had blossomed during the fall, the plants exchanged for the painfully pruned bushes along the perimeter of the home. Some of the hardier mums were still in bloom but being dusted with an early snow. Come the spring, more of the boxwoods would be gone, and flowers would be in bloom there once more.

Maggie and Owen strolled down the aisle first, their smiles so joyous that they filled the room with brightness despite the growing gloom of the snowy December day. Tracy and Andy came next. Andy winked at her playfully, but the smile on Tracy's face was forced and didn't quite reach up into her eyes.

Emma and Carlo hit the aisle next, looking perfect together. Her pale skin, reddish hair, and pixie-like features complemented Carlo's handsome, chiseled face and dark hair and eyes. As much as Emma might deny the whole happily ever after, hers was standing right beside her.

But then Jonathan's breath hitched in his chest as Connie and her mother came to the center of the aisle. *She's so beautiful*, he thought and couldn't take his eyes off Connie as she hurried down the aisle, apparently as eager as he was to be married.

He stepped forward to take Connie's hand from her mother but couldn't wait another minute to show her just how much he loved her. He wrapped his arm around her waist and kissed her, earning applause and laughter from those gathered for the ceremony. Dudley barked excitedly and raced around them in a circle, clearly happy.

After he released her, she reached up and wiped away the traces of her lipstick from his mouth, and Dudley took a spot between them, a grin on his puppy face.

"You're very impatient, Mr. Pierce," she said, but her smile was bright, and her gold-green eyes sparkled with pleasure.

"And you, soon-to-be Mrs. Reyes-Pierce, are irresistible."

"Which means we should start this ceremony and get you both wed," the priest said with a stern but playful glance.

"We definitely should," they said in unison, joined hands, and stood close together as the priest began the introductory rites for the wedding celebration.

The words were a blur, since Jonathan was so focused on the woman beside him and the fact that she would soon be his wife. So much so that Connie had to squeeze his hand to prompt him for the traditional "I do."

At her strongly voiced "I do," it was all he could do not to drag her close for another kiss. His hand shook as he slipped the wedding band on her finger, and Connie's hand was none too steady either. The priest continued with the blessing of the rings and after, they recited the Lord's Prayer together before the nuptial blessing. Finally, happily, the priest said, "You may now kiss the bride."

He did, hauling her tight against him and digging his fingers into her artfully arranged hair to hold her tenderly as he kissed her. She kissed him back but withdrew at the minister's warning cough. Smiling, she said, "I love you, Jon. As long as we're together, we will always be home."

Grinning, he nodded and said, "Always, Connie."

UNTIL THERE WAS US

New York Times and *USA Today* bestselling author Samantha Chase continues her beloved Montgomery series

Megan Montgomery has always been careful…except that one time she threw caution to the wind and hooked up with a sexy groomsman at her cousin's wedding. But that was two years ago. Why can't she stop thinking about Alex Rebat?

Alex has been living the good life. He loves his job, has a great circle of friends, and doesn't answer to anyone. But now that Megan's come back to town, Alex hopes he can convince her to take another chance on him…and on a future that can only be built together.

"A fun, flirty, sweet story filled with romance."

—Carly Phillips, *New York Times* bestselling author for *I'll Be There*

For more Samantha Chase, visit:
sourcebooks.com

About the Author

New York Times and *USA Today* bestselling author
Caridad Pineiro is the author of more than fifty novels
and novellas and has sold more than one million books
worldwide. Caridad writes romantic suspense, military
romance, contemporary romance, paranormal romance,
and vampire suspense. Caridad is also a Jersey Girl who
loves to travel, cook, and spend time with family and
friends. Visit her at caridad.com.

MUST LOVE BABIES

Bachelors find themselves with unexpected bundles
of joy in this heartwarming series from
award-winning author Lynnette Austin

Brant Wylder is a bachelor and loving it. He's found the
perfect location for his shop restoring vintage vehicles:
Misty Bottoms, Georgia. Supporting his family and
running the shop, he's convinced he doesn't have time for
a relationship. Until he meets Molly Stiles.

For Molly Stiles, it's nose to the grindstone establishing
her bridal boutique—not the time to meet Mr. Right.
But Molly can't help her attraction to Brant. And when an
accident leaves his seven-month-old nephew in his care,
Molly won't turn her back on them.

"Romance that has it all!"

—Fresh Fiction for *Every Bride Has Her Day*

For more Lynnette Austin, visit:
sourcebooks.com

Also by Caridad Pineiro

AT THE SHORE
One Summer Night